(For more acclaim, please turn page . . .)

TO
DIE
FOR

JOYCE MAYNARD

A SIGNET BOOK

SIGNET
Published by the Penguin Group
Penguin Books USA Inc., 375 Hudson Street,
New York, New York 10014, U.S.A.
Penguin Books Ltd, 27 Wrights Lane,
London W8 5TZ, England
Penguin Books Australia Ltd, Ringwood,
Victoria, Australia
Penguin Books Canada Ltd, 10 Alcorn Avenue,
Toronto, Ontario, Canada M4V 3B2
Penguin Books (N.Z.) Ltd, 182–190 Wairau Road,
Auckland 10, New Zealand

Penguin Books Ltd, Registered Offices:
Harmondsworth, Middlesex, England

Published by Signet, an imprint of New American Library,
a division of Penguin Books USA Inc. Previously appeared in a Dutton
edition.

First Signet Printing, January, 1993
10 9 8 7 6 5 4 3 2 1

 REGISTERED TRADEMARK—MARCA REGISTRADA

Printed in the United States of America

PUBLISHER'S NOTE
This is a work of fiction. Names, characters, places, and incidents either
are the product of the author's imagination or are used fictitiously, and
any resemblance to actual persons, living or dead, events, or locales is
entirely coincidental.

For the voice at the other end of the telephone, my agent and friend—and an irreplaceably astute reader—Robert Cornfield. With love.

ACKNOWLEDGMENTS

In that lonely period when a person is consumed with the writing of a book, no individual is more valuable than one who can read what the writer has produced and offer guidance. A handful of such good and trusted friends read or listened to portions of this manuscript and offered thoughts and criticism that helped immeasurably. I particularly want to thank Ernest Hebert, Bill Barton, Vicky Schippers, Audrey LaFehr, Graf Mouen, Susan Herman, Lynn Pleshette, Bob Carvin, and Bill Oster.

Well she grew up hard and she grew up fast
In the age of television
And she made a vow to have it all
It became her new religion
Oh, down in her soul, it was an act of treason
Oh, down they go for all the wrong reasons

—from the song
    "All the Wrong Reasons"

PART

I

PART

1

Carol Stone

Just to give you an idea of Susie. What a go-getter she was, right from the start. I can remember back when we lived on Sunrise Lane, her standing in front of the mirror, giving weather reports. She couldn't have been more than three years old at the time. I mean, this girl had a goal in life, and the determination to pursue it. You know how some little girls say they want to be fairy princesses or ballerinas when they grow up? That wasn't Susie. Right from the start, she had her feet on the ground and she knew what she wanted. I remember one time, we were watching the "Today" show. This was way back, when they still had Barbara Walters, for goodness sake, and my Susie's pointing to her on the screen telling me, "That's what I want to be someday, Mommy. I'm going to be on TV."

And now of course, she is. Every night. It's just not the way we pictured it. God, look at me. They said this mascara was waterproof. I'm writing a letter to the company.

And she was good at it too. Earl and I can show you her tapes. We got one of the first home video cameras they made—back when you still had to carry around a battery pack—just so we could tape Susie's broadcasts. She had this news show—"Suzanne's World." You've never seen anything so cute. She'd report on what was going on in the neighborhood—so-and-so got a puppy, so-and-so's grandparents came to visit. But the way she did it, it was just like a real TV newscaster. "Now back to you, Faye," she'd say, at the end of her report. Faye was the anchorwoman. Earl ran the camera. But Susie was the star.

Back in those days, she was always self-conscious about her nose. Which I always thought was fine just the way it was. But it was typical of Suzanne that she started planning for the plastic surgery from—what?—fifth grade? Sixth at the most. We finally got it taken care of when she was twelve, but in the meantime, she worked out all these little tricks for deemphasizing her nose with contour brushes and so forth. Every time we'd take her picture, she had this certain angle she liked to tilt her head. I'd show you, but after the operation she up and threw away every one of those old portraits, if you can believe it.

If you want to know the truth—and we never told Suzanne this, naturally—Earl and I were sort of upset after the swelling came down from her surgery. Maybe her nose was a tad bigger than average in the first place, but the new one was awfully small, and kind of tilted up. Earl said we should sue, but how would that have made Suzanne feel? The main thing was, she was happy.

And popular? I'm telling you, by the time that girl was thirteen, Earl had to have another phone line put in for Susie's calls. We had boys knocking on the door just to get a look at her. Older boys, too—seventeen, eighteen—asking her out when she was still in junior high. Of course Earl and I said no. We always ran a tight ship. Not that Susie would have done anything, anyway. This was a young lady with a head on her shoulders. "You know, Mom," she used to tell me, "I just don't have time for a lot of dating. I've got to think about my future."

Not that she was antisocial. We're not talking about some sort of hermit. I'm telling you, this girl had activities every day of the week. Monday, cheering practice. Tuesday, yearbook. Modeling class, Wednesday nights. Church youth group—if you want to know how ridiculous all this is, let me tell you: she was real active in that. Susie even started a chapter of Students Who Just Say No at the high school. Got right up there in assembly in front of the whole school and made a speech. Cool as a cucumber, like she'd been doing it all her life. Well, of course, she had.

Earl and I never missed watching her cheer. Lancaster High didn't have that good of a team, but I'm telling you, you never saw better cheerleading. Suzanne was the captain. They had these little maroon skirts—maroon and yellow, those were the colors. Suzanne hated them, but what can you do?— and yellow sweaters with a big L on the front. I remember the day they got the uniforms. Suzanne didn't think the hem on hers was quite right, so she redid the whole thing. That was Suzanne for you. Always a perfectionist. Always the highest standards. You couldn't say gymnastics was her specialty, but you've never seen a person work so hard on the splits. Every night, when she was on the phone, she'd be sitting there, on the floor, working on that full split of hers. I don't need to tell you she got it, now do I?

It was always hard for Faye. We knew that. Here's Susie with that cute little figure of hers, a natural blonde, boys coming round at all hours of the day and night. And there's Faye starving to death on some new liquid diet. Life isn't always fair, what can you say? There was our Suzanne getting straight As, and Faye struggling to keep a C average. Suzanne making the ski team. Faye breaking her leg on day one. And then there was Faye's skin problem. The money we spent on dermatologists.

But Faye was always proud of Susie. I can still see the two of them, Faye pushing Susie down the street in that little stroller of hers down Sunrise Lane, barely out of diapers herself. Telling everyone, "That's my baby sister." She just adored Suzanne. Well, who wouldn't?

So it was no surprise when Larry Maretto started calling her up. I can't tell you he seemed any more determined than some of the others. But maybe because he wasn't in school—he was working at his folks' restaurant—and Suzanne had graduated from college with a degree in media communications and landed a part-time job modeling at the Simpson's over at the mall while she pursued a position in the media field. They were both ready to start thinking about settling down, I guess you could say. Not that she fell all over him or anything. But she didn't turn him down, point-blank, like she always used to before.

You couldn't say she was head over heels. Suzanne never got that way. She was always practical. But she let him keep calling and coming around. And things just slowly developed. I can't even say when it happened, but before you know it, Larry's coming by the house every night after work, to take her out, sending flowers, the whole bit. Next thing we know, she's telling me, "Mom, we need to go shopping for a wedding dress."

Earl and I had always pictured Suzanne settling down with more of a college type. So I have to admit that at first we had our doubts about Larry, and we told Suzanne as much. But for the first time in her life, it didn't seem to bother her, making a choice that didn't exactly please us. It was almost like she was finally having her own little adolescent rebellion or whatever, with this long-haired rock-and-roll drummer of hers. "All my life I've been doing what you and Dad wanted, Mom," Susie said to me. "This time I'm making my own choice."

And in the end of course, Larry won us over too. Anyone could see he was nuts about her—sending her flowers, writing her poems, songs even, that he played for her on his guitar. Delivering this pizza to the house one night, with her name spelled out in olives. Then giving her that puppy of course. A Lhasa apso. You could tell he was a hard worker. He'd been working in the family business since he was twelve or thirteen, and Earl and I both felt confident that he was done sowing his wild oats and now he was ready to make something of himself.

It was a beautiful wedding. Susie wore this cream-colored silk gown with little seed pearls down the back. She copied her veil from this picture we had of Maria Shriver. Suzanne kept a scrapbook of all the big network newswomen. She could tell you anything you wanted to know about those women—where they got their first news anchor job, what their shoe size was, I'm telling you. So anyway, she had a Maria Shriver wedding veil.

When Larry first started coming around, he had this long hair. Don't get the wrong idea—he was always clean, but they were just kids, you know. They liked listening to rock music and going dancing at clubs and so forth. Larry had a motorcycle. Although I have to say he always wore a helmet, and he made sure Susie did too.

But by the wedding, they had all that behind them. Larry had sold his motorcycle and cut his hair. His dad made him weekend manager down at the restaurant. I mean, you've never seen such a change in a person in such a short time. Suzanne was sending out job applications to TV stations, and finally, right after the honeymoon, the cable station here in town took her on, which was a real breakthrough. She wasn't in front of a camera yet on a regular basis, but it was a beginning, something for her résumé. And you knew it was only a matter of time before she'd move on to something bigger. Larry was behind her a thousand percent.

By the time they got engaged, Suzanne and Larry had saved enough to put a down payment on a cute little condominium. They picked out furniture, carpeting, dishes, you name it. If you want to know how much Larry loved Suzanne, let me tell you: His wedding present to her was a Datsun 280 ZX. Suzanne said that was the same kind of car this reporter drives that's on Channel 4 all the time. I forget her name.

They went to the Bahamas on their honeymoon. We all got postcards, how beautiful it was, how happy they were. That was June. July 1, Suzanne started her new job and I guess she was a little let down. Her boss had promised her that she'd get a crack at some on-camera work, but it turned out what she did was more in the secretarial line. But Suzanne's not the kind to give up easily, as you might guess. So when it turned out what they had in mind was not in the reporting line, exactly, Suzanne just took it upon herself to make something of her position. She asked the station manager if she could produce a documentary, on her own time, about the lives of a group of local teenagers—the kind of problems and pressures young people confront these days. Follow them around for a couple months, get to know them, and get to where they trusted her enough to bare their souls, if you will. It was going to be an exposé of teen lifestyles, sex, drugs, the whole shooting match. And that's how it all started. This giant mess.

Mary Emmet

I was supposed to have an abortion. Sixteen years old, Eddy off to Woodbury with no forwarding address two days after he got the news, my mother and dad on unemployment, calling me a whore. No way I was going to get to keep this baby. I had the appointment all set up. I even got a ride over to the clinic that morning. "Don't come home without blood in your underpants," my mom told me. A real softie, that one.

We got there early, so I told Patty, my friend that drove me, to drop me off a couple blocks away. I'd walk the rest. It was May. A real sunny day and the black flies hadn't come out yet. I stopped at a park—not even a park, just a playing field—where this Little League team was practicing. A bunch of little squirt boys and a coach that looked like he was somebody's dad. And over on this bench a little ways away, the moms sitting by a cooler, handing out Hi-C and calling out to their kid when it was his turn at bat. Some of them had littler kids too, playing in the dirt. This one mother was pregnant, only not like me. She was showing. Wearing this shirt with an arrow pointing down at her stomach that said FUTURE ALL-STAR. They were all laughing and talking. One had a baby in her lap and it looked like she was nursing him. I guess she was married to the coach, because he came over to her one time, when the kids were taking a break, and gave her a kiss. Not a french kiss or anything, like Eddy used to. This was the type kiss a husband and wife give each other. Just a peck on the cheek, but I saw that and I thought to myself: He doesn't just want sex out of her. He loves her. They're a family.

I knew it wasn't likely that this little amoeba or whatever that I had in my stomach was going to be some big baseball player, or some guy that discovers the cure for cancer. But one thing was for sure. He was my best shot at somebody that would always love me. And he'd be all mine.

There I am. A total fuckup at school. My parents hate me and you know Eddy wishes I'd jump off a bridge. I'm not smart and I'm not pretty, and I'll never get further than sponging ketchup off the tables at some fast-food restaurant. This baby I got is the most precious thing I ever had, and I'm going to let somebody stick a tube in that sucks it out of me and flush it down the toilet? I must be an even bigger idiot than my father tells me.

I tell myself there are people that have a million dollars, but they can't have a baby. They fly all over the country having operations, getting sperm donors, hiring women to have one for them, getting doctors to try and fertilize their eggs in a test tube. And here I am, I pulled it off without even trying. It's the most important thing I ever did or ever will do, most likely.

I sat down on the bench, behind the mothers. I guess I sat there a long time. Thinking about all the same stuff I'd been over a million times already: How am I supposed to pay for the diapers and stuff? How will I ever get another boyfriend if I have a baby? What happens if my dad kicks

me out of the house? It's not like I'm going to be
driving some station wagon and talking about trips
to Disney World like these mothers. I don't even
have the money to buy my kid a baseball glove.
Who am I kidding, thinking I could be someone's
mother?

This little guy with real thick glasses comes up
to bat. He's a shrimp. The batting helmet keeps
falling down over his face and he's all choked up
on the bat. Then I see something's wrong with one
of his arms. It's shriveled up and it looks like some
of the fingers are missing. You can tell the kids on
the team aren't that wild about him either. The
mother that's keeping score or whatever mutters
something about how his father was drunk when
he dropped this kid off. One of the others says he's
always sticking his hands down his pants and she
wouldn't make any bets on him wearing underwear. Lucky her son wears a batting glove. "You'd
think it was enough we had him for soccer," she
says.

Frankie, his name was. A little guy that had less
than nothing going for him.

OK, I say to myself. It's up to you, Frankie.
Strike out, I'm heading straight over to that clinic
to plunk down my two hundred dollars. Get on
base and I'm having the baby.

First pitch they throw him, Frankie swings and
misses. Second pitch, same thing. Then he lets
maybe a dozen good pitches go by. Just stands there
grinning, while you can see the dad that's pitching
getting pretty fed up. "Come on now, Frankie," he
says. "Other kids need to get a turn."

It's like he doesn't hear. He keeps waiting as one
perfectly good ball after another sails across the

plate. Nice easy balls. Ten, maybe fifteen more pitches.

The kids are yelling at him now. "Funky," they call him. Mothers shaking their heads, looking at their watches. Me, I'm barely breathing.

"OK, Frankie," says the coach. "This is your last shot." He releases the ball. Not even a good pitch like those others. It's way outside. No way is Funky connecting with this one. In my head I'm already climbing up on the table, putting my feet in the stirrups.

He does this little dance, and then he swings like no swing you ever saw, dips the bat low. Taps the ball. Just barely, mind you. You figured the pitcher had to get it, the way the ball wobbled over to him, only it bounced off his glove and past him. Fell to the ground and rolled right between the second baseman's legs.

So I skipped my appointment at the clinic. Decided then and there to have my baby. And that was my son Jimmy.

But here's the trick life hands you. You get this kid all right. You love him to death. And just like you figured, he loves you too. You weren't wrong when you figured this child was going to be the most precious thing you'd ever be handed in your life.

But the joke's on you. Because once you get this child, what can you do about it but wake up every morning, waiting to see what dreams won't come true today? Before long, you stop having the dreams altogether. If you're smart you do.

Jimmy was three weeks old before I could bring him home from the hospital on account of how little he was. Four pounds, two ounces, when he was born. They had him in an incubator.

I'd stand there in the nursery, holding him in my hands, him with this little shirt on that came off my old Tiny Tears doll. His skin was almost transparent, with these blue veins showing through. Legs like chicken wings. No hair, no eyelashes. Fingernails barely sprouted. He was so little he couldn't even cry. Just made these little squeaking sounds, more like a puppy than a kid.

It was no picnic. My folks wouldn't let me come back home, so I moved in at Patty's, put Jimmy in day care when he was five weeks old, got my job at Wendy's, the three-to-eleven shift.

You think about all this stuff you'll do when you have a kid. Taking them to the carnival to ride in those little boats. Get their picture taken with Santa, make sand castles at the beach. You picture yourself being one of those mothers pushing the stroller down the street, pushing your kid on the swings. Passing out the Hi-C at baseball games. It never works out like how you pictured. You only have enough tickets for him to ride the little boats four times, and then you got to take him home only he's crying for another turn. He's scared of Santa. Your one afternoon off all week to take him to the beach it rains. Or you're just so tired by the time you get home, you got barely enough energy to stick the frozen pizza in the microwave and turn on the TV.

He was always a good boy, Jimmy. Nights I'd be at work, he'd fix himself supper, get himself to bed even. He learned pretty young not to ask for much, so I hardly ever had to say no. I mean he always loved dogs, but he always knew we couldn't have a puppy.

Third grade, he wanted to join Little League. Not that he knew the first thing about baseball. It's not like this was a boy that got to play catch with his dad every night after supper. He just watched games on TV and got the idea in his head that this was his sport. What could be so tricky about running around the bases, you know?

So we signed up for the league. I paid my registration money. We bought him a glove and a bat and I even took him down to this field near our apartment to throw him some balls. Not that I could throw worth beans. But you did the best you could.

Comes the Saturday morning of the tryouts, he takes a bath, wets his hair down, changes his T-shirt three times, he's so excited. Down at the field, when I fill out the papers on him, and they ask who he played for last year, I write down "Never been on a team before." The guy in charge looks surprised. "Most boys his age already have some experience," he says.

"Well this one doesn't," I say. You got to start somewhere.

I see a couple of the mothers rolling their eyes, like "What kind of people are these?" and you know they take one look at me and figure out my whole story: She got knocked up when she was a teenager. No dad in the picture. Kid's a loser.

When Jimmy's turn comes to bat, they throw him all these pitches, and he never manages to hit one. Finally they set up the T for him, and he kind of taps it. They tag him out. One of the mothers on the bench that doesn't know this is my son says, "Jesus, let's hope the Orioles don't get that one."

Jimmy stuck it out that season, but he never

signed up for a sport again, and we never discussed it.

I should've known, that day on the ballpark, heading over to the abortion clinic. Frankie got on base all right. But what happened next was the real story. Next batter up hits a single, and Frankie's an easy out at second. No way that kid was ever going to score in baseball or in life.

The game's rigged. Doesn't everybody know that yet?

Earl Stone

I remember Carol and myself bringing her home from the hospital, in this little pink dress and booties, and Carol saying to me, "You'll be walking this little girl down the aisle someday."

"Who's ever going to be good enough for her?" I said. I guess every father thinks that.

Back when the kids were still in high school and junior high, even, we started putting money aside for their wedding day. Faye too, of course, although she hasn't found Mr. Right yet. But you knew with Susie it was only a matter of time, and probably not a lot of time either. She isn't the kind you'd ever want to see in some bargain basement gown either. Suzanne always went for quality.

The things you think of, when the day actually comes. I mean, here you've been dreaming and planning for this moment, and now it's finally there. You're walking in the church and it's like it was just yesterday she was up on that stage singing "High Hopes." You remember the time she had scarlet fever and you stayed up with her all night, trying to bring the fever down by putting her in the tub every couple hours. Family trip to Washington, D.C. Her twirling her baton in the Fourth of July parade, and this friend of mine leaning over to me and saying, "Watch out for that daughter of yours, Earl. She's going to be a heartbreaker."

She never gave us a minute's worry. Never the drugs. Never the late nights staying up waiting for her to come home, and she's past curfew. Only worry she gave us was that she pushed herself too hard. "Ease up a little, Susie," we'd say. "It's not the end of the world if you get a B. Nobody's going to die if you don't make captain of the cheering squad." But of course, she always did make it. Every goal she set herself, she attained it.

Do I need to tell you her mother bawled like a baby, watching her come down the aisle? It's the day we'd looked forward to all our lives. I never felt such pride. And her, she's got that ten-million-dollar smile. We never even needed to get her braces.

As she gets to the pew where her mother's standing, she turns to Carol and blows her a kiss. "Thanks, Dad," she says to me. I want to tell you. It was too much.

And there's Larry, standing there at the altar, waiting for her, looking like he's about to bust himself. And Faye of course, the maid of honor. Always so proud of her little sister.

When the priest asked, "Who gives this woman to marry this man?" Carol squeezes my hand tight and we both say, "We do." Just like we're one person, one voice. That's how we felt.

There was kind of a funny moment there when the priest said to Larry, "You may kiss the bride." And of course she still had the veil partly covering her face, so he had to lift it up and push it back over her face. Only he had a little trouble finding the edge. You know how it is when you keep trying to get one of those Glad bags open, and you just can't get the edges separated? Of course after a few seconds he got it and everyone laughed and he kissed her.

"Ladies and gentlemen," says the priest. "May I introduce to you Mr. and Mrs. Larry Maretto." Everyone clapped. The two of them just stood there for a minute or two, just to give everyone a photo opportunity.

Have you ever seen a nicer-looking couple? Wouldn't you just think, to look at them, they were headed for a wonderful life?

Jimmy Emmet

It wasn't my idea. It was Russell got me into it. Always was a peckerhead.

It's, I don't know, September, October maybe. October I guess, because I didn't have my license yet. Got my license November 8, day I turned sixteen. Man I'd been waiting a long time for that day.

We're outside school, having a smoke, when she pulls up in that Datsun of hers. Steps out like some chick in a commercial—first all you see is her legs in those high-heel shoes. Didn't even see her face right off, just that leg. Fuck if that doesn't give you a boner, says Russell.

Her nose was kind of funny, but to me she still looked pretty. And knew it. She bends over so her rear end's in our face, reaching for her damn briefcase or some shit. Then she just stands there a minute, leaning against her car, and she runs her tongue over her lips, like you know women do because they saw it in a movie and they know it makes guys hot.

And then she heads into the school, tossing her hair when she passes us, wiggling her butt, the works. "Some cunt," Russell says to me, loud enough I bet she heard. Not that she let on. "Wouldn't I like to bang that?"

Me, I'm just standing there letting my cigarette

burn down. She was close enough that I could smell this perfume she was wearing. But you know, she might as well've been heading to Mars, for all the hope I had of getting in her pants. I'm fifteen years old at this point, and I know I'm never going to have a piece of ass like that. They'll strut by you with their I-got-the-pussy attitude, but they'll keep on walking. I might as well be a piece of dog shit.

She shows up at our health class that morning. It turns out her name's Mrs. Maretto, and she's some TV reporter making a video about teen life. She wants to interview a bunch of kids about their thoughts on all these subjects like, How Do You Feel About Using a Condom? and Do Your Parents Understand You? She's looking for volunteers to work with her for the next six months. I tell Russ, "I dare you to talk to her." He says, "OK, I will." I should've known better. Russell's not what you could call the quiet type.

The next day we're out there having our smoke and her car pulls up again. "By the way," says Russell. "Looks like you'll be spending some time with Mrs. Hard-on." Turns out Russell signed me up for this video project of hers.

I go straight for his balls, but of course he's ready for that. "Fuck," I say. "Why'd you go and do that for?"

"It's about time you picked up some brownie points at this scumhole," he says. "You might even get your name on the announcements or something." Then he laughs, because as long as Russell and I been going to this fucking school, the only place our names ever came up was in the detention list. They might as well make a rubber stamp with Russell Hines and Jimmy Emmet on it, because we're always there. Dependable as shit.

I didn't plan on showing up for this video gig.

Just because my name's on her list doesn't mean I'm Joe Student all of a sudden. Only what happens is, I guess nobody else signs up and she's desperate. Most likely she told her boss she's going to make this video and she's got the equipment and shit, and no kids. Or just me. Now probably the asshole says they're going to bag the whole deal, but she don't want to do that on account of she's wetting her pants thinking about this being her big break that's going to make her famous. Meanwhile my guidance counselor's having a hard-on of his own that I'm finally showing an interest in extracurricular activities. He figures he's got to encourage the little fucker. Or words to that effect. Then she comes back to Russell and says listen, why don't you join our video project? And old Russell, thinking this is going to be a gas, says, "Sure, Mrs. Maretto. That sounds interesting. I wouldn't miss it."

She says to meet her at Pizza Hut after school, so we can get to know each other. We make a plan, Russell and me. We're going to give the chick a hard time from day one, fuck with her head a while, then split. We figure we're her little project. She can be ours.

But when I show up that first day, it looked different all of a sudden. I'm the first one there, and she's sitting in this booth with a new notebook, and she's got these papers all copied out, one for each of us, and she's even typed out all this stuff on her computer with roman numerals. An outline or whatever you call it. And it hits me, I don't know, that she's been busting her tail over this, like it really matters. She calls me James and she even shakes my goddam hand. And when I shake her hand back, I can feel it's trembling like she's nervous. Which it never hit me somebody like that would be.

The other times I saw her she always looked so pretty and perfect. Up close, I could tell some things I never saw before, like that she was so skinny she had this safety pin in her skirt. This is dumb, but I remember she had a zit. Nothing major, just a place on her forehead where you could tell her skin broke out, and she'd tried to cover it up with makeup only it didn't work. And even though she didn't look so pretty then, it hit me that she was more like a kid, wobbling around on those high heels of hers. She actually thought I was tough shit.

She had this diamond ring. Jesus, I'm thinking, this chick is married. She's a TV reporter and everything, and she still gets zits.

"So," she's saying, "I think this will be a stimulating look at the sociological and psychological ramifications of being a young person in the nineties" and blah blah blah. And she's saying she just knows we can make a dynamite documentary. And I'm looking at Russell, who's come in by this time, and he's staring straight at her tits, and she knows that too, and when she gets to the part about being excited he grins. Real quiet, I say to him, "Fuck off man. Lay off her." Which I never in a million years figured I'd say. A guy like me, I mean.

But there was something about Mrs. Maretto. I didn't just want to fuck her. I respected her. I liked her. I didn't want her thinking I was just this jerk kid that all he cared about was humping some girl. More than anything I wanted her to like me. Not that I let on to Russell, naturally.

What I said to Russell was, "I'd kill for a piece of that." But at the time, it was only meant to be an expression.

Suzanne Maretto

Put yourself in my shoes for a moment. All my life I've been dedicated to achieving certain goals in life, and I've pursued those goals. I worked very hard to get where I was. I never used drugs. Always maintained my appearance. I never got into any trouble. Look at my high school record, and college. I graduated with a 3.9 average. I have always believed that life is what you put into it, and that it is every person's God-given right to be all that he or she can be. For myself, I wanted to be happily married, with a home and a fulfilling career. A mere six months ago I had attained those things, and I was working to build an even more exciting future. Now everything I had is lost. I'm twenty-five years old, and I'm a widow.

I know what Larry would say if he were here today. "Don't let it get to you," he'd say. "Life isn't always fair, Suzanne, but we have to make the best of the hand life deals us and move forward from here." He would say, "I have faith in you, Suzanne. I know everything will work out." "Look for the positive aspects instead of dwelling on the negative." And so I am trying to do that. Larry is gone forever, and nothing will bring him back to us. But I can't give up on my life, just because he's gone. I'm a fighter.

This whole thing is like a movie on television I can't turn off. Sometimes I still wake up, forgetting it actually happened. I look across my pillow, expecting to see Larry lying there asleep. Then I remember. It's not just a bad dream.

I had gone out to an audition for a position at a television station over in Woodbury that night. Arts and entertainment reporter at WNTK. I hold a bachelors degree in Media Communication from Sanders College. One reason I always try to cooperate with the press, the way I'm doing right now, is because I've been a journalist and broadcaster myself, and I always planned a future in television. I owe it to Larry as well as myself to make that dream a reality someday. Just because a person you love dies doesn't mean you're dead too. I'm still very much alive. And I still have dreams. I still have a future.

Just to give you some idea of how things were between Larry and I, I had talked to him just a few hours before the audition. And he was so excited for me. He knew how much this job meant to me, and because it was important to me, it was important to him. Looking back on that conversation now, I realize it was the last time I ever spoke to him. His last words to me were, "You go in there and show them, Suzanne. I know you can do it."

It was a very important night for me. I'd worked hard on my presentation, which included a sample movie review and a weekend roundup of fun activities for families. I know I did well on my interview too. Everyone was impressed. After I played the video of my weather broadcasts at my present job, they even clapped. Naturally nobody was going to make a commitment that very day, but the station manager gave me this look, as he was shaking my hand, before I left, which I knew meant he was looking forward to my coming aboard. "Very nice material, Suzanne," he said to me. "Very nice." I'll always remember the way he squeezed my hand as he said that. You knew he was sincere.

So naturally I was feeling good as I drove home. Thinking about the new job and all. And especially looking forward to telling Larry. Knowing how proud of me he'd be. He was always my biggest fan.

It was another dream come true. And the whole time I was driving home, I was thinking to myself, Larry will be so happy when I tell him. He'd been out late himself that night, at the restaurant, but I figured he'd get home before me, and when I got to our condo I saw I was right, because his car was parked out front like always. Only the odd part was, Larry always left the house lights on until I got home. It was just after ten o'clock, but our house was completely dark.

Still, nothing could have prepared me for what I found when I opened the door. There was Larry lying in a pool of blood, like John Lennon or somebody. Our home had been totally ransacked. There were stereo components lying in the middle of the floor, and a box of my jewelry spilled on the rug, and furniture turned over, like there had been a fight. I figured Larry must have come in just as this burglary was being committed and surprised the criminals. It's one of those situations of being in the wrong place at the wrong time, that's all.

So they grabbed him, and struggled. Larry was a very strong, very athletic person, so I think there had to be at least two of them to hold him down. Anyway, there he was. You know the rest. Lying there, with blood all over his head, and blood dripping on our new carpet. I took one look at him and knew he must be dead. Looking at him, I remember thinking, He'll never know if I get the arts and entertainment reporting job. It would've made him so happy.

I've been trained in crime reporting, so I kept my head. I knew I should get out of the apartment right away, in case the criminals were still there. Also I knew better than to disturb the body. At Sanders I worked as a reporter for the college radio station, and I was present at numerous crime scenes. I know how important it is to leave everything the way you found it. Even in a crisis, you never stop being a journalist. That's just the way I am. It doesn't mean I don't feel the same things as other people. It's just my professional training coming through.

Right from the start, I tried to cooperate with the police in every way, to assist them in finding Larry's killers. It won't bring my husband back. But it's important to those of us who loved him that we see justice done. The police have been doing a terrific job. Just incredible.

I don't blame the police for what's happening now. It's their job to explore every avenue, consider every possibility, no matter how ridiculous it might seem. In a murder investigation, you've got to listen to everybody, even if they have a reputation for getting into trouble. Even if they're the kind of people everybody knows are mixed up with drugs and crime. Which applies to both of those boys, heaven knows. I mean we're not exactly dealing with a bunch of Eagle Scouts here.

Jerry Cleaver

One day last fall, we came into first period and our health teacher said, "We have a very important guest here this morning, a representative of our local television station who has asked to have a few words with you." Just when I'm ready to space out, up she steps. That woke me up, let me tell you. I mean, this wasn't any Kim Basinger we're talking about, but she was definitely an improvement on Mrs. Finlaysson.

She was wearing this little skirt with suspenders, and these lace-up boots, and the tiniest feet. Lacy stockings. Her hair in a ponytail. "I know you'll want to give Mrs. Maretto your attention, students," says Mrs. F. Like there was ever any doubt.

Then she tells us about this video she's making for the cable station. "Adults are always sounding off to kids," she says. "This is your chance to tell them what's on your mind." It wasn't so very many years ago she was in high school herself, she says. Even if she did seem like an old married lady. Which of course she didn't.

The show was going to be called "Teens Speak Out." She'd be spending time at the school for the next couple months, interviewing kids. She wanted to really get to know a group of us, hear our thoughts on drugs, sex, rock music, peer pressure. You could just see all the guys, especially, rolling their eyes when she said that. Like they were really going to sit down in front of a TV camera and tell their deep feelings about sex.

She knew it too. "Listen," she said. "You don't have to worry about your anonymity. We have this special device I use on the sound equipment that scrambles your voice. You can have your back to the camera. We can even speak in private, off camera, and I'll just report on some of what you tell me. Think of this as your opportunity to let the older generation understand what makes you tick."

By this time it wasn't just the guys that were making faces, it was just about everyone. There's this little wave of snickering going on, people shooting each other looks or giving the person in front of them little kicks under the desk. One real popular guy, Vic, that plays center on the varsity basketball team, raised his hand and asked her, real innocent like, whether they'd need permission slips from their parents before talking to her. "That won't be necessary," she said. You got the impression she was the type person that could never tell when someone was pulling her leg.

When she said, "OK. Now I'd like to take the names of the people who would like to talk with me, so we can set up a time to get together," nobody raised their hand. She had this clipboard with her name on the front in gold letters, and she just stood there, with her pen uncapped, waiting to write down names, only there weren't any. You could see her looking around the room, trying to make eye contact with someone. One guy burped real loud. One of the girls took out her cheering sweater that she was sewing a letter on and started stitching.

"You know, I used to be a cheerleader myself," Suzanne says. "Back in the dark ages." Then she kind of laughs, only nobody else does.

Mrs. Finlaysson called on a couple of people at this point, the usual good-citizen types teachers always count on to cooperate at moments like this. No luck.

"It's too bad," she said. "Mrs. Maretto has taken time out of her busy day and everything." Chick's still standing there, holding the clipboard. She was looking so young. It almost looked like she was going to cry.

That's when old Lydia raised her hand. I figure Mrs. Finlaysson was so used to her never saying anything she didn't even get what she was doing. "Yes, Lydia," she said. "Can I help you with something?"

"I just wanted to sign up," she said. "To be in the TV show."

"Well, that's more like it," said Mrs. Finlaysson. "I'm glad to see someone with a little school spirit. Someone not afraid of speaking her own mind."

Lydia wasn't exactly a trendsetter, of course— her with that frizzy orange hair of hers, and those crossed eyes that you never knew where to look when you were talking to her. She was the only one in the whole class that gave her name. You knew right then this project was Dork City. Later, when we heard that Russell Hines signed up Jimmy Emmet, for a prank, I almost felt sorry for this reporter chick. And then Russell got roped in himself. I guess that was it, just the three of them. Not exactly your representative sampling of all-American teenagers.

Faye Stone

I was four years old when Mom brought Susie home from the hospital, but I can still remember the day. I had chicken pox, so my face and hands were all covered with scabs, and of course they wouldn't let me touch her. But I remember leaning over the bassinet and looking in at her, all wrapped up like a present in this little pink blanket. My dad used to worry that her nose looked big, but to me she was perfect. The minute I saw her I knew she was going to be the favorite.

You get used to it. It's not like I spent the next twenty years expecting people to stop my mother on the street and say, "You have a beautiful little girl there"—meaning me instead of Suzanne. It's not like I was sitting around waiting for some modeling agency to put my picture in its file. When you know you're not cheerleader material, you don't try out for the squad. Not unless you're really dumb, you don't. And I'm not. Not cheerleader material. But not dumb, is what I mean.

So what you do if you're smart is you join the fan club. I'd push Susie around in her stroller and people would come up to me and say what a cute baby sister I had, and wasn't I a good big sister. When she put on her tap routines, I'd be the announcer. How I got into hairdressing in fact was from all the years of doing Suzanne's hair. I'd sit there for hours, just trying out the styles. Hot rollers, crimping, french braids, we tried them all. She's not really blond anymore, incidentally. I've been coloring it for her for years now. You notice those highlights? I did that. Some salons just use a cap and pull the hairs they want to peroxide through the holes, you know. But I prefer the foil technique the big salons in New York use. It takes a lot more time painting the hairs one at a time like that. But it comes out a lot more natural looking.

She was always so tiny, just like a little doll. I remember sitting in the tub with her one time, seeing her ribs. I mean, we always took our baths together, but this was the first time I ever noticed them I guess. And I screamed, because I didn't know what they were, and I thought something was the matter with Susie.

You should've seen her in her twirling outfit. Baton, tap, you name it, Susie did them all. Even when she was just three or four, she loved an audience. A lot of the kids in her dancing school would just freeze when it came time for the recital. But not Susie. If she could've performed every night she'd be happy. I can still see her standing in front of the mirror, practicing her curtsies and blowing kisses. She'd walk around the house holding the curling iron like it was a microphone, saying, "Thank you thank you thank you. . . . For my next number I'd like to do such and such. . . ."

When she was oh, six maybe, or seven, she worked out this tap routine to "High Hopes." You know that song, about the little ant that's trying to climb up this rubber plant? Well she won first prize in this talent show, and my folks brought her to the city for the finals. My mom took her around to all these talent agencies and had these professional pictures taken. She even tried out for a Stop & Shop commercial. Suzanne was always convinced it was her nose that kept her from getting the part, but for months after that we'd hear her doing the ad, around the house. "Stop and Shop means freshness for less. My mom says you just can't beat those prices. But me, I love the bakery-fresh jelly doughnuts." To this day I can remember the words.

Oh, not just that commercial either. She did Honey Nut Cheerios and saggy panty hose, Golden Dream Barbie, Johnson's Baby Shampoo. She had, like, a whole repertoire. Whenever my parents had friends over, I'd be the announcer and Susie would perform her ads.

Around sixth or seventh grade we got the video camera—one of the first they came out with—and that's when Suzanne got into news. She'd have me tape her so she could watch her performances and work on certain problem areas, like licking her lips and saying um. It's a very competitive field, video journalism. And she figured it's never too early to start. She knew what she wanted by then, so why wait around to start developing her skills, is what she said. We were all so proud of her.

By that time there were a lot of boys after her naturally. Even older guys, in my class, would ask me about my sister. She went out with them sometimes, but I don't think anybody ever got anywhere. Even then Susie was more interested in her career.

I think that was partly why Larry was able to get where he did with her in fact. He was her biggest fan. He was the first guy that came along, that paid her even more attention than our dad. And believe me, that wasn't easy. The other thing about

Larry was, he was the first person that got Suzanne to let her hair down and have a good time. He was such a funloving kind of person himself. He brought out a side of Suzanne you never would have known was there. Kind of a wild side.

I was her maid of honor. It was a beautiful wedding of course. I did her hair in these french braids, with little tendrils going down the back of her neck, and sprays of pearls and voile woven into the back. You couldn't take your eyes off her. I was bawling like a baby, naturally, and so were my mom and dad. I can still see Larry standing there, like he can't believe she's his. I could show you the tape.

After an event like that, there's always a certain amount of letdown of course. So many months of planning and preparation, and then it's over in a matter of hours, and you've got to get down to regular life. I remember going over to their condo, a couple weeks later. Once they'd got back from the Bahamas, and she was sitting there with a whole row of Mr. Coffees on the counter, writing thank-you notes. "It was all over so quick," she told me. "It seems like something else should be happening."

She had her résumé printed up, listing her modeling experience at Simpson's and all the workshops she'd taken and her communications degree of course. We all thought it looked so impressive, going way back to her talent show award and the cheerleading championship. Which tells something about a person, after all. Their ability to stay cool under pressure and so forth. She had professional pictures taken and everything. We even included one of her videos in the package she mailed to some of the better places. Channel 56 and Channel 38 and so forth. But she never heard back, except a form letter saying they weren't looking for a reporter at this point in time, but they'd keep her name on file.

You've got to hand it to her, she didn't give up. She went to ad agencies, to see if anyone was looking for somebody to do commercials. She contacted some agencies, looking into modeling, and she certainly was pretty enough, but I don't know, maybe she was too short. Finally she went to schools. One or two offered her a job in the office, you know. But then WGSL said they'd give her a job in news. Once she started it turned out mostly what they had in mind was typing and answering the phone, same as the others, but like she said, "You make out of something what you put into it." Larry had this little nameplate made with his own money that said SUZANNE MARETTO, STAR REPORTER, and a clipboard with her name embossed in gold. I remember him telling me he'd sneaked in and had it waiting for her on her desk the first day she went to work. That was Larry for you.

Of course I knew about the teen life video project. We all did. "I'm working with these disadvantaged kids," she told me. "I really think I can make a difference in their lives. Isn't that what it's all about after all?"

Plus, if she got her report on the air, of course, that would be a real feather in her cap. You knew one way or another Susie was going to get her big break. You thought maybe this was it.

My sister with a sixteen-year-old hood? Don't make me laugh. Listen, if you want to know the truth, Suzanne was never that interested in guys, period. I mean, she might like to meet a Tom Brokaw or a Dan Rather, but she's not the type to get all excited about, you know, the sex part. I feel funny saying this and I'm only telling you because certain accusations have been made, and I think if people knew what she was like it would help prove her innocence. Jumping into bed with some kid would have about as much appeal for Susie as changing bedpans in a nursing home. It just wouldn't be her thing, you know? Even as far as doing it with Larry was concerned, she told me one time she wished there was some pill you could buy to just get that part taken care of. One time she told me it grossed her out, seeing him all worked up and sweaty, crawling all over her. And he was a nice-looking guy, in reasonable shape, even if he did put on a few extra pounds after the wedding. So you can just imagine how interested she'd be in some skinny kid that smelled of clams or whatever.

I'm not saying there was anything wrong with my sister. She loved her husband. They had future plans. They had a perfect life. She's just not the kind of person who would have anybody murdered because she was in love with somebody else. She was too serious about her career and whatnot. She had too much going for her to mess it all up over some guy.

Jimmy Emmet

It goes like this. It's a school day, but we're down at the clam flats. Place we go sometimes, smoke weed, get laid. Place is dead. You know how it gets. You just want to get some shit going. See what happens.

We get to talking about this video business. Russell's making comments about Mrs. Maretto. "Mrs. Tight Cunt," he calls her. I mean even Russell, I don't think in his wildest dreams he ever figured we'd get anyplace with her. It was Lydia we figured on sticking it to.

The girl had a face like the whole dog pound put together and a body to match. "But it's all the same between their legs," Russell says. You knew she'd never got laid. We figured it was about time somebody tried. I mean we'd be doing her a favor.

So we drive by school right around seventh period, thinking we'll catch Lydia when she's leaving and tell her we want to talk about Mrs. Maretto's video and shit. Then we'll take her down to the beach. Smoke some dope. Jump her bones.

Only when she comes out she's got Mrs. Maretto with her. We were just going to cut out, forget the whole thing, only Mrs. Maretto sees us. No mention of how we hadn't got around to going to school that day. Only she's got the script to the video started and she needs us to give her some reaction shots or something. Don't ask me what that meant.

I'm just thinking I'm going to tell her forget the whole thing. I mean, this was definitely not my scene, you know. "James," she says. "I think you've got a good voice for the job." And then she mentions some guy on Channel 4 that she thinks I look like him.

"Listen," she says. "Since you guys are free now, what do you say we go over to my house and pick up the script and do some work right now? I was just going to give Lydia a ride home anyways."

I say I don't know. Seems like we got someplace to go. Something about Mrs. Maretto, she just got me so nervous. She was too pretty, is all. But Russell there, he grins at her and says, "Sure, that sounds stimulating," or some crap that just about makes me piss in my pants.

"Russell," she says, and she's handing him money. "Why don't you and Lydia just stop by Domino's and pick us up a pizza, and James and I will go on ahead to my condo? Lydia knows the way."

You could tell Lydia wasn't too thrilled about this, and Russell neither. I mean, the guy had a reputation. As they're pulling out of the parking lot I see her buckling her seat belt in Russ's pontiac. I mean, the girl's scared shitless. And me, I never rode in no TV reporter's car before neither.

She puts a handful of Tic Tacs in her mouth, asks if I want some gum. No thanks I say. Turns on the cassette. Some heavy metal shit. That was a surprise.

We don't say nothing, just drive. She's banging her hand on the steering wheel, staring straight ahead. From the side view she kind of looks like when they were handing out noses they forgot to call her name, but she's got these real nice tits, and I'm thinking, man, lucky she can't read my mind right now.

"You like Aerosmith?" she says.

I don't have no stereo or shit, but I just say, "Yeah." You know she's trying to show you how cool she is. Like she's just another fucking slob like the rest of us.

"You have a girlfriend?" she says. I say nobody special.

"Well why not?" she says. "Cute guy like you."

I can't think of nothing to say, so I just sit there with this boner that won't quit.

"Don't you ever go dancing?" she says.

I tell her I don't know how to dance. "Well," she says. "I could teach you." By this time we're at her what-do-you-call-it, condo. "Condom," Russ used to call it. Funny guy.

She unlocks the door. I never been in a place like this. Furniture all matching. Pictures of waves and shit on the walls. Place smells like a fucking flower bed. Little dog comes over and starts jumping up trying to grab my balls. Alls I needed.

She takes off her shoes. The place has this carpet on the floor. I mean it's so soft you wouldn't need no bed to fuck in. You could do it anyplace. Which in the end we did.

She turns on the stereo. It's more of Aerosmith or Motley Crüe maybe. I never listen to the words to songs normally, but you kind of felt like whatever it said right then, that would be her message to me. Which in this case was "Ten Seconds to Love." Jesus Christ, I'm thinking. Is it my imagination or does this chick want to ball me?

But she's just dancing. Not real wild. Just mov-

ing back and forth. Come on, she says. Try it.
You'll never get a girlfriend if you can't dance.

So I take a step forward, then back again. Wishing Russell would hurry up and get here, only also
thinking about what if he didn't. What I could do.
Crazy stuff.

"My husband won't dance," she says. "I mean,
we used to, but now that we're an old married couple he's changed. I guess he doesn't think he needs
to anymore.

"It's funny," she says. "I can remember thinking
once a person was in their twenties they might as
well be a million years old. And now I'm there
myself. Only it feels like it was just the other day
I was putting on my cheering uniform. I was a
cheerleader you know."

"No shit," I say.

"Yeah," she says. Then she does this little routine. Right there in the middle of her living room.
The splits and everything.

"We were division champions," she tells me.
"Third in the state finals. Really gross uniforms
though."

This is when I hear Russ pulling up out front.
It's easy on account of that car needed a muffler
bad.

"Hey," she says. "Where'd you get the tattoo?"
She's talking about this skull I got on my arm. Russ
and me, we all got shitfaced one night and did it.
Never believe anyone tells you it doesn't hurt.

"Little Paradise Beach," I tell her.

"I always wanted a tattoo," she says, and then
she kind of giggles, like she's sixteen or something.
That's when Russ and Lydia walk in with the fucking pizza.

Suzanne Maretto

I guess this is what you get for trying to give a few disadvantaged youngsters the opportunity to do something constructive for once. I mean, I've always been an idealist. I see the potential in a situation. I look for the best in a person. I'm one of those people that thinks the glass is half full, not half empty.

So to me, the way I saw it my high school life video was a great opportunity not only to prove my own abilities in my chosen field, but also to provide these youngsters with a true learning experience concerning the media. More than that even, I saw myself giving them what you might call a positive life experience too, by showing them a positive role model who cared about them and their lives. I was so excited to think about one of these kids maybe using this as the launching pad for a whole new way of life, where they'd reach for something better. Larry and I used to talk about how all it takes is one person who cares to turn a person's life around. I thought maybe I could be that person.

That's one reason why I brought the kids over to our place. I wanted them to see how some people live. Give them a lifestyle to aspire to, beyond spending the rest of their life digging clams and shacking up with their 250-pound first cousin. If you know what I mean.

Yes, I gave James a ride in my car. And went out and bought an air freshener the next day, just to try and get the smell out of my Datsun, incidentally.

The minute he got in the car, he started in with all this what I would call suggestive talk about his various girlfriends and so forth. It's "F" this and "F" that. This is the kind of person we're dealing with here. I guess just because I listen to contemporary music he got the idea anything goes. I set him straight on that, or tried to. Then when we got to my place—Larry's and mine—he walked right over to our stereo and turned it on, without asking or anything. I had an Aerosmith CD in there I remember. To give him something to identify with, you know. Although to tell you the truth, the kind of music I prefer is more along the lines of Billy Joel. I saw Christie Brinkley once, incidentally. When I was in New York City, on a Women in Media workshop, and she walked right past me, just as I was coming back to my hotel. She's every bit as gorgeous in real life.

Anyway. He took off his shoes, right there in the middle of my living room, and started dancing, I guess you could call it. With these very sexually explicit moves. I told him, "James, you need to remember we're here to work on the video project." He asked me if Larry and I ever went dancing. I made a point of telling him what a wonderful marriage we had, and that we did a lot of activities together on the weekends. Dancing being one of them.

He suggested that maybe I could teach him how to dance better. He'd seen a picture I have in my front hall of me in my cheerleading uniform. He said he figured from all my cheering experience I'd be a good dancer. I explained to him that cheering is more a precision sort of thing. People don't understand how much practice and choreography goes into a single cheer. Where dancing is more loose and free. We were the division champions, the year I was captain. Third place in the state, in spite of those awful uniforms. Maroon and yellow, can you believe it?

But I have to admit I told him I'd give him a few pointers sometime. You have to reach them on their wavelength, you know. Reporters such as myself have to show our subjects that we're people too, if we want our subjects to open up to us. I couldn't seem so perfect that he just wouldn't relate. It's a fine line.

He had a tattoo on his arm. A skull or a devil, as I recall. I remember thinking we'd have to be sure he wore something that would keep it concealed, if we had him on camera. Something like that could really give viewers the wrong impression. I wanted people to sympathize with these kids, not write them off as a bunch of hoods, even if that is what they turned out to be.

But the point of the tattoo is how I came to see it. Because after he'd been dancing around my living room, he said he was sweaty, and he took off his shirt. Which is how I came to see the tattoo.

First he took off his shirt. Then he came up behind me, while I was putting something in the microwave. He grabbed me by the arm and turned me around, hard. Then he kissed me. And then Lydia and Russell walked in with the pizza.

Lydia Mertz

The first time I saw Mrs. Maretto I thought she must be a new student, not a teacher. If she was a student, she'd be homecoming queen for sure. She'd be the most popular girl in the entire school.

And her clothes. Everything was always perfect, not just for some special occasion, but just every day. Later on, after I got to know her, she taught me that's an important trick all the newswomen know. You dress every day like you might be going to the White House. Because you never know who might be watching you. You never know when your big chance might come along, so you've always got to be ready.

Say she was wearing a peach-colored dress with little purple specks on it. You knew she'd have purple earrings on. Her shoes might be tan, but she'd have little peach-colored bows on them, or her stockings would have this pale, pale peach-colored tint. And if you looked close you'd see that instead of regular eyeliner, it was purple.

I never would've dared speak to her. But then she came into our health class and explained how she was going to be interviewing kids for this TV special she was taping, and she needed some volunteers to work with her. I wouldn't have thought of it if they were looking for someone that had to be smart or pretty or anything, but they said they wanted just regular kids. It didn't matter who you were. And I guess I figured it would be nice to just hang around her a little, maybe. I never dreamed we'd get to be friends like that. I figured someone like her would have a jillion friends.

Who she reminded me of was Princess Diana. Or that girl in Wilson Phillips, the skinny one. She had this certain way of pulling on her earrings when she was thinking about something. Or when she'd sit down, instead of crossing her legs like most people would do, or just sitting there like a total jerk, forgetting about whether anybody could see your underwear, like I might do, she always crossed her ankles.

You wouldn't believe all the things she knew. Like did you know, when you put on makeup under your eyes, to cover up the circles, you always want to apply it in an upwards direction? "Just because we're young doesn't mean it's too soon to start fighting gravity," she told me.

Never cut your cuticles, or they grow back twice as thick as before. That was another one. There's no such thing as drinking too much water. Keep a pack of Tic Tacs in your purse wherever you go. Whenever you have any doubt about your breath, pop one in. She was the one who told me I should bleach my freckles. I never would've thought of that. She even got me doing these exercises, to uncross my eyes.

"This is great," she said, when I signed up to be in her video. She said she'd be working pretty close with this group for the next couple months and it would be good to have someone she could share some girl talk with.

I told her I never did anything like this before.

She was so nice. She told me that was fine, at least I wouldn't have any bad habits. She said she'd teach me everything she knew, like a big sister. She had this perfume on. In the end she gave me my own bottle, I loved the smell so much. Pavlova. They named it for a famous ballerina.

Of course I heard about Larry right away. For one thing, you couldn't miss her ring. It was such a big diamond. Plus she kept their wedding picture on her desk.

And in the beginning she was always saying how great everything was. How lucky she was, what a romantic guy she married, how he was always bringing her flowers and presents and stuff. One time he surprised her over the weekend with a whole bedroom set. Another time it was a sheepskin cover for the driver's seat in her car. Or they would've gone away to Atlantic City for the weekend. Or to some real romantic hotel in the mountains with a heart-shaped bathtub. They seemed like the perfect couple.

The only other people in the video were Jimmy and Russell. And they were always such total washouts. I mean, they'd show up stoned, or one of them would walk in and say something really dirty about some girl he was with over at Little Paradise Beach the night before. They'd slump into their chairs with their hands on their, you know, between their legs. There was Mrs. Maretto, acting like she was having lunch with a couple of senators, only it was Russell Hines and Jimmy Emmet sitting there instead, scratching themselves. But she always did what she told me. She acted like you never knew who might come in, who might be watching that might make a difference.

This video we were working on. The idea was to

take some kids, meaning us, and get to know us and our inner feelings and stuff. So a big part of the time she wasn't filming us or anything, because like she explained, first we had to really get to know each other, get to be friends. So this one day she invited me to come along with her to her aerobics class, just Mrs. Maretto and me. She let me wear this extra sweatsuit of hers that she said was too big for her, and took me into the special locker room in her health club and everything. We took our showers side by side, which made me feel kind of weird on account of how she was so skinny and I'm such a total mess. I held my stomach in, but still.

After the shower, we went in the sauna together, and then she brought me in this hot tub where you sit naked, just letting the water swirl over you. I'd never been at a place like this before.

All of a sudden I look over at Mrs. Maretto, and she's crying. "Larry doesn't understand why my work is so important to me," she says. "I could never explain my career to him. I come home from a day like this, where we've done all this great talking, and I got such terrific footage. And he doesn't even ask me how it's going."

Well I didn't know what to do. Right in the middle of the hot tub, seeing Mrs. Maretto crying like that. She wasn't going crazy or anything. I mean, she splashed some water on her face right away and that looked like the end of it. But after, in her car, driving me back to my house, it was like she became a different person. She starts telling me all sorts of stuff. How he never wants to party and go to clubs anymore. He just wants to stay home and watch TV. How he wants to have kids and she's still on the pill but she can't tell him because he says it's time to start a family, and Joan Lunden has kids but look how fat she got for a while there, and besides, she was already famous when she got pregnant, so were Jane Pauley and Deborah Norville. Nobody has kids first.

I didn't know what to say, but I didn't have to say anything, she just kept talking. How it was all a big mistake, getting married. She didn't know it would be like this. They used to have a lot of fun, but now she just felt like this old married couple, that their life was behind them. He wants her to be home. But if she's ever going to get ahead, now's the time she has to really hustle. She's in a very competitive business and you can't afford to lose time, when you're twenty-five years old, and you're still just doing cable. And how this video project was supposed to be her big chance, but the boys are such losers she'll never be able to make anything of it, and even if she did, what difference would that make, because Larry would never leave his folks' restaurant, even if NBC called up and offered her "The Sunrise Report." You don't know it, she says to me, but right now is the best time in your life. It won't ever be any better than it is right now, when everything's still ahead of you. Which made me kind of sad myself because how it was right then was not very great. But also, I felt so, you know, special. That she'd be telling me this stuff. That she would talk to me like that, you know. Just like a couple of girlfriends. I would've done anything for her after that.

Chuck Haskell

Larry and me got to be friends in third grade. He was my neighbor across the street. We hung out. Rode bikes, tossed a ball around, the usual. That guy was good at every sport he tried.

Junior high, I started playing bass and Larry picked up the drums. I think he mostly figured it was a way to meet girls. He never was that good. But we had a lot of fun hanging out in his parents' basement fooling around. Us and these two other guys, one on lead guitar and one on rhythm, and there were always a couple of girls hanging around, wanting to shake a tambourine or sing. We called ourselves The Suckers.

Besides the band I couldn't say he had any special interests. I mean, the guy liked to party, liked to go off-roading when he had the chance. He might light up a toke, but nothing major. He was just what you'd call a fun guy. Easygoing. Always ready for a good time. Loved his folks. Loved dogs.

Sure he dated. The guy wasn't queer. But no one serious in high school. He was just having a good time.

After we graduated, Larry started working full time at his folks' restaurant and I got kind of serious with my band. Playing clubs over at Little Paradise Beach, even in the city sometimes. I guess you'd call us your basic metal band. Man, you want chicks? Let me tell you. Get a guitar.

He saw Suzanne at the mall one day, handing out perfume samples, and he said that was it, love at first sight. He still wore his hair long back then. She was real cute, that blond hair and all, although it always kind of freaked me out the way you'd be talking to her and you could see right up her nostrils. They started going out pretty steady right off.

I remember this New Year's Eve party they were at, just a couple weeks after he met her. She had this video camera with her, and she was going around asking people their New Year's resolutions, like it was going to be on the news. Everybody was loaded, basically. Guys were saying stuff like, "Ball a lot of girls," or, "Get laid in a convertible." You get the idea. But Larry, his resolution was, "Find someone really special and settle down." I remember because everybody laughed when he said that. It was such a weird thing for a guy to say, and especially Larry, who always seemed like such a party guy. And he kept going on about all this other stuff, how when he found the right girl, he'd buy her the biggest diamond and a sports car and he'd take her out dancing every Friday night. "I want to make Mrs. Larry Maretto the happiest woman in America," he said. "Maybe the universe." Poor jerk meant it too.

And like I said, a lot of people laughed hearing him talk that way to the camera. Maybe Suzanne did too, I don't know. But I figure he made enough of an impression, because who do I see the very next weekend, dancing over at Shooters? Suzanne and Larry. And he's looking at her like he's hypnotized. Which I guess he was.

After a month or so, I guess she told him they

were getting too serious, she still wanted to date other people. I'd run into Larry at the gym, and he'd be by himself, just mooning around. This was a guy that was ready to party seven days a week, and now he's talking about saving up to make a down payment on a condo. He tells me, "Sooner or later, Chuck, you got to grow up and think about your future." And it's looking like his future is Suzanne, he says.

He buys her a dog—a puppy, don't ask me what kind. Alls I know is, the goddam mutt never shuts up. She names it Walter, after Walter Cronkite. She had a thing about anchormen she told me. Get this: anchormen and heavy metal stars. "One thing I know," he says. "If Peter Jennings or David Lee Roth ever called up Suzanne and asked her to meet them their hotel or someplace, she'd be out of here." Well, my girlfriend's pretty crazy about Axl Rose. But I don't know. You like to think you can count on a person. To hang around.

Anyways. Come April, maybe, Jeannie and me cook up this plan of driving down to Florida. Don't laugh, but Jeannie wants to see Disney World. Larry hears about it and says how about if him and Suzanne come along, they both got vacations coming. So the four of us take off for Orlando, drive all night, make the trip in two days, that's how crazy we were.

Most of that trip we took to Florida is kind of a blur. We worked our way through a lot of six-packs on that trip. All except Larry, actually. Who was never that big of a drinker.

Suzanne on the other hand. She was a real maniac on the trip. I'd never seen her like that before—and never did again, I can tell you. From the minute we left town and hit the highway, it was like she was let out of jail. She wanted to play this Aerosmith tape over and over, super loud. Every other word out of her mouth was fuck. Fucking drivers, fucking traffic, fucking New York Thruway. In the middle of the night one time, somewhere in Pennsylvania, she actually mooned a toll booth operator. You wondered if she was on drugs only she wasn't. Larry hated that stuff. Even grass.

He was so much in love with Suzanne though, I don't think he cared how dumb she was acting. He just kept trying to kiss her, make out with her. We took turns but mostly they sat in the front seat on account of he was in the best shape for driving. One time she actually had her face in his lap, if you know what I mean, while he was in real bad traffic. You could tell he was embarrassed. "Not now, Susie," he'd say to her. "Wait till the motel." She just laughed. Come to think of it, that trip was about the only time I ever heard her laugh.

Once we get there, we do the whole bit. Ride those little boats where they keep singing "It's a Small World." The teacups, the pirate ships, this 3D Michael Jackson movie they got. Suzanne gets her picture taken with Mickey Mouse. Larry buys one of these Goofy hats with the ears flopping down. Suzanne kids him about it, but you can also tell she doesn't like it. She keeps trying to get him to take off the damn hat. He doesn't want to. "You look stupid," she says. "You look like a nerd." He takes off the hat. But right then I remember thinking it was like we're back in third grade and he's this little boy again.

We stayed at this nice hotel, the four of us. Larry was making real good money at the restaurant at this point, so he said, It's on me. Room service, Jacuzzi, cable in the room. The works. Sirloin steak for dinner. Banana daiquiris like they're going out of style. I mean, we were going strictly first class.

Our last night in Orlando, Larry buys Suzanne these two stuffed dogs, and they're hugging each other. Like one is him, and the other one's her. Then we go see the fireworks over at Epcot Center, and Larry and Suzanne are making out pretty good while these fireworks are exploding all over the place. I guess you'd have to say the whole thing was about as romantic as it gets. Must of been, because after, when the four of us were heading back out on the monorail, Larry holds up Suzanne's hand, and she's got this big diamond on her finger. "What do you think of this?" he says. The whole thing makes me a little tense, you might say, on account of Jeannie's right there, and I know she's thinking, OK, where's my ring?

But we took their picture, the two of them, with the stuffed dogs. I've still got the picture, if you want to see it. That's more the way I remember Larry, before he got all serious and cut his hair. Grinning like he always was back in those days.

But the thing that got me—well now, of course, looking back, it seems more important than it did at the time—was the way she only held his hand while Jeannie was taking the picture. The minute the flash went off, she let go.

Joe Maretto

I don't get it. I keep trying to figure out what went wrong. Because at every step along the way, things just looked so good. And now this.

Angela and I went steady right through high school. I never looked at another girl. That's God's truth. She was all I wanted.

I wasn't looking to set the world on fire. She didn't need to find herself or any of that. What we wanted was to take over my uncle's lunch counter, get a nice home, have healthy kids, raise them right. Someday sit in the den and watch our grandchildren open their Christmas presents, knowing we'd done a good job. Does that sound like too much to ask?

We did it by the book. No fooling around before we were married. First two years we were married, we lived with her folks, so we could save up for the down payment. We moved into this house the day Kennedy was shot. Our daughter Janice came along nine months later to the day. And Larry two years after that. So we had our boy and our girl. Angela stayed home with the kids, like mothers did in those days, and I worked like a dog at the restaurant. Nights, weekends, I didn't complain. I had two healthy kids and a lovely wife. They were worth it.

Angela was just great with those kids, you ask anyone. Homecooked meals every night, you could eat off the floor. Janice wanted skating lessons, Angela drove her an hour each way to the rink. Same thing with Larry's Little League games, and then those drums. By this time the restaurant was doing real good, we got our liquor license, put in the bar. Running a restaurant in this part of town, big Italian clientele, I'm not saying we didn't have one or two fellows among our customers that may have been on the wrong side of the law on occasion, but we kept our noses clean. We always ran an honest, family-type establishment. A lot of the time I'd be working, but Angie never missed one of the kids' events at school. And always had the right thing to say if Janice didn't get invited to a dance or maybe Larry struck out or fumbled a ball in the field. Larry may not have been a natural athlete, but you never saw a bigger heart in a player, or a kid that tried harder.

I'm not pretending the teenage years were a picnic. Janice had her skating to keep her out of trouble, but Larry was always such a friendly guy, always going someplace, he had some friends that maybe wouldn't have been Angela's and my choice. Long hair, guitars, drums, the whole bit. Larry's only problem was, he trusted everybody else to be as decent as he was. But I trusted him too. I knew he had his head screwed on right, and sooner or later he'd buckle down and get on with his life. Which he did.

Angela and I had always planned on Larry going to college, but when he graduated high school, he said that was it. What are you going to do? He starts tending bar down at the restaurant. We tell ourselves now's just not his time yet. His time will come.

Then he met Suzanne, and it seemed like that was going to do it for him. That little blonde had enough ambition for the two of them. "You know, Dad," he said to me, not too long after he met her, "Suzanne's going to go far in the world.

"You wait and see," he says. "One of these nights you'll turn on the news in the den and it'll be Suzanne up there on Channel 7. And she'll be coming home to me."

He said being around her gave him a reason to make good himself. He was always telling us things Suzanne told him, how you've got to have a goal in life. Whatever it is you want, you can attain it, if you try hard enough and believe in yourself. You have to think positive. Don't ever doubt yourself, and don't get distracted looking over your shoulder at the other guy. Just be the best you can be, or be all that you can be. Go for it. Now I'm probably getting it confused with some commercial. But you get the idea. And I'm telling you, it all sounded pretty good to Angela and me. It seemed to us like Suzanne was giving Larry just the kick in the pants he'd always needed, to get somewhere.

Six, maybe eight months after he'd met her, Larry comes up to me real serious one night, says he needs to have a talk with me, man to man. He's been thinking about his future, and he's set his priorities. A person can't get anywhere just having fun all the time. He wants to make something of himself, and not just party the rest of his life. All the things I used to tell him, only now he's telling them back to me.

The bottom line was, he'd cut his hair and signed up for a night course in accounting. Told me he wanted to learn the restaurant business properly, so he could take over the place one day and make me proud. "I think I got a future in this line of work, Dad," he tells me. Well, I could have told him that. A person would come into the bar just to be around that boy. You trusted him. He listened to what you said. He'd make you feel he cared, which he did.

"OK, son," I tell him. "Show me you mean business and I'll make you weekend manager come fall. I won't treat you no different than if you were somebody else's boy, though. No special favors. Business is business."

You should've seen how serious he was about the whole thing, right from day one. Sold his drums. Went out and bought a briefcase, and a diamond for Suzanne. Handed out our matchbooks every time he walked in a door. People were telling me they'd run into Larry somewhere and before they could even spit it out to say, "How do you like those Red Sox?" he'd be asking them, "You give any thought yet to where you're holding your company Christmas party this year? You tried my mother's lasagna recently?" He's hiring bands, got a comedy night once a month, ladies night at the bar. And so forth.

Next thing I know, my son's close to doubled our business, Saturday and Sunday nights. No college degree, but the guy's golden. He takes the bonus I give him and puts a down payment on a condo. The place on Butternut Drive.

All this time, Suzanne and Larry were engaged, although what with his night hours and her job at the mall, sometimes days went by he didn't see her. Angela used to say she couldn't understand it how two young people in love could be apart that way. My wife's more what you might call the romantic type. But by my way of thinking, those two kids were just being sensible. Before a couple starts their life together, they need to have their ducks in a row.

He gave her the Datsun for Christmas. Nothing was too good for that girl, as far as my son was concerned.

They were married in July, and she gets this new job at a cable TV station. He kept his nose to the grindstone. They lived just around the corner from us, but we didn't see that much of them to tell the truth. He worked long hours, and she was always out with her girlfriends or taking some workshop on how to improve your vocabulary or get ahead in the career world or some such thing. One time I remember Angela called her up and she couldn't talk because she had this wardrobe consultant there, looking over her clothes, to tell her what she should wear. "I just found out I'm a summer, and all my clothes are winters," she told Angela. "I beg your pardon?" says Angela. She called it getting her colors done. Said it would help her in her career. All I know is, finding out she was a summer cost my son a couple hundred bucks, and that was before she even went out to buy all those new outfits. She told us on television, everything's got to be perfect. "The camera never lies," she said. Well I don't know about that.

Carol Stone

I don't normally watch daytime television of course, but I have to admit I was tuned to "Wheel of Fortune" when Suzanne called to tell us she got the job. I admit it, I think Vanna White is a real sweetheart. Not so much in the brains department, of course—not like Suzanne. But she's got this presence that practically comes right through the screen and into your living room. Like Suzanne always said about Vanna, "She understands the camera. It's like she was born on TV."

"You better be tuned to Channel 37, Mom," my little girl told me. "Because from now on, that's my station."

"You got the job!" I said, and then I started screaming like I'd won the "Wheel of Fortune" myself. Earl was upstairs in his den. To hear me carrying on, he must've thought someone had been murdered.

"I knew you'd get it," I told Susie. "I've been thinking positive." Which was the case. All that morning I was picturing her, sitting at a desk in front of a microphone, reading the news, interviewing celebrities, and so forth. Ever since she was a little girl, basically, I've been visualizing that scene. And now it was finally coming true.

I said she'd be needing some new clothes. We'd

better make a trip over to the mall. Then her father got on the extension. We were both just so proud of her. Who wouldn't be?

We asked her when she was due to start. You didn't want to miss her debut, that was for sure. She explained to us that she wouldn't be on camera right away. A person had to put in their time, getting orientated. They were planning to start phasing out the guy they had reading the news, but he had seniority. They couldn't step on too many toes, you know? But it was only a matter of time before our Susie would be the main on-camera talent. Well, as far as her father and I were concerned, she was always the main talent. The rest of the world just took a little longer to recognize that fact, was all.

"At first I may have to do a little filing and typing," she told us. "But that's only temporary. I just know that once the station manager sees what I can do, he's going to give me my big break."

"Sure you will, honey," Earl told her. Suzanne could always get a man to do what she wanted. No one knew that any better than her daddy. When Suzanne set her mind on something, she got it.

Ed Grant

One thing you've got to understand: This isn't some NBC affiliate I'm running here. We're talking local cable, broadcast range forty, fifty miles tops. Your church holding a bake sale? Senior class got a car wash going to raise money for a trip to Washington? We'll put it on the air. This is the station to watch, if you're interested in a public service short on how to do the Heimlich maneuver, or you want to know if school's going to be cancelled on account of snow.

You couldn't exactly call it a news show, what we produce here. But three times a day we broadcast what we call our community events listing. Such and such an organization is holding introductory square dancing lessons. So-and-so lost their kitten. That kind of thing.

The job I actually advertised was your basic secretary, gal Friday position. Girl I can send over to Dunkin' Donuts for coffee, type me up a memo to the oil company saying they made a mistake on our last bill. That kind of thing. We're talking minimum wage. No benefits. Kind of job you give a gal with nothing but a high school diploma, that's just biding her time till her boyfriend pops the question.

Then Suzanne Maretto shows up for her inter-

view. She's got this little suit on, with a bow at the
neck, and she's carrying a briefcase. High heels,
hairdo like she's just come from the beauty parlor,
a nose kind of like a cartoon character, I'm telling
you, George and me—he's the cameraman, sound
man, all-purpose studio technical crew—we just
shot each other a look when she walked in the door.
Like, I think you got the wrong idea, sister.

I told her that too. First thing she does when she
comes in my office is shake my hand really hard
and look me dead in the eye. You got the feeling
she must've taken a class one time where they told
her that made a good impression, but she didn't
quite get it right. Then she hands me this résumé
she's got listing all her college broadcasting experience, video credits, workshops she's attended, what
have you. She's all wired up, like she's been psych-
ing herself all morning. "Here's a list of my refer-
ences in the media field," she tells me. "I
encourage you to contact any or all of the people
on this list for confirmation of my credentials." Et
cetera et cetera.

I wanted to stop her then and there and explain,
this wasn't that kind of job. She was overqualified.
I was looking for your basic gofer. But it was hard
getting a word in edgewise. You had the feeling she
had this speech all set, and if you interrupted in
the middle she'd have to start it all over again from
the top.

So I just sat and watched her. You had to admire
the kid, she was trying so hard. And here she actually thought I was some kind of media bigwig, and
my two-bit job might actually be a stepping-stone
in her career. I can still remember the gist of how
she finished off her little speech there. "In our fast-
moving computer age," she says, "it is the medium

of television that joins together the global community, and the television journalist who serves as messenger, bringing the world into our homes, and our homes into the world." She had a line in there about Paul Revere, and how the television journalist carries his or her news across the countryside, bringing us all together. "It has always been my dream to become such a messenger," she says—looking me in the eye again. "I look to you now to make that dream a reality." End of speech. You kind of felt like you should applaud.

"Listen, Suzanne," I tell her. "Sounds like you've got a good head on your shoulders. You're ambitious and nice-looking and you got a lot of natural poise. You seem like you're the type that might really have a future in broadcasting. But I got to tell you, you won't find that future here. This place would be a dead end for you. Not a beginning."

Now it's her turn to just sit there. She's got her legs crossed at the ankle. Hands folded in her lap. Briefcase propped against her chair leg. Up close I can see it's imitation leather. And something else I'll always remember. Her makeup, you know that liquid foundation stuff women put on? Up close, you could see how she only applied it out as far as her jaw line, so her neck and under her chin is a different color, like she has on this peach-colored mask. For some reason, seeing that made me kind of sad. Sorry for her, almost. All of a sudden she didn't look so pulled together after all. You had to wonder if maybe she was about to cry.

"Take my advice," I told her. "Go to Mansfield. Go to Troy. Find a network affiliate." It wasn't till later I found out she tried all those places before she came to me. They turned her down.

"I just need to get my foot in the door," she says.

"A person has to start somewhere. I've had this dream all my life, and I've just got to pursue it."

"Working here won't be pursuing your dream, believe me," I told her. "I'm looking for a person to run errands and type memos. Minimum wage."

"At least I'd be working in my field," she said. "Just give me a chance. You won't be sorry."

So I did. And I have to say, she was the best gal friday we ever had, for a while there anyway. Up until she got too big for her britches and started spending all her time trying to get a job in a bigger market. I'll tell you one thing: She was the only gal friday I ever had who showed up to work carrying a briefcase.

Babe Hines

OK. I'll tell you, save you the trouble of asking. My grandmother married her first cousin. Had two sons never grew no teeth and three daughters, one leg six inches shorter than the other. Youngest one, that was my mother. She married her great uncle, on my grandfather's side. Had two sons never grew no teeth, one daughter, leg six inches shorter than the other one, and me. My only problem is, I don't got no money and I don't got no whiskey. Tide's coming out though. Figure on raking me some clams and soon's I get paid, you can bet where I'll be going. You want to know about my son Russell, I'll tell you.

First day Russell goes to that school over there, he's real happy. Riding the bus and all. Comes home and tells me he needs a lunch box. "Every other kid in his class got a lunch box," he says. "Every other kid in his class got a dad that don't rake clams for a living," his mother tells him. "You carry your goddam brown bag and be glad there's Spam in it." Next thing you know, he's got a note in his pocket. Teacher wants to talk to his mother and me. Says our son don't know his alphabet letters. Don't he watch "Sesame Street"?

First problem is, I tell her, we don't got no TV.

Next problem, no electricity. Is she beginning to understand?

Russell, it takes him longer. He wants to go play with these kids, over in Lancaster. Wants to join some kind of team they got over there. Wants a dollar for a field trip, a dollar-fifty to have his picture took. Wants to sell me a Santa candle, come Christmastime. Wants a goddam shirt with some kind of cartoon character on the front, don't ask me why. He says his class is singing these songs over there in the gymnasium, and can we go listen. And what am I supposed to wear to this concert of yours, says his mother. You ever think of that?

Now my boy may not be no egghead, but he finally figures it out. That school over there, they don't have nothing in it for him. What they teach him over there I can tell you in two sentences. Shit happens. Life's a pisshole.

Fourth grade, maybe fifth, note comes home. Ain't I concerned to know my son's been skipping school? Can't say I been losing sleep over it. Red tide now, that's a problem. Two months, clams all over the flats, but who's going to eat them? Then the tide clears and the rain starts. Ever try Purina Dog Chow casserole?

Seventh grade some girl gets knocked up, and they say Russell done it. Boy takes after his old man. At least it's not his sister. Not his cousin, even. Baby's legs come out, both the same. "Not bad," says his mother. "Keep up the good work."

Russell, he's just been marking time till he's old enough to quit school and get his clamming license. And when he does, he won't get no grief from his mother and me. All my boy ever got out of school was a bunch of letters from the principal. That and this TV reporter woman, thinks she can get a couple of young boys to do her dirty work for her, do old hubby in and leave her hands clean for counting the insurance money.

I'll say one thing about Russell. Ain't no liar. Reporter's husband kicks the bucket around February, I guess. Ten days, maybe two weeks later the cops start sniffing around, asking questions. Murder took place on the good side of town, but it don't take long before they make it out to the flats naturally, on account of the reputation, and of course my boy's a prime suspect on account of he's got a record in the first place, plus he knew the guy's wife.

So I ask Russ what's the story here. We may not have your regular father and son talks, but we got our moments, and he tells me straight. "Ernie," he says. "Could be I was in on this murder business."

"Spit it out," I say. So he does. Maybe it was my boy pinned the poor sucker on the floor, but it wasn't my boy that pressed the gun up against his head. Alls he did was rough the guy up a little and drive the car, afterwards, just like she told him to.

And the way I figure it is, someone's gonna tell. And whoever it is that gets to the cops first, that's the one they lay off of, before they start screwing the others. "It's every man for himself out there," I say. "Don't you go treating that buddy of yours any better than he'd treat you, because if you don't squeal on him he's sure to squeal on you."

I take him over to the cops myself. Seemed like what you might call the fatherly thing to do. Of course I knew when we walked in the door what they was all thinking. Here comes a Hines. What'd they do now?

So Russ, he told them. Told them about the girl there, getting her mother's gun, and Jimmy, that fired it. And how the TV reporter dame put them all up to it for her old man's insurance money. For Russ it was money. Jimmy, he got his payment between the sheets. He was sticking it to the reporter, if you can believe it. A college graduate and all, but when the lights go out she's no different from nobody else. Fucks like a mink.

They put a warrant out for Jimmy, and they took my boy Russ into custody too. Well, we figured on that. He'd of ended up there sooner or later, the way he was going. Maybe they'll go easy on him, on account of confessing, and let him out sooner. Not that it's any picnic out here neither.

Earl Stone

She was my little princess. Everybody said it. Even when she was a tiny baby, the age when all most of them want is their mother, our Susie was Daddy's girl. Saturday mornings, Faye would be home watching cartoons or playing with friends or something, and Susie would climb up in my lap and say, "Where we goin' today, Daddy?" It didn't matter if I was going to play a few holes of golf or just head over to the barbershop—she just took it for granted she'd be coming along. She'd sit on the back of the golf cart, over at the club. Afterwards I'd always take her for a soda. "Just you and me, Daddy," she'd say. Those blue eyes of hers. How could you ever say no?

And she never let us down. Some of our friends would tell us about their kids—on drugs or hanging around with a rough crowd, dropping out of school or what have you. Our Susie was honor roll all the way. Never stayed out past her curfew—in fact, she usually got home early. "Ease up," we'd tell her. "Nobody will die if you get a B once in a while." She never gave us one thing to lose sleep over.

You love all your kids. It's not a question of that. But there was always a special bond between Susie and me, I won't deny it. When she was little she used to say when she grew up she wanted to marry me. Once she got older, and she understood things better, she'd still say, "How'm I ever going to find a guy like you, Dad?" Most of the boys in her school were just too immature, she said. Even as a kid, she had goals and ambitions. She didn't have much respect for anyone that didn't. I mean, that girl was going somewhere.

To think of her sitting in some women's prison. It's too much for her mother and me. Especially knowing it's Susie, who has always been so delicate and sensitive. Susie's just not used to that type of people. She wouldn't know how to take care of herself. She's such a little lady.

Janice Maretto

I was working as a waitress at my folks' restaurant one afternoon, just waiting on tables. This was a couple years back, before I went on the road. I was living at home, saving up money to go study in Lake Placid. Larry was playing drums in a band and picking up extra hours at our folks' place between jobs. Which were never that plentiful for him, if you want to know the truth. That afternoon he and a couple of his friends had been hanging out at the mall, I guess. Looking at records and stuff. He comes running in the door and announces to everybody in the whole place, "That's it. I'm in love."

Well it turns out she'd been standing in front of some department store, giving out free perfume samples, and they got to talking. This was a woman's perfume mind you, but Larry went over and said, "Let me have a squirt of that stuff." Then he pretended he liked it so much he came back a couple minutes later, said, "Let me smell it again." I guess he was so knocked out, he ends up buying the biggest size bottle she's got. "Whoever you're buying this for, you must be really crazy about her," she says. "You're right about that," he says. And then he hands her the bottle. Right there in the middle of the store. That was my brother for you. Hopeless romantic.

"You got to meet this girl," he tells me. "She's the most perfect girl you've ever seen. And smart too. This job she's got right now is just temporary, while she finds her niche in the media field. She's going to be the next Barbara Walters."

"Right," I tell him. My brother always had a million girlfriends hanging around. A different one every week. Girls were always falling hard for Larry. It actually bothered him, because he said he hated to hurt their feelings. He liked a lot of people, but there was never anybody serious.

I was curious to see this person, of course. And not particularly impressed, to tell you the truth, when I laid eyes on her. Which I did just a couple days later when he took me over to the mall to meet her for myself.

"The little runt?" I asked him, while we were waiting for her to finish up with some customer. "Suicide Blonde," I called her. Dyed by her own hand.

"She's just so delicate," he said. "So fragile. You look at her and you just want to take care of her. For the rest of your life."

"Listen, Lar," I told him. "I've known girls like her before. I can spot them a mile away. Under that soft voice and those thin lips of hers she's hard as nails, trust me. She's the kind that's had guys falling all over themselves to get next to her all her life."

"She looks so pure," he said. "She looks like a china doll."

"Right," I told him. "You ever try making it with a doll? They don't give a lot back."

He didn't pay any attention of course. All I know

is, my brother, who was too shy to tell a person if they forgot to pay for their drink, was dialing up some florist shop in the Yellow Pages arranging for them to deliver a dozen long-stemmed roses to her that afternoon. For the message, he wanted it to say, "To my future bride. I'd die for your love."

Suzanne Maretto

Larry and I were so very much in love. You know that song about someone being the wind beneath your wings that Bette Midler sings? I had them play that at Larry's funeral. Because that was Larry and myself.

There was something about him so innocent and vulnerable. He was like a little boy in a way, that always saw people in a good light, always seemed happy. "You're too much of a worrier, Susie," he'd say to me. Myself being a more intense kind of individual I guess you could say. Always giving a thousand percent. Always pushing the outside of the envelope, while he was content to go with the flow.

"Just take it easy for once in your life," he'd tell me. "You don't need to work so hard all the time." He was always trying to get me to get an ice cream cone, call in sick for work, skip my aerobics class. I remember the first time we slept together, I got up before him, to make sure I had my makeup on and my teeth brushed, you know. And when he woke up, he said, "You didn't have to do all that. I like you just the way you are."

"You don't know what I'm really like," I told him. I mean, I'm one of those people that feels like they're naked until they put on their mascara. "Believe me," I told him, "if you knew how I really look when I first wake up you'd have nightmares."

"One of these days I'm going to find out," he said. "One of these days I'll get to meet the real you. And I know I'm going to love her just as much. Probably more." That was Larry for you. A real romantic.

Charisse La Fleure

You don't remember them all, of course. No way a person could do that, as many little girls as I get, clattering up and down these stairs in their tap shoes year in year out. I've been doing this going on eighteen years now, and let me tell you, the faces start to blur after a while. Faces of the kids, faces of the mothers. Which year it was you did All-America Salute for the spring show and which year it was Gay Paree. All you can bet on is some kid was sure to get out there the night of the show and freeze. Some kid was bound to start giggling. And somebody had to wave to their mother.

But Suzanne now—I remember her. And would even if all this hadn't happened. There aren't a lot like her around.

Not that she was much of a dancer. She had a cute little body all right. She just didn't have the feel of it. There are some people, they might weigh 300 pounds or they've never taken a dance class in their life, but you put on a record, and they just can't sit still. They've got to move. It's in their blood.

Suzanne was more what you'd call a technician. Every step executed just right. Always knew her combinations. And you never worried about her panicking in front of an audience either, the night of the recital. Far from it. Suzanne loved an audience. From the minute she stepped onstage to the minute she stepped off, it was like the smile was glued on her face.

She took tap from me three, maybe four years, but once they get to be thirteen or so, they lose interest. She switched over to my modeling class in high school. Never could have got too far with it, of course, being as short as she is. But like she told me, no matter what you do in life, it's important to present yourself well. Besides, we all knew her ambition to be on TV. A competitive field like that, a person's got to have everything going for them they can, and Suzanne really seemed like she did too. I mean, this was a girl that said she didn't like to laugh because it gave you wrinkles. This was a girl that wound Saran Wrap around her thighs before she went to bed, to sweat off extra water weight. She told me once she put Vaseline on her teeth to make them shine in the spotlight.

One thing I'll always remember about Suzanne. You never met a person with a worse sense of rhythm. She could be sitting in a crowd of people, all clapping in time with the beat, you know, and she'd be clapping on the offbeat, without fail. The girl just could not get the feel for music.

Applause now, that was a different story. I remember coming into my studio one time and finding her there before class. She was standing in front of the mirror, smiling that fifty-thousand-watt smile of hers, blowing kisses. She never even noticed I was there.

Ed Grant

From the minute she started working at the station, Suzanne was cooking up plans to get on the air. She'd ask why didn't we have a weather girl? Who did the news when Stan went on vacation? What about us doing broadcasts of local high school sports events, with a live host? Only instead of some jock doing it, our gimmick would be, we'd have this cute little former cheerleader standing in the locker room. Viewers would eat it up.

"There's such a thing as budgets," I'd tell her. "You have to spend money to make money," she said. Did we want to make something of this station, or just stay in the same place forever, never changing? Didn't I have any dreams?

That's young people for you. Still thinking they're going to set the world on fire. "To tell you the truth, Sue," I told her, "staying in the same place sounds good enough for me."

She always got to work before me. By the time I'd sit down at my desk, there'd be a memo from Suzanne, all typed up on the computer, in duplicate, with a copy for our marketing guy. One day she'd be proposing a weekend roundup spotlighting upcoming entertainment events. With her as the reporter, naturally. Reviewing plays and movies and so forth. Another time she had the idea for doing this kiddie show in the mornings, with a studio audience of preschoolers, and games and songs and stories for the kids at home to follow along with. And guess who as the hostess?

Her being a newlywed, you might figure she'd just as soon coast along for a while, not push too hard. Save her energy for back at home, you know? But not Suzanne. I remember this one weekend she and Larry took off for some little inn in the mountains, heart-shaped tub, the works. Monday morning, she's sitting at her desk same as always, when I get in to work. Has a whole stack of proposals and memos typed up for me already, ideas that came to her while she was away, she said. Jeez, that's not the kind of ideas that would come to me in a heart-shaped tub.

Couple months after she came to us, I let her read the weather reports, twice a day, just to get her off my back. But once she got a taste of being on the air, she couldn't get enough. Instead of easing up on me, after that she just came on stronger than ever.

So by the time Suzanne came to me with her idea about making a documentary about the lives of teenagers—following this one group over a period of a month or two, hearing what was on their minds—it seemed like my best bet was to make sure she stayed occupied. We had a minicam at the station she could use. She said she'd do all the camera work and editing herself. What did I have to lose? I figured it would keep her out of trouble.

Lydia Mertz

At first I got to admit, I thought Jimmy was a creep.
Like Russell. They hung out and everything, so
knowing the way Russell is, I figured Jimmy would
be the same. But once I got to know him I saw he
was a totally different kind of person.

Like for example, Russell was only into Suzanne's video project to make trouble. You knew
that from the word go. Suzanne knew it too, she
just didn't have any choice on account of nobody
else but me and Jimmy were signed up. And maybe
that's the way it was for Jimmy at the beginning
too. Only with him you could tell it changed. It got
to be he really wanted to do a good job. Partly because he was into it. And a lot because you just
knew to look at him that he was nuts about her.
Who wouldn't be?

So we got to be friends. I mean, he'd never let
Russell know he cared about this, but Russ hardly
ever showed up anymore anyway. And once Russ
wasn't around, Jimmy got into the video, thinking
up ideas and really thinking about the subjects we
talked about, instead of just jerking Suzanne
around like Russell used to. He said if he could be
anything in the world it would be a veterinarian, I
remember that. Before he started spending time
with Suzanne he said he just figured he could

never really do something like that. He always
screwed up. But she made him feel like he was
really worth something after all. She had him
studying these vocabulary lists, so he could talk
better. One time I even saw him reading one of
those little books you get at the supermarket, *The
World's Greatest Love Poems* or something like that.
He didn't want you to know it, but he had a sensitive side. You could talk to him. I'm not saying he
would ever be my boyfriend or anything, but he
was my friend.

Like one time, after we'd been working late on
the video, Jimmy asked me if I wanted a ride. I
couldn't believe it. I mean, apart from that time
when Russell gave me a ride, no guy ever drove me
anyplace. And that time was just because Suzanne
made him. And he's a pig anyways.

But this time it was Jimmy's idea. I mean I knew
he didn't like me or anything, except as a friend.
But still.

He wanted to talk about her. Suzanne I mean.
"Mrs. Maretto," he always called her. He wanted
to know all this stuff like what was her husband
like, and did she ever mention him, meaning
Jimmy. By this time Suzanne and I were real good
friends. Just like sisters. She told me her deep
thoughts. Like that time when I saw her cry in the
hot tub.

And the truth was, she never had mentioned
him, but you could tell he was hoping she had, and
I didn't want to hurt his feelings, so I said yes. I
said she liked him, and she told me he had a lot of
talent.

"I never saw anybody so pretty," he says. "It's
like she's an angel. Everybody else seems like dog-
shit next to her."

Of course I knew that included me, but I'm used to that. I was just proud to be her friend. I mean, imagine a person like her, that was going to be a television personality some day, wanting to be with a person like me? The whole thing was like a dream.

Joe Maretto

You drive yourself crazy, looking back. You ask yourself, Why didn't I see something was wrong? You just lay there, going over and over it in your mind when you're supposed to be sleeping. Angela and me, we both take medication now. It's not like we fall asleep anymore. We just take this pill to knock us out a few hours, so we can get up again in the morning and go through another day of hell all over again.

So I think back to Larry and Suzanne, of course. It's like I'm switching the channels and I'm trying to find the one that has my son and his wife on it, so I can watch for a while. Knowing what I know now. To see if there were clues.

It was after he'd started managing the bar for us weekends. I took him out to the track with me one night. Father-son thing, just the two of us. That's what it's all about, right? We were sitting in the lounge. And he said to me, "She's the kind of girl a man dreams of, Dad." He said just knowing she'd be home at the end of the day waiting for him, he felt like he could do anything. Sell Chinese yo-yos. Run for president. Anything. He was going to be a success in life.

"All I want to know, son, is does she love you and stand by you?" I asked him. "Because pretty won't last forever. Pretty looks good on Saturday night, but where's she going to be Sunday morning? Is she going to be a faithful companion? Will she make a good mother for your children? These are the questions."

"You should see her with that puppy I gave her, Dad," he tells me. "It's like he's a baby. She's got him his own little bed. She even cooks him special dinners."

I asked him if he felt like he could trust her that she wouldn't be looking at other men. With a woman like that you've got to ask the question, because you know other men are going to be looking at her. The opportunity is always going to be there. So the question is, What's she going to do about it? And especially with this career business. She'll be out in the world, maybe even up on the damn television for the world to see. "Your mother was always home," I told him. "And call me old-fashioned, but in my opinion that's where a man's wife's meant to be."

He laughed when I said that. "This is the nineties, Dad," he told me. "Women aren't content anymore to just stay put. They've got to get out there in the world. They've got to have their own identity. It's not enough for them anymore just to clean the bathroom and bake lasagna."

"Your mother did plenty besides that," I told him. "You watch what you're saying, young man." Now I'm sorry it happened but I actually got a little hot under the collar when he said that.

"Don't get me wrong, Dad," he said. "You and Mom have a great marriage and all I hope is Suzanne and I can do that well. It's just different nowdays. The fact is the other night, we were sitting around watching TV and Suzanne made me a batch of brownies. Don't ask me how a person can mess up a box of Duncan Hines where all you have to do is crack an egg and stir in a little water, but she managed it. Chocolate flavored cardboard, that's what came out of the oven."

"She can learn," I told him.

"Right," he says. "She can learn how to put a frozen dinner in the microwave and take the pizza out of the box. Lucky we own a restaurant."

I mean, we were just kidding around.

Then he gets real serious, and I almost think there's tears in his eyes. "You don't know how wonderful she is," he tells me. "And knowing a girl like that would choose me makes me feel like I've got something to live up to. Like I've got to buckle down and make something of myself down at the restaurant. I'm going to spend the rest of my life making her happy she chose me. I'll never let her go."

Janice Maretto

Of course all he ever said about Suzanne to our parents was what a great person she was, and how much in love they were. But he told me—back when they were first going together—she was real horny too. I mean, these two didn't just do it in the backseat of his car. Larry told me they used to make love in the storeroom at the restaurant, and at the beach, at night, and one time she even took him up to her room at her parents' house, with them right downstairs watching TV. "She looks so prim and proper," he says. "But you should see how she gets. She's so wild and passionate." He was actually worried about keeping her satisfied. That's why he came to talk to me, in fact. I mean, we never had a conversation like this before, but he said he was just so anxious to please her. He wanted my thoughts on how to keep a woman happy. "Just be yourself," I told him. "If that's not good enough for her, that's her problem."

Back when they were dating, they used to go to this place in Woodbury, The Hot Spot, where you could rent a hot tub room for an hour, with a CD player, a TV, VCR, the works. I guess every room at this place had a different theme, like Hawaiian, Wild West, The Big Apple. He called me up this one morning. "You should have seen Suzanne and me in Jolly Olde England," he says. She brought along a video of *Beaches,* her favorite movie. They had champagne and strawberries. "You wouldn't believe some of the things we did, Jan," he told me. "I thought they only did that stuff in the movies."

Another time, I guess he took her into Boston to see a Red Sox game. Not that she was this big sports fan, but of course my brother was, and you got the impression she figured this was a cool thing to do—like afterwards, she'd enjoy working it into the conversation, "When I was at Fenway last week."

It was kind of a chilly day, late in the season, so I guess he brought along a blanket to put over them, and she starts unzipping his pants under the blanket, feeling him up. Anybody knows Larry knows when he's watching a game that's what he wants to do, watch the game. Plus I guess he felt pretty self-conscious. I mean this was in the bleachers and everything. Even with the blanket over them it must've been pretty obvious what was going on. He tried gently to get her to lay off, but she didn't want to. She told him this story she heard, about this ball game at the Skydome in Toronto. I guess there's this hotel there, where some of the rooms look right out over the ballpark. And this one time—a night game—the Blue Jays were playing, and all of a sudden you can feel the attention of the crowd shifting from the diamond to this one picture window in the Skydome hotel, where this couple's going at it, with the lights on. Before long you got—what?—50,000 people maybe, all eyes on these two people screwing their brains out, and hardly anybody's even following the game anymore.

Larry told me, when he heard that, he was thinking how awful that must've been for those two people, when they found out. How embarrassing. But for Suzanne the point of the story was how she'd like to drive up to Toronto some time and catch a game. She told him she wanted one of those special rooms in the Skydome. "Just think," she told him. "We'd be more famous than the ball players."

Chuck Haskell

After the wedding I didn't see so much of Larry. I'd call him up to go four-wheeling or just to hang out, but he'd be tied up, furniture shopping. "Married life," he'd say. "What are you going to do?"

He didn't talk about her that much, and she wasn't around that much either, from the looks of it. I'd stop by and he'd be home watching a game or working on his truck but not her. She'd be out shopping with her girlfriends or over at her mother's. He said he figured she felt more at home at the mall than in their bedroom. He joked about it, but you know, it made me wonder. Especially when she started working on that video of hers, and it seemed like she was always off someplace with her students.

Who ever knows what goes on behind closed doors? But if I was taking bets I'd have to guess things weren't that hot between the sheets anymore over at Butternut Drive. A girl like her, she just figures she can ride her face around for the rest of her life. It's the other ones, that don't seem like they've got so much going for them, that really put out for you. Her, she'd always be wondering how her hair looked.

What do I know? Larry never said boo. I mean, I knew the guy eighteen years, but we never talked about personal stuff. It was always, you know, how do you like those Sox? How do you like those Celtics? He could be hemorrhaging to death and he'd tell you, "I'm fine. How's by you?" That's guys for you.

Everything just looked so perfect over there. I mean, the condo and the dog and all the trips they took, and her always dressed so fashionable, and their house always neat, and him doing so good at the restaurant. They were making plenty of money. Had a nice home. They just looked golden. I remember saying to them one time—one of the few times I saw them both together—that they could be in a TV commercial. She looked like she might be one of those wives that uses Ivory soap, and her husband writes in to the company to say how soft her hands are. I said someone should write in to some company about them. And the next week he told me she'd done it. Got him to write in to this shampoo company, to say how great her hair smelled. "Who knows," she said, "they might put us in a commercial."

I asked her one time if she ever heard back. She said yeah, but all they did was send her a free bottle of conditioner.

Angela Maretto

I'll tell you what kind of a boy this was. This was a boy that one time, when he was eleven years old, took his paper route money and sent it to Africa for the starving children. This was a boy that, the night of his senior prom, he stops by the nursing home with his date to visit his grandmother. You want to talk Mother's Day? I'll give you Mother's Day. This boy, on Mother's Day, sent me one long-stemmed rose for every year he'd been alive. Last year it was twenty-three. Now that's as many as it will ever be. You tell me—does a mother get over something like that?

Even when he was a baby he was good. Slept through the night, first night we brought him home from the hospital. Even before we had him toilet trained, he used to apologize when I had to change his diaper. I kid you not. "Sorry, Ma," he'd say to me. His big sister taught him how to say, "Better luck next time." "Better next time," he'd say to me. Could you be mad at a boy like that?

Oh, he was an altar boy. But he never planned on being a priest, like so many of the other altar boys. Even when he was five, six years old, and people would ask him, "What are you going to be when you grow up?" his answer was always the same. "I'm gonna cook spaghetti and pour beer at

my pop's restaurant." Never a fireman. Never a
policeman. My boy was going to make the best egg-
plant parmigiana in town.

Larry never gave us trouble with girls. He was
always a gentleman. The girls loved him, naturally—who wouldn't? And he liked the girls too.
But like he always said, "You and Pop come first,
Ma. Any girl for me, she's gotta be a girl for my
whole family."

Now I won't say we didn't have our moments.
What parents don't, I ask you? One time we got a
note home from school, Larry's gotta do his homework. He says you don't need algebra to work in a
restaurant. So his father and me had a talk with
that boy. "You sure you don't want to go to college,
Lawrence?" I ask him. "Because you know, you say
the word, your pop and I will come up with the
money, same as we did for Janice's skating." We
may not be wealthy people, but our children never
lacked. Never was there something they asked for
that we didn't provide. And never did they abuse
our good faith either.

But no, he wasn't a college man, and we made
our peace with that. We knew our Larry would
earn an honest living at our place, and one day it
would all be his. The customers adored him. Not
just the young girls but everyone. "How's Larry
doing?" they'd ask me, if a couple weeks went by
they didn't see him. "You should see my grand-
daughter that's visiting from college," they'd say.
"She'd be a nice girl for Larry."

He was always polite. Never made them feel like
they weren't good enough. Only he kept his dis-
tance. Never got serious once, until she came along.
The little blonde. A model, he called her, meaning

she gave out free samples at a store. Not Italian, that's for sure.

"I got to tell you something, Ma," he said to me one time, when the two of us were tending bar, a week, maybe two after he met her. "This is the girl I'm going to marry." By this time he'd sent her the roses, took her out for dinner, but you didn't want to think it was serious. I mean, these two had nothing in common. P.S., she was older. Two years. Not that she liked to let on.

"She's a cutie all right, Larry," I told him. "Reminds me of Nanette Fabray." I mean, you don't have to be Sigmund Freud to know it's a bad idea to try and discourage them. That only fans the flames. "I bet she's a college graduate too," I say. Her father running a car dealership and all.

Oh yes, he says. She went to college over in Somerset. Honor student, sorority sister, the works. She's heading someplace, this one. We'll be hearing from her, you can just bet on it.

"Let me tell you something, son," his father tells him. "The cute ones, the pretty ones, they aren't always the best bet for the long haul. Look for a woman you can grow old with."

"What are you saying, Joe?" I ask him. "You saying I didn't ever cause your heart to skip a beat, round about 1962? You telling me all I ever was to you was somebody's ma?" I can say these things to my husband on account of what a good relationship we got. I know he's crazy about me. He knows I know it too. I just like to give him a hard time now and then.

"You're the exception, Angela," he tells me. "Everybody knows that. But how many times in a century is a boy gonna find a beautiful woman that's a beautiful mother too? And since I found one, how many more times can it happen? Tell me the odds lightning's gonna strike twice."

"Well," he says, "all I know is this is the girl for me, Dad, and come summer, you'd better get your good suit cleaned because there's going to be a wedding."

Couple weeks later he brought her by the restaurant. You could tell he was nervous taking her around. He shows her the baseball trophies from the team we sponsored, shows her the ice-making machine. Takes her into the cooler even. "Here's the ladies' room," I hear him telling her. "Here's a picture of my sister, the year she placed second in the eastern division junior figure skating competition, compulsory figures. . . . One time we had Tony Conigliaro sitting here, right on this very bar stool," he says. "And you know the guy that does the muffler commercials, that says 'You show us a better deal, we'll install your muffler free of charge'? He sat right there in that corner booth."

You could tell she was trying not to laugh, when he said these things. This was a worldly type woman. She probably never met a boy like Larry, that couldn't tell a lie to save his life. She probably thought he was nuts.

I'm still trying to figure out why she decided to marry him. I mean, no question, she could've found other guys. I'm not saying Larry wasn't a wonderful catch. Best husband a girl could ever find for herself. And it's true, he worshiped the ground she walked on.

But what was she looking for out of him? That's the question I lay awake nights asking myself. Why'd she have to go and marry my son?

Suzanne Maretto

The first thing I thought when I met Larry was Tommy Lee. The drummer for Motley Crüe, you know? Not that Larry wore an earring or snake tattoos naturally, but he had those same dark, brooding eyes, and he used to wear his hair pretty long. Before he got serious about the restaurant business and everything. He even used to play drums, although he sold his drum set when we got engaged, to pay for my ring.

As a matter of fact, people used to say I was a little like Heather Locklear, too. The one that used to be on "Dynasty"? She's Tommy's wife. And of course I took that as a compliment. Her eyes are brown and mine are blue, but I see what they mean. She's also blond of course, and petite like myself. And like Heather and Tommy, Larry and I were two individuals from very different walks of life—her, this major television personality, hanging around with people like Linda Evans and John Forsythe, and Tommy Lee, with a ring in his nose, and making these videos that are so crazy they won't even show them on MTV. But underneath, you can tell he's just a big teddy bear, who loves Heather to death. If you've ever read any interviews with him, you know how much he keeps her on a pedestal.

Larry was the same way about me. I mean, from the day we met he just worshiped me, and showed it. He was an old-fashioned guy in lots of ways: sending flowers, opening car doors for you. That kind of thing. He used to say, no matter how long we were together, he wanted to make every night of our life like it was our senior prom. He was a true romantic.

The first time I introduced Larry to my parents, I know my father, for one, was a little shocked. Not just the hair—which was pretty hard for my dad to understand, being an old Air Force man—but Larry's whole carefree attitude. He was the kind of guy that would say, "Hey, you want to jump in the car and drive to Florida?" And he meant it.

Myself having been a very different sort of individual all my life, that aspect of Larry was actually very refreshing. I guess you could say I'd been so focused on my career and so forth, I hadn't always taken time to stop and smell the roses. One thing Larry really knew how to do back then was have fun. It was like we were a couple of kids. In fact, I felt like more of a kid when we started dating— and I was in my twenties then—than I had when I actually was a teenager. Young at heart, I guess you could call him. He was one of those individuals who reached for the brass ring in life.

I could've chosen to marry someone more successful in the career arena. Which frankly was what my parents advised me to do. Myself having a college degree and so forth, and Larry coming from what you might call a more ethnic background. "You don't know what you're getting into, Suzanne," my dad said to me, when Larry and I first started getting serious. "His family could be mixed up with the Mafia or who knows what."

That's my dad for you. No matter how old I am, I'm still his little girl. Nobody was ever going to be good enough for me, as far as he was concerned.

It was ironic, what happened in the end. I mean the way Larry turned into this superresponsible, straight, business-orientated person that believed in all my parents' goals of home and family, working hard and getting ahead. He even took up golf. That wasn't the Larry I knew. Although, of course, I was so proud of him, to see him get so motivated.

We used to go dancing a lot. Friday nights, when he wasn't working, we'd head over to this club we liked, Dandelion's, where they had a good DJ and a nice crowd. Certain places you go—Little Paradise Beach, for example—the music may be great, but there's an element that goes there—how do I put this? They may be perfectly nice people, but they don't have a lot of education, don't have goals. All they can think of is drinking and partying. While Larry and I, and the couples we socialized with, had our eyes on the future. We wanted a little something more out of life than to get drunk every weekend and come into work Monday morning with nothing more to say than how much beer they drank Saturday night. You know the type.

But at Dandelion's you knew you'd rub shoulders with a different kind of clientele. These were people who skied and played tennis and went into Boston to have their hair cut. When Phil Collins was on tour, a bunch of us hired a limo to drive us down to Worcester for the concert. We may have been young, but we cared about the better things. One couple ran a clothing store. Another girl we used to see a lot used to be an executive assistant at *Vogue* magazine in New York City. She rode up on the elevator one time with Paulina. The model?

Who is married (speaking of unlikely romances) to Ric Ocasek. And have you seen what he looks like? We're not talking Rob Lowe. You think about the two of them maybe having kids someday, and you have to worry what they'd look like. But yet, they're so much in love.

Larry and I also came from two very different worlds. There he was, from this kind of old-fashioned, traditional Italian family. You've met his mother, right? She's a sweetheart, but you know what I mean. Every time some cousin of hers gets a cold, she publishes one of those letters to St. Jude in the newspaper. She served me this bowl of soup one time, some special recipe from the old country I guess. And when I got to the bottom, what do you think I found lying in my bowl? A chicken's foot. Claws and all.

Whereas my family is what you'd call up with the times. My mom is a career woman. She takes care of herself, keeps in shape. The two of them fly to Las Vegas every winter. Take in a show on Broadway at least twice a year. *Les Mis*. Liza Minnelli.

We had our two sets of parents over for dinner at our condo together one time. A very elegant meal. Martha Stewart. Expensive wines, appetizers—and I don't mean chips and dip. You could see the Marettos were out of their element. In fact, I have to say, the entire evening was uncomfortable. Our families had so little in common. But for Larry and myself, our love formed the bridge. He wasn't just my husband. He was my best friend.

He was a more laid-back sort of individual than myself. He was the kind of person that if you gave him a choice between going to a concert or staying home and watching the Celtics on TV, he'd just as soon choose the game. But once you got him out, you knew how much potential he really had. That's why we were a perfect couple. I had the motivation that acted as a catalyst for him. He used to say being married to me made him want to accomplish more for himself than he did before. He started listening to things like the Pachelbel Canon. Buying socks that weren't white. Taking these accounting courses and restaurant management seminars. He had a tape player installed in his Firebird so he could listen to motivational tapes. This was a guy that used to live from one party to the next, and now his whole orientation became getting ahead in the business, buying a home, life insurance, taking up golf even. Life's funny. I married a rock drummer and ended up with a younger version of my dad.

Carol Stone

Suzanne called me up one morning. Things had quieted down by this time. She was working hard down at the station, Larry was managing the restaurant on weekends and taking an accounting course at night on top of that. They were busy with the puppy of course, always the puppy. And they'd bought this cute living room set, sectionals. White, naturally. Try talking a pair of newlyweds out of a white sofa, that haven't started a family yet. They just can't picture what lies ahead.

"I got this great idea last night while I was lying in bed," she said. "I'm going to give a dinner party. For the two sets of parents. You and dad, and Larry's folks."

Now, my daughter was never exactly Betty Crocker. I'll never forget her making quiche this one time, back when she was in high school. She just stuck a hunk of cheese on top of the prebaked pie crust and poured a little cream and egg mixture on top. Said she figured it would melt and blend in, once she put it in the oven.

But the other thing about Suzanne is, once she sets her mind to doing something, she does it. And not halfway either. So you knew it wasn't going to be any take-out pizza dinner she'd be serving us, or even spaghetti or hamburgers. You knew you were in for a gourmet experience.

"I don't know, Susie," I told her. "Joe and Angela seem like nice people, but they don't have that much in common with your father and I." I mean, Joe Maretto wasn't exactly the kind of person you could sit down with and say, "Did you read that article in yesterday's *Wall Street Journal*?" I doubt the man has held a golf club in his whole life, unless maybe he keeps one behind the bar at that restaurant of his, to use on unruly drunks. The other thing I didn't want to mention to Suzanne was, these people are Italians. They know their food—as you have only to look at Larry's mother to realize. I didn't want to see Suzanne getting in over her head. Didn't want to leave her open to criticism, you know, when this really wasn't her forte.

"Don't worry, Mom," she said. "I already bought a recipe book. It's by this woman named Martha Stewart who's a real expert at entertaining. There's plenty of pictures."

So it was all set. The four of us were going to Larry and Suzanne's Columbus Day. This was two, maybe two and a half weeks' notice, but you know Suzanne. Always the perfectionist. I doubt a day went by she wasn't on the phone to check on some detail or other. Could she borrow my crystal wineglasses? How about Grandmother Miller's lace tablecloth? What did I think of pear-filled crêpes and barquettes with leek chiffonade for appetizers? I won't even get started in on telling you all we went through over the main dish: should it be Italian, knowing the Marettos, plus the fact of it being Columbus Day? Or did she want to steer clear of Italian food? In the end she went with a pesto—goat cheese—sun-dried tomato lasagna recipe of Martha

Stewart's, with raspberry orange soup for the first course. She was going to have these little individual radicchio leaves with smoked quail and currant sauce and coriander on the side.

What kind of wine? She went out and bought a book about that. I can't even remember what she ended up going with, red or white. But whatever it was, you knew it was the right choice.

Day of the dinner, Suzanne was a nervous wreck. This is just the six of us mind you—all family. But that didn't matter to our Susie. She might as well have been cooking for President Bush. Everything had to be just so. And it was.

Larry was so proud of her. Anyone could see that. "Can you believe my wife?" he said, when he was taking our coats. "All I can say is, Julia Child better look out or she could be looking for a new job."

"How about that idea?" said Earl. "You ever think of introducing a cooking-type show on that cable station of yours?"

Suzanne was looking a little tired. She didn't say anything. She still had tarts or something in the oven she had to keep checking on.

So we all sat ourselves down on this new sectional sofa of theirs. His mother couldn't get over the color. "All I can say is, the first thing I buy you, when your first child is born, is a set of plastic slipcovers," said Angela.

"This is the new style, Ma," says Larry. "You don't put slipcovers on a sectional."

"Yeah, well furniture styles may change," she told him. "But I'll tell you one thing that doesn't, and that's what babies do in their diapers. And it doesn't always stay in their diapers either."

Larry serves us cocktails. They have swizzle

sticks, napkins with their names printed on the corner even. I tell you, these kids had thought of everything. "So, Pop," he says. "How's it going down at the restaurant?"

"Pretty much the same as when you were there yesterday," his father says. Then we all just sit there.

"Have you lost weight, Angela?" I say. Not that she was looking exactly svelte, but you wanted to keep the conversation going.

"Who knows?" says his mother. "I don't step on the scale, the scale doesn't step on me."

"Speaking of weight," says Earl, "have you seen that Delta Burke, on 'Designing Women'? First she gets married, and next thing you know the woman's bursting out of all her clothes. Every week you tune in the show, she's a little fatter. Good-looking woman, too."

"Think that would ever happen to you, honey?" says Larry, and he gives Suzanne a pat on the rear. One thing I happen to know Suzanne never liked is that sort of thing. Certain gestures you can save for the bedroom, you know?

Suzanne doesn't say a word. She's dishing out the soup I think.

"Well I just want to say for the record, that if Suzanne ever did pack on a few extra pounds like that Delta Burke, I'd love her just as much. There'd just be more to love, is all."

"In my business you have to be very careful about your diet," says Suzanne. "The television camera puts an extra ten pounds on everyone. So you can't let your guard down for a minute."

"Well I for one plan to let my guard down tonight anyways," says Larry. Who looked like he'd been packing on a few extra pounds himself since the wedding, if you want to know the truth. "Can you believe the spread my girl put on for you guys?"

We sat down to eat. I tell you, this was quite a meal. Though I'm not sure whether the Marettos fully appreciated it.

"Skinny little buggers, these quail," says Joe. "I guess they were out of chicken, huh."

Lydia Mertz

We were at the mall this one time. Just hanging out, you know. Looking at the records and stuff. We're walking past this store called Victoria's Secret that sells fancy lingerie, and Suzanne says, "Hey, let's go in here."

It was just for fun, you know. I wasn't in any rush to get home, hear my mom yell at me for not spending more time watching TV with her or something. Suzanne said Larry was off riding ATVs with his friends. So why not?

I never was in a place like this before. First of all, the way it smelled, which was all flowery from these baskets of potpourri they put all over the place, and perfumes and soaps. Everyplace you look there's lace pillows and satin and flowers. Real feminine. There's negligees and silk robes and these slippers with feathers all over the front. If you want to look at yourself, it's not a regular mirror, they've got this mirror with gold all around the edges.

I'll give you an example. Say you wanted a bra. You wouldn't just look for your size and go pay for it. They've got twenty million styles, all different colors, with lace and pearls stitched on in different places, all hanging on these special gold hangers, and if you can't find something you like hanging up, they have special drawers with sachets and more bras in there. They even have that old-fashioned kind, like Madonna sometimes wears, that's strapless but it fastens in the front and it goes all the way to your waist. I wouldn't wear something like that, but it looks really good on her.

"Come on, Lydia," Suzanne says to me. "Let's get you a pair of panties. You choose anything in the store. My treat."

I tell her I don't need anything. I mean, these panties cost nine, ten dollars. Each. "I got enough underwear," I tell her.

"But nothing like this," she says. "You feel different when you're wearing lingerie like this. You feel beautiful."

"It's not like anybody'd even see it," I say. "Except my mom, and she'd just figure me having underwear like that must mean I was going all the way with someone and then she'd give me a hard time about it."

"So hide them," Suzanne says. "Let it be your secret. Everybody needs a few secrets in their drawer." That's when she shows me the garter belt. "This is what I'm getting," she says.

I didn't even know what it was exactly, except you see them in pictures sometimes. Only I don't look at those kind of magazines.

She tells me it's how they held up their stockings in the olden days. Before panty hose.

It makes me feel kind of weird, knowing she's getting the garter belt. It wasn't the way I pictured her.

"You'll understand someday, Liddy," she says to me. "When you meet someone."

It was pretty. It had these little pink roses stitched on the place where you hitched the stockings on, and little silk ribbon bows. They wrapped it up in pink tissue paper for her and put it in this little box with flowers on it, like it was a present for someone. Only it was for her.

There was this man and woman there at the store, same time as us. About the same age as Suzanne and Larry. She wasn't as pretty as Suzanne, but you could tell he was crazy about her. He kept picking out bras and stuff for her to try on. I mean, he'd run his fingers over the fabric like he was testing it or something. You almost felt embarrassed watching him, it seemed so personal. But you also had to envy her. Knowing there was someone that felt that way about her. Even though she was a little chunky.

They were in front of us at the counter where you pay. I guess the stuff she bought must've come to a couple hundred dollars, the amount of panties and stuff she was getting. After they added it all up, he just handed the girl his charge card. She kissed him—french kissed—right there in the middle of the store.

"He really knows how to treat a woman," Suzanne said to me. "But I bet you they aren't married."

Chuck Haskell

Thursday afternoons, Larry and I used to go down to the Y, play a little pickup basketball, take a shower, go out for a couple of beers. It wasn't a team. Just a bunch of guys blowing off a little steam.

I remember this one time in particular. We're sitting in the sauna after the game. Us and these other two guys we used to play with sometimes. Single guys, like me.

"Man, did I hit the jackpot last night," one of them says. You know the way guys talk. "Chick could've kept going all night, like she hadn't been laid in a year."

So then I say something about the girl I'd been out with, you know? I mean, half of the stuff you say is made up, and everybody knows it. You just like to talk big. It's part of the game, same as dribbling the ball or making foul shots. Just a bunch of guys screwing around, no big deal.

So this other guy, the first one, he starts telling us how this particular chick liked to do it at her parents' house when they were downstairs watching TV. And this other guy starts talking about this chick he knows that likes to be tied up. I say my girlfriend likes it the normal way, "just often is all." "How often?" says the guy with the tied-up girlfriend. "Three, four times a night," I say. "Man, it's a sacrifice, but what can you do?"

All this time, Larry's just sitting there, not saying much. Then this one guy, he turns to Larry and says, "So, how's it feel to be an old married man? Your old lady keeping you happy?"

And then he does a funny thing. He gets up off the bench and wraps his towel around him. "Why don't you guys just grow up?" he says. "You think that's all there is to life? Let me tell you, there's more to it. There's such a thing as love and commitment." I don't remember the exact words, but that was the gist of it, anyway. Real heavy and serious. Like the guy couldn't take a joke. Which generally he could.

After he left, Buzz, this buddy of ours that did it at his girlfriend's parents' house, he turns to me and says, "Jeez, what's with him?"

Richie, this other guy, says to blow it off. "Sounds to me like he just hasn't been laid in a while," he says. "Just because the package looks good doesn't guarantee it'll be so great on the inside."

Angela Maretto

There was this time the kids came over for dinner. No special occasion. It was just something we did every now and then. Joe made rigatoni and I baked an almond cake that was always one of Larry's favorites. She didn't bake, herself. Not that I'm blaming her for that. There are worse crimes. As we all know.

Anyway, they came over the house five o'clock, maybe five-thirty. Larry and Joey got a beer and went in the den to watch the end of the basketball game. She and I were in the kitchen. I mean with Janice off on the road with the Ice Capades it was like Suzanne was my own daughter. We'd talk about everything. If she was wondering should she cut her hair or something, she'd call me up. Did I think blue curtains would be nice in the bathroom? She'd sooner call me than her own mother.

We were having a glass of wine. There wasn't much fixing to do for this dinner—just pour the dressing on the salad, that was it. So we were just sitting there at my cooking island, sipping our wine and talking. And I said to her, "Have you two given any thought to starting a family?" Their anniversary was coming up and all. They had this beautiful condominium, and he was doing so well down at the restaurant. They were really on their way.

"Oh," she said, "I don't know about that. It's so complicated, you know."

Well no, actually, I didn't know it was so complicated. It always seemed pretty simple to me. You love someone. You get married. You have a family. "What do you mean 'complicated'?" I said.

"With my job and all," she told me. "In my field a woman with young kids has two strikes against her. Especially when she's just starting out."

I asked her what she meant. "Say you're covering a big story like, maybe, Princess Stephanie's getting married over in Monaco," she says. I'm trying to act like I know who this Princess Stephanie is— which I don't. "Right," I say. "I'm with you so far."

"So they have to send—in addition to the on-camera talent—a hairdresser and a wardrobe person, and a camera and sound crew. A satellite. You wouldn't believe how many people it takes to put together a major network news remote broadcast.

"And what if the reporter has a baby? Does she leave it home? Maybe, but can you imagine how expensive it gets hiring that kind of round-the-clock help? Not to mention, who do you find that you can trust?

"Or say you bring the baby along. But then he gets chicken pox or something, and he's throwing up all over the place. Maybe he even gives his mother chicken pox, and she's got to go on camera in front of millions of people, with these chicken pox all over her face.

"Or maybe you haven't had the baby yet. You're just pregnant. And there's all these people at the wedding, the jet set, in their designer dresses and everything, and you're big as a house. Do you remember how Jane Pauley looked when she was cov-

ering the wedding of Prince Charles and Lady
Diana? It was gross."

"Gross," she said. I still remember that part.

"Well I don't know," I said. "I always loved how
it was when I was expecting. I never felt so
fulfilled."

"But that's not even the worst," she says to me.
"The worst is after the baby's born, when you
haven't lost the weight yet. And you've got all this
blubber and these boobs out to there, without even
the excuse of being pregnant anymore." Then she
mentioned this other woman I never heard of,
Christina Ferrari. I remember her name because it
was the same as the car. Christina Ferrari used to
be a cover girl, she said. In addition to hostessing
some TV show. Don't ask me what.

After that I didn't know what to say.

"Larry and I really value our freedom to pursue
our other interests," she told me. "Couples that are
tied down to kids can't just up and take off for the
weekend to go skiing or something." But I knew
she couldn't be talking for my son when she said
that part. Because you just knew Larry was dying
to be a father.

"Well," I said, "there's a time and a place for
everything." And around then was when Joey came
in saying whatever happened to dinner? We didn't
talk about it anymore, and I guess I just figured,
she's young, you know. She'll come round.

After supper, I remember, we were looking
through some of our old home movies. Joe had just
brought all our old Super 8s in to have them trans-
ferred to video. Janice's ice shows, and Larry in his
first jv basketball game and so forth. There was
this one of me giving Larry his bottle when he
couldn't have been more than six, eight months old.

And Larry puts his arm around Suzanne and says, "Someday that's going to be us, honey." And she looks at him and says, "Listen. If you wanted a baby-sitter you should've married Mary Poppins."

Suzanne Maretto

They say Connie Chung left her job with CBS voluntarily, but I have my own theory concerning what happened there. This whole story that it was her biological clock ticking, and she wanted to devote herself full time to getting pregnant and having a baby. It just doesn't add up. In my opinion, the network wanted to get rid of her, and this was just their way of giving her a graceful exit.

Who would give up a career like that to have a baby, when they could adopt? That's what Barbara Walters did, and look how fabulously everything worked out for her. As she herself puts it in her autobiography—which is one of the most inspiring books I ever read, incidentally—whenever she has any regrets about the time she missed, staying home with her little girl, seeing the first steps, whatever, she remembers: If she'd been home watching those first steps, she would have missed out on her historic interviews with Henry Kissinger and Barbra Streisand and that Egyptian president, what was his name. The one that got shot. You can't have everything. Life is full of trade-offs. But when all is said and done, who would really trade a bunch of dirty diapers and drool-soaked clothes for a career like that?

Not that I was closed off to the idea of having kids with Larry. Listen, nobody gets more gooey over kids than me. Little booties, little smocked dresses, all the cute stuff they make now. It's enough to make you want to adopt a whole orphanage.

Which was always an idea of mine, to tell you the truth. As I told Larry, why do we need to have our own baby when the world is so full of kids who need good homes? Just a while back, I saw this special about Romania, and I want to tell you, you wouldn't believe what's going on there. I mean, it was almost too disgusting to watch. Some of the children were older or handicapped, and naturally you have to be very careful with a country like that, that you aren't getting one with AIDS. But some of the little girls were real little dolls, too. There was this one, big eyes, skinny little arms and legs. You just wanted to reach right through the TV screen and pick her up.

The way I figured, so long as we were adopting, there was no rush either. I wouldn't have to take time off for pregnancy, or worry about getting out of shape and then having to work so hard to get the weight off like Joan Lunden did. Plus, if we adopted in a place like Romania, we could maybe pitch our experience for a half-hour special. Bring along a camera crew, let the viewers at home live through the whole process, start to finish. I bet if we did something like that, the phone would be ringing off the hook, at the station, with people wanting to know how they could do it too. It would make you feel good, knowing you had an influence in so many people's lives like that. And I mean, when you're in broadcasting, you do. Whether you know it or not. Dan Rather changes the part in his hair on Monday, and by Wednesday half the men in America are changing the part in theirs. When you think about it, it's awe-inspiring.

Ed Grant

Suzanne had been working for us and doing the weather show ten, twelve months, when we got the notice about the Northeast Regional Cable Television Operator's Conference, over in Mansfield. Stuff like this usually went straight in my circular file. I mean, who needs to pay a couple hundred bucks to eat rubber chicken and sit through a day and a half of workshops on how to increase advertising revenues or liven up your test pattern?

But Suzanne got all excited when she saw the brochure. "So," she says. "We're going to have to pretape 'Senior Chat' and the Sunday morning show, if we plan on being gone over a Saturday night. I'd better get onto that."

"Whoa there," I tell her. "Who says we're going anyplace? I never go to this conference myself, and I sure as hell don't send my employees."

"Well you never had me working for you before either," she tells me.

"Look, Suzanne," I say. "I know you're young and you're full of ambition and energy. That's great. You may even have some talent in the field. But you're not going to turn this dog of a station into anything more than what we're running here. The potential's just not there."

It was like she didn't hear me. "So," she says.

"We'll need to book a couple of hotel rooms. Lucky I just bought a new suit."

"You think an event like this is free?" I ask her. "Think again."

"I'll pay half of my registration fee," she says. "It'll be tax deductible. Career development." Then she starts reading off the names of the different optional workshops you could attend. The keynote speaker is a news anchor from Troy, New York. Suzanne says she wants to be sure she gets to meet this woman. That would be a perfect type of market for her.

I could've said no, of course. But past a point I didn't have the heart. "OK," I tell her. "I don't have the stomach for these conferences, but you go for it if you're so goddam eager. God forbid I'd try and get in the way of the next Connie Chung."

"I knew you'd say yes in the end," she says. Come to think of it, this was one of the only times I ever saw her smile, that she wasn't on the air.

"I pity the poor guy that ever tries to say no to you," I say.

"Nobody ever does," she says.

Suzanne Maretto

There are some individuals I could mention that will probably tell you I'm some kind of cutthroat, ambitious bitch. I'm not naming names, but I know people talk. And right now what they're probably saying about me is what a pushy ball-busting woman I was down at the studio. They're saying I was full of myself, thought I was so great.

Well, what if I did? Since when did it start to be a crime to have a little confidence and self-esteem? If I didn't blow my own horn, who else was going to do it for me?

I may not be some bra burner, but I'll tell you this. Nobody gets on a guy's case just because he knows he's good and says it. If a guy tells his boss he deserves a raise, or a more responsible position, it earns him points. But you take someone like me, and just because I'm petite and blonde, I'm supposed to be some shy, retiring little decoration in the corner, never making any waves, never going after any more than what people give me. So when I didn't behave that way, they call me a ball buster.

It's true, I went into our station manager's office and told him I wanted to be made the news anchor within six months. Yes, I pushed him hard, to send me to the cable TV conference. I told him I wanted to produce a segment about the lives of a bunch of high school kids from the wrong side of the tracks. You think if I hadn't done that, Ed was going to stop by my desk some morning and say, "Hey, Suzanne, suppose I let you use a minicam for a few days, to make us a report on teen life"? Not likely.

It's a dog-eat-dog world out there. You have a goal, you're a fool not to go out there and pursue it. Because I'll tell you something: If I don't go after what I want, there's always going to be someone else who will. And if there's a prize out there for the taking, it might as well be mine.

Ed Grant

She bought new luggage for the trip to Mansfield. Had her hair highlighted, got herself a new briefcase. I'd be willing to lay odds she even started going to a tanning parlor a week or so before the big event. I mean, this was the dead of winter, and all of a sudden Suzanne's looking like she's just got back from Hawaii.

One morning when she was bringing in the coffee—which was still the most important part of her job, if you asked me—I commented that her husband must be looking forward to this little getaway. Two nights in a nice hotel with his bride, indoor swimming pool, Jacuzzi, king-sized bed. "Oh," she said, "Larry's not coming on this trip. I thought it would be best not to have any distractions, knowing I'm going there for business reasons."

She was doing her homework all right. Looked up the keynote speaker, Casey Anderson, in our *Who's Who in Media* guide, so she'd have some idea of her interests. Even sent a couple of introductory letters to five or six station managers who were signed up to attend, letting them know she'd be there and she was looking forward to meeting them and perhaps sharing her tapes with them.

One thing I got to say for Suzanne. She never

concealed from me the fact that she had bigger fish to fry, never pretended she was going to grow old at WGSL. "Someday you'll be able to point to me up on the screen and tell people you gave me my start in broadcasting, Ed," she'd say. "I'll never forget you for that."

And she knew it was fine by me, too, that she was looking for a better job. Having Suzanne around was kind of tiring, if you want to know the truth. She was so wound up, you had to keep thinking up jobs for her to do. So all of us at the station looked forward to her big break almost as much as she did.

Day she left for Mansfield, George, our sound man, tied a bunch of tin cans to her bumper: "Mansfield or bust." It was a joke, you know. We watched her go out into the parking lot, to her car, to see her expression. Nothing. She gets in her car, turns on the ignition, like there's nothing out of the ordinary, backs up, and turns around. Still no reaction. I mean, those cans must've been making one hell of a racket, but she just drove off down the road, never stopping. Way I figured it, she was just so focused on the damn conference she never even noticed, probably drove the whole three hours to Mansfield like that. I like to think of her pulling into the parking lot at the Mansfield Marriott like that. Mrs. Big Shot Weather Girl. With her tin cans clattering.

Lydia Mertz

I used to come over to her condo three, four times a week. Not just when we were working on the video. Just to hang out. Try on clothes, do each other's hair, listen to tapes. God, we could talk all day and never run out of things. I'd tell her anything.

She knew about Chester, my stepfather. She was the only one I ever told about that. "You got to just block that out of your memory," she told me. "Pretend like it never happened and before you know it, the whole thing will be like a bad dream." She said that's what she did. Just focus on the good stuff. Things make problems in her life, it's like her brain's a TV screen. She changes the channel.

That was the day she told me things weren't going so great with her and Larry. "I don't know, Liddy," she told me. "I think I might've made a mistake, getting married when I did. Cutting off my options like that. I was thinking twenty-four was so old. But you know Diane Sawyer was close to forty when she let herself get tied down to that movie director guy. And look at her career. Plus, she chose someone that could really support her career, help her along." You know what Diane Sawyer's husband, the movie director, did this one time, Suzanne told me? He didn't think they were hanging the lights around her the right way. So he went over to the TV station himself, and fixed them just the way they should be, to make her look better. "That's what I call love," she said. "Imagine a guy that would know to do that for you. Larry, he thinks all they have to do is turn on a spotlight and start the cameras rolling. I mean, he's a nice guy and all, but he doesn't know a thing about television.

"And another thing," she said. "He's just so boring. All he wants to do is sit around watching TV and talking about what we're going to name our kids."

She told me she met this guy, at the TV conference she went to in Mansfield. He was a station manager or something like that, somewhere in New York State. This guy could've been a model in GQ, she said. He had this hair, not all gray, but at the temples, so he didn't look that old, just distinguished. He was married, but his wife wasn't there. He told Suzanne they weren't getting along. They'd be getting a divorce soon, they were just waiting till their kid got into prep school.

"We had so much in common, Liddy," she told me. "It was like I finally found someone that spoke the same language as me, someone that cared about the same things I did. It was like I'd known him all my life."

She said she didn't mean to hurt Larry, but after she got back from the conference, all of a sudden everything he did just started grating on her nerves, like fingernails scraping across a blackboard. The way his pants were always too short. The hair in his ears. The way he'd leave his socks on the sectional sofa. He just hung around all the time, she said, never doing anything but watch TV.

He'd been putting on weight too. "Love handles," he called it. But Suzanne called it fat.

"It's horrible," she said, "when someone's crazy about you, and you wish they wouldn't even touch you. Night after night I tell him I'm not in the mood. But the truth is, I don't think I'll ever feel like doing it with him again. And the worst part is, he doesn't even get mad. He's just like this dog that follows me around drooling."

Not that her puppy Walter ever drooled, she said. But Walter was one dog in a million.

Hal Brady

To be honest, I wouldn't have remembered her at all if you hadn't come up here asking these questions. In my job, I go to so many conferences. I've met so many young women like her, they all start to blend together: Reasonably pretty, reasonably bright girls who want to grow up to be Barbara Walters. Look at, what's-her-name, Fawn Hall. One minute Barbara's interviewing her about her involvement with Oliver North. Then Barbara's asking her what she's going to do next with her life? And what does old Fawn say? "I want a job like yours, Barbara." I mean, at this point the woman's more rich and famous than most of the people she interviews. Used to be kids growing up had dreams like cowboy and movie star, fireman, ballerina. Now it's "television journalist."

This one—you say her name is Suzanne?—may have been a little more driven than the average, a little more hungry. Hard to say, there were several of her kind swarming over the Marriott that weekend. Girls in man-tailored suits with their video cassettes in their briefcases that you know would give you their room key in a minute for the chance at a job—any job—at any station. But what would be the point in taking them up on it?

I'll be honest with you: I haven't always con-

ducted myself like a complete Eagle Scout at these
conferences. My wife and I—we've been going our
separate ways for years now, and both of us look
the other way now and then. It's not some high-
flung notion about the sanctity of marriage that
would keep me from having a quick fling with a
girl like your little Suzanne Maretto there. It's total
apathy. More than apathy, actually. Boredom.

They look attractive enough, understand. They
even know the moves—they may put their tongue
inside your ear and run their hand down the front
of your pants in a way that makes your body hungry enough. They know the way to look at you—a
certain blank, open-mouthed, wet-lipped look—as
though they've been so carried away by your ex-
traordinary magnetism and power over them that
they've become total sexual animals. They breathe
heavily, they make little noises as though they're
beyond words—beyond thoughts even. They appear
to have more orgasms in a half-hour period than
my news hour has commercials. They're skillful
too: they've read books on the subject, or magazine
articles anyway. The last girl who took me up to
her room at one of these conferences kept a bottle
of creme de menthe next to the bed and took a big
sip from it right before performing oral sex. It was
a unique sensation, I have to admit.

But what they're doing, these girls, is performing, and nothing more. They're auditioning,
same as they would in a sound studio, with two
cameras pointed on them and someone holding up
the cue cards. I can't pretend I haven't enjoyed the
performance now and then, but frankly it gets old
fast. There aren't that many new tricks left, and
the ones I haven't seen by now, I don't really need
to. As for Suzanne Maretto in her cheap suit and

her push-up bra—not that I remember, understand, but I can guess—she was strictly a beginner. There are girls in this business that could tell Suzanne Maretto to go audition for "Romper Room." And I don't hire *them* either.

Joe Maretto

I don't know what happened at that TV conference Suzanne went to, back in the winter, but I'll tell you one thing, she was a different person when she came back. All of a sudden, everything was wrong with her life. Nobody was good enough. Nothing we did was right.

I remember having the two of them over for dinner, my son and his wife, a day or two after she got home. She starts in raving about the wine they served at the banquet. Not the kind Angela and I serve at the restaurant. This was some fancy stuff. Who knew? Main thing was, it was expensive, and it was better.

And the meat they served. You never tasted better. It came on a little bed of, not lettuce, but had we ever heard of endive? She's talking to a guy that's run a restaurant twenty years and she wants to know have I ever heard of endive, like they maybe invented the stuff in Mansfield.

And the workshops she took. Now she knows how backward the station she works for really is. Their lighting, cameras, everything. Might as well be from the dark ages.

She met this anchorwoman, Stacy Something-or-other. Stacy, Casey, who remembers? Point is, to hear Suzanne talk this woman hung the moon and several of the minor planets. All evening it's "Stacy says this" and "Stacy says that." Angela and me, we're in the kitchen, fixing the coffee, and she says to me (my wife doesn't usually talk off color, but she has a real mouth on her now and then), she says, "Next thing we'll be hearing Stacy pees champagne and shits gold."

But that wasn't the part that got to us. The part about these television people, one step removed from the saints, we could just laugh that off. It's the way she was treating our son that hurt. Picking at him, nonstop. Pointing out the calorie count in every piece of food he puts in his mouth, giving him this look. "Your pants are too short, Larry," she tells him. "We've got to get rid of this polyester shirt. It makes you look so cheap. And it's getting a little tight on you too, I might add.

"Don't you think Larry would look good in a beard?" she says to Angela.

"I think he looks pretty good just the way he is," Angela tells her.

"Oh, well, sure," says our daughter-in-law. "Only he's got this receding chin situation, and a beard would conceal it better."

I can see Angela's eyes go real dark when Suzanne says this, but I give her a look like, keep out of it. This is Larry's business, not ours.

Only Larry just takes it. Never fights back. Never says a word. "I guess I could give it a try," he said. "Just so long as you wouldn't mind scratchy kisses." Then he nuzzles up to her, like a big teddy bear.

"Not now, Larry," she says. I tell you, that dog of hers got more affection.

Lydia Mertz

We were over at Suzanne's condo this one time. I mean, it had got to where I was over there more than I was at my own house. Larry was always off at work, and Suzanne and me were best friends.

We were doing our nails. She was doing my nails, is more like it. And all of a sudden she puts down the emery board and looks at me and says, "Do you think Jimmy Emmet's cute?"

That took me by surprise. The truth was, I had a crush on Jimmy Emmet. I mean, there were guys more well built than him, and plenty of guys a lot more popular. But he had this gentle face. I used to sit behind him in Government, and I'd stare at his hair. He had this cowlick. I was always wishing I could reach out and pat it down for him. And he had these beautiful brown eyes, with long lashes, almost like a girl. Sad eyes, but sensitive too.

"Search me," I said. "I never really thought about it one way or another. Cute enough, I guess. Why?"

"I think I'm falling in love with him," she said. Just like that.

"Jeez," I say. "What are you going to do?"

It was one of these hopeless situations, she said. Where two people are just meant to be together, only they can't. Here she'd gone and married Larry, thinking he was Mr. Romantic rock drummer, and he turned out to be this stick-in-the-mud workaholic that wants to join the country club like her dad and turn her into a housewife. They were going to have this exciting life, going to concerts and partying and stuff, and now all he wants is to stay home and have a bunch of screaming babies. Where Jimmy loves her for herself. Jimmy's wild and exciting. Dangerous, of course. Almost like Bonnie and Clyde or something. She knows he's young. Knows it's crazy. But they've got this fire burning between them. She hasn't told him what she feels but she can tell he feels the same about her. There's this electricity between them. You can sense it.

"I can't believe it," I say. "I just can't believe it."

She asked me if I'd suspected anything. No, I said. Never.

"What about other people?" she said. She figured there were probably a lot of people talking about her—talking about the two of them. She was scared to death the school principal would find out. Or her boss over at the TV station. And then word would get to her parents, and Larry's parents, and Larry. And everything would be such a mess. She wanted to know what I thought, what were people saying? And how did I think she should handle the talk?

"Nobody talks about you," I said. I said that to make her feel better. Only for some reason, I don't think it did.

PART

II

Lydia Mertz

My real dad took off before I was born. My mom doesn't say much about him and I don't ask. "You get your ears from him," Ma says. They stick out.

When I was little, we lived in an apartment up over my grandparents, Bubby and Pops. Ma had a job working at the paper mill, second shift, and the rest of the time she had to rest up. So mostly it was Bubby and Pops that took care of me.

Bubby was mean. If you peed in your bed she made you lie in it. She didn't get around much on account of her varicose veins, but she had this little water gun with ammonia in it. If I touched something I wasn't supposed to—squirt—she'd shoot me. She had good aim too. Always went for one of my eyeballs.

Pops was nice though. He was scared of Bubby too, so he'd have to sneak off if he wanted to say something to me. He taught me poker. "She'll be good at that, little liar like her," says Bubby.

I always wanted a set of paints. At school they'd only let you have three colors at a time and you had to share and the other kids always forgot to clean off their brushes between dipping in the black, say, and the yellow. So the colors always got all cruddy. I was careful with my brush, and I tried to show the other kids how to do it, so we could keep ours nice, but they never paid attention. They just smushed all the colors together till it just looked like throw-up. So naturally the teacher got mad, and never let us have any of the really pretty colors like hot pink or purple.

My seventh birthday, Pops bought me a set of poster paints. Every color in the rainbow and enough brushes so you didn't even have to wash the same one off to paint a different color. Best birthday I ever had.

I took real good care of those paints too. I only painted small pictures, so they'd last longer. If there was some big area to fill in like sky or grass, I'd water down some of my paint, so I wouldn't use it all up. I did this one picture of Pops, I still remember it. In real life he used a walker, but I made him sitting on a horse, with a lasso in his hand. To me he was a hero.

Another time I was making this picture of our whole family. Big this time, even though it was going to take a lot of paint. I started it before I went off to school in the morning so I left my paints out on this tray I used till I came home in the afternoon, to finish. It was turning out so good I didn't want to rush it. I even made Bubby smiling.

When I came home that day, my paints weren't there anymore. My picture was, but not my tray of paints. Pops was taking his nap I guess. Just Bubby sitting in the kitchen, listening to "PTL Club."

"What happened to my paints?" I asked. "They were right here on the table when I left for school."

"Darn tooting they were," she said. "And what was I supposed to do with a dozen little jars of paint dripping all over the place all day? You think we're living in Santa's workshop?"

"Where's my paints?" I asked her. Then I saw.

Instead of all my little bottles, with the blue and the green and the purple and that, she had the big three-quart pickle jar on the counter, and it was full of this throw-up-colored stuff. She had my brushes soaking in ammonia. I knew better than to say anything. Just went to my room, like Pops did.

After Pops died, Bubby got real funny and had to go to the county home. That's when Ma met Chester, that worked as a nurse there. I never heard of a man nurse before, but Chester was.

He was the first person since Pops that was nice to me. Chester used to give me rides in the wheel-chair. Gave me the extra Jell-Os. Called me Princess.

I was real glad when he started coming round our place. It got to where he was over there most of the time, on Ma's day off, and then he started sleeping over. He kept his razor in the bathroom. He even brought over his Lazy Boy chair, for TV watching, and this pet parrot he had since he was in the service, that was like twenty-five years old named Rat Fink. Rat Fink didn't have a cage, he just perched on the back of the Lazy Boy chair eating seed out of this bowl Chester kept handy for him and dropping the husks on the floor. But I didn't even mind that, just Dustbustered up the mess like Bubby was still there watching me.

It seemed like maybe we were going to be a happy family after all. Me and Ma, Chester and Rat Fink, kind of like on "The Brady Bunch." We'd go to the movies sometimes, and bowling even. Saturdays we always went out for pizza, like a real family. Nights sometimes, real late, after Ma came home from the mill, I'd sometimes hear the sound of their hideaway bed bumping against the wall. I'd think, good. He's going to stay around.

One night when I was coming out of the shower with my towel wrapped around me, Chester came over to me. Ma was at work naturally, so it was just Chester and me.

"Come here," he says. "Let me dry your hair."

"That's OK," I say. "I got a blow dryer."

"You got to be careful with those things," he says. "They dry your ends right out." Still, I didn't like the idea much. I was eleven, twelve maybe. Just starting to develop. You feel self-conscious.

"I do this for the old bags at the home all the time," he says. "Massage their scalp, stimulate the blood vessels. It's the big thrill of their week." Now he's unwinding the towel off my head, and working his fingers through my hair. "Sit," he says. I do.

At first I feel uncomfortable, but then I start to like how it feels, the way he works his fingers into my scalp. I get so loose I almost forget where I am. The radio's on. Chester always listened to this station where they just played polka music.

"You got real pretty hair," he says. "I like your freckles too. And you're starting to get yourself a nice body." That part was nuts and I knew it. "I'm fat," I say.

"I like my women soft like a pillow," he says. "Laying on top of your mother is like laying on a brush pile."

After that it's like I'm watching a TV show, not my own life. He starts rubbing my neck, then my shoulders. He takes off my glasses. Then he's lifting the bath towel off my shoulders and working his fingers into my back. "Let's see your little titties," he says. I turn around and show him.

He tells me I'm beautiful. All day long at the nursing home he's scrubbing old dried-up, shriveled bodies, he says. "You're my fresh peach," he says. "I could eat you." And then he starts sucking on me, making these slurping sounds. There's this little trickle of drool I can see, running down my stomach. I'm wondering if the Brady dad ever did anything like this. I can't believe the Brady girls would let somebody put their finger up inside them. I can't picture Mrs. Brady letting him put it in her mouth. On the other hand, I never would've pictured Chester doing it either. So who knew anymore what might happen when nobody's watching?

It lasted as long as one polka. Less, even. When it was over, he just pulled up his pants and handed me the towel. "I'll bring home some of that coconut conditioner we use at the home," he said. "For next time. Smells real good."

That's when I noticed Rat Fink, sitting on the back of her chair as usual, giving me the evil eye. "Lucky she don't talk, huh?" says Chester.

And I never talked either. Three-and-a-half years he was doing it to me nights my ma went to work, I never said a word. Even after he left, I couldn't tell her it was good riddance. We were better off. All I said was, "I sure don't miss that bird."

Jimmy Emmet

She came up to me in the hall that day. I was just getting some stuff out of my locker, heading out for a smoke, and all of a sudden I turn around and there's Mrs. Maretto standing there. "I've got a wild idea," she says. "My husband's out of town on a business trip and I don't have anything to do tonight. How about taking me to that tattoo parlor over at Little Paradise Beach?"

I didn't know what was going on. The whole thing seemed so crazy to me I just burst out laughing. "You kidding?" I say. One thing about Mrs. Maretto, though. She wasn't what you could call a joker. I don't think I ever saw her smile.

"I thought it might be interesting," she says. She was thinking she could maybe film a report, like, you know, an exposé or whatever you call it, on the tattoo business. She said, "Why don't we just take a drive on over and check it out, anyway? We wouldn't bring a camera or nothing. Just kind of scope out the scene." Plus, she loves skee ball. And maybe I'd win her one of those stuffed dogs.

I said I didn't know. I mean, if she wasn't a hot-shit TV reporter, I'd sure think this person wanted to get me to ball her. But she's married, and old. Real pretty, but what does she want with me?

She drove. I'm sitting there in the passenger seat,

listening to that Aerosmith tape of hers again. She's chewing gum and pounding on her steering wheel. It was the same scene all over again. The music. The boner. Only this time she drives to the beach. She parks the car and we head over to the board-walk, her and me. I'm thinking, what am I fucking doing here? It's perfect. It's just what you always dreamed would happen, but when it does you're scared shitless.

We play a couple rounds of skee ball. She buys some cotton candy, which we share. Jesus, we even had our picture took in one of those machines you sit in and make faces, three for a dollar. The thing is like a phone booth, real tight, so she ends up on my lap. In one of the pictures she puts her two fingers behind my head, to make like the devil sign you know? And then all of a sudden she's kissing me. Right when the flash goes off.

"I love these type of places," she says. "They always make you feel so crazy. Like you're sixteen again."

Which in my case I am.

After that, you knew we were both thinking about the same thing, but nobody's saying nothing. She buys some fried dough. I try to get these darts to hit a poster of David Lee Roth or Van Halen for her, but my head's so messed up I don't come close.

"I bet you don't think I'd really get a tattoo," she says. "I bet you'd dare me."

Shit, at this point I just wanted to be out of there, I was so freaked. "They've got this kind of tattoo that washes off after a few days," I say. "You could get one of them."

No, she says. She's talking about a real one. Like Motley Crüe, but more feminine.

"It hurts," I tell her. "They tell you it don't, but they're lying."

She says she had an operation one time and they told her she had a high pain tolerance. She's kind of laughing, like she's drunk. Only she's not.

We head over to the tattoo parlor, down by the beach. There's no other customers, so this dame comes right up to us and says, "Can I help you?" Mrs. Maretto says, "I want this rose over here."

"Fine," says the chick. "That's a very popular one with the ladies. Twenty-five bucks."

"You wait out here," she tells me. So I do. Though I got to tell you, I wanted to just run. But I didn't. I mean, where was I going to go?

After twenty minutes, maybe twenty-five, she comes out. She's not in such a light mood anymore, and you can tell it hurt. She pays her money. "Well," she says, "I did it all right."

"Far out," I say. Knowing that's what she wanted me to say. We start walking again, toward the beach.

"So," she says, "don't you want to see it?"

"I guess," I say.

"OK then," she says, and we step off the board-walk to this place on the sand where nobody's at, just some old closed-down arcade and a couple of kids making out way down the sand. It's like I'm dreaming.

She unbuttons her shirt. She's got this little pink lace bra on. She don't have much chest on her. She's like a little kid, practically.

She pushes the bra down, so one tit's mostly showing. Then I see it. A rose, like she picked out. "Well," she says, "don't you want to fuck me?"

Suzanne Maretto

I know you're wondering about the tattoo. OK, I'll explain. It's the dumbest thing I ever did. But there's an explanation.

As you know, I was working with these kids on the video. I mean, Russell was an animal, there's no other word for him. But James actually showed some promise. And then he said he didn't want to do it anymore. He was dropping out of the group.

He said he just couldn't get excited about sitting in a chair talking. And you know, given what I know about education, it made some sense to me. You have to reach them on their wave-length, you know? It's like how certain teachers might play a Bruce Springsteen song in English class. Just to draw the kids in with something they can relate to. And that's what I was trying to do too.

So I said to him, "OK, what would interest you then?"

He had no response of course. Everything you get from these kids, you've got to really work to get it out of them. Which I have to add is certainly what the police must have done. He's not what you could call a talkative individual.

But I didn't give up either. "What do you like to do in your spare time?" I asked him. "Where did you go on Saturday? Tell me some of your favorite extracurricular activities." Of course I understood it wasn't going to be the debating society or anything. I was ready to take whatever little scrap he gave me, and run with that.

"I went to Little Paradise Beach and got a tattoo," he said. He said he had one already, but on Saturday he went and got another. And then he showed me. A snake on one arm. A skull on the other. I mean by this point he was flexing his muscles and so forth to impress me. Anybody could see what was going through his head, but I was strictly ignoring it. I was just trying to reach him on a teacher-student basis. See what made him tick, so to speak, so I could help him.

So I told him that was very interesting, and I thought it was the perfect subject for a segment on our news broadcast. An exposé of the tattoo industry, you know? You could talk to people that got tattoos about why they did it, and talk to the tattoo artist or whatever you want to call it, as to his method. Does it hurt? Is it dangerous? What's the most interesting tattoo request he ever had? Really, the more you thought about it, it was a great subject.

James was still off on this other track. He'd say things like did tattoos turn me on? Did my husband have a good body? If I made any mistake, it was just caring too much about his welfare, instead of being more careful about protecting my husband and myself. But you know I was very idealistic. These kids come from a really rough background. And I felt, if I can just use my talent to save one of them, then that's reason enough for being put on this earth. So I just pretended not to understand what he was trying to do. I kept my focus on the video aspect.

I said, "Listen. Why don't you and I go over to Little Paradise some afternoon and check out the scene ourselves? We don't even have to bring a camera or anything." This would be strictly research, initially. And then just to get him to agree I said I'd take him out for a hamburger while we were down there. I mean I'm hardly the only reporter who ever took a kid out for a burger.

That clearly got him interested. All right, he said. He was free that very afternoon. And as it happened, Larry was out of town at a restaurant equipment show. So I said fine. We could take my car. And that's how it got started.

Once we got to the beach he kept wanting to stop at these game booths and things. Didn't I want to throw some darts? How about playing a couple of video games. He even tried to get me to buy this fringed T-shirt with some Harley-Davidson slogan on it. But I just paid no attention to what he was doing. And finally we got to this little burger joint. He got a cheeseburger. I ordered a salad and a beer. That's where I got into trouble.

I should've known better. I don't drink. I don't even like beer. One glass and I can get sick to my stomach practically. But I was just trying to make him feel like I was, you know, a regular person. Someone he could relate to on his level.

I guess I ended up having two or three beers with him, and they must've hit me like a ton of bricks, especially since I hardly ate anything. In any event, I can barely remember what happened after that, except to say that clearly I got drunk. I'm not proud of this. But you know, I only weigh 103. It doesn't take much to knock me flat. The next thing I knew I was walking out of the tattoo parlor and to my horror I had a tattoo. On my chest. It's the most ridiculous thing that could've happened to me. But there you have it. I suppose I should at least be grateful it's a rose and not a skull like his.

I guess he drove me home. I don't remember much about that either, except that I recall saying good-bye to him and telling him he'd have to figure out his own way home from our place. I didn't let him in our condo of course. I was just sick at this point. Sick about what had happened, and sick period. It was the worst night of my life. Up until, you know, finding Larry I mean.

But as a matter of fact the worst part came later. Not simply explaining the tattoo to Larry. He was really sweet about that. He knew of course that he had no reason to mistrust me. We were so much in love. To him it was just a funny story. "My wife the tattooed lady," he kidded me. He said if I ever quit my job at the station I could always join the carnival.

The worst part was from that night on, James wouldn't leave me alone. He'd gotten this crazy idea that I was interested in him, and he just wouldn't take a hint. In his twisted mind we hadn't gone to Little Paradise Beach to research a project. We'd gone on a date, if you can imagine. He kept coming round our condo, trying to see me, and leaving me these notes when I wasn't around. I wouldn't even want to repeat what some of them said. He'd call me up at home, late at night even. I'd see him and Russell driving past at all hours. Mornings, when I got to work, he'd be waiting for me out in the parking lot with some obscene comment to make, naturally. And of course the worst part was his knowing about the tattoo, and where I'd gotten it and so forth. And knowing that if I went to the authorities about it—which I really wanted to do—then it would come out that I had the tattoo. Which would look bad.

I was in a terrible bind. And of course the person I confided in was Larry, who was not only my husband but also my best friend. And being the way he was, I can imagine now what he must have done about it, although he never told me. I think he must have called James up and told him to stay away from his wife. That would be so like Larry.

But by that time, James must have just been obsessed with me. He couldn't stop. He got the idea that the only thing standing in his way, the only thing preventing him from being with me was Larry. So naturally, as a person accustomed to using violence as the solution to problems, it wasn't a very big leap to the next idea. Kill Larry. And make it look like a burglary. And then when he got caught, tell the police that the whole thing was my idea, because he had this fantasy that we were lovers.

Let's face it. What would I want with someone like him? I came from a good family. I had a good job. I had Larry. We had our whole lives ahead of us. A golden future.

Have you ever been up close to James? He might be a cute enough kid, but do you know what he smells like? Dead clams.

Jimmy Emmet

I never told no one this. People all thought I was so tough. Hanging out with Russell and shit. Him that had a kid before he was fifteen. So people figured I had to be the same way. Like I was Mr. Fuck. But she was the first one I ever did it with. The only one.

You think about it all the time. Everyplace you go, it's on your mind. Russ and me, we'd sit on the beach smoking and watching tail, and we'd talk like, "Maybe I'll go stick it in that one." "Yeah," I'd say. "I sure could go for some wet pussy right now." You talk big. Sometimes I'd even point to one and say I think I done her one time, over at Little Paradise, behind the pier. Should've heard her screaming for more. And Russ says yeah, he might've fucked her too, her and her girlfriend there together. It's hard to remember. Now I'm wondering how much of it he made up. But at the time it never hit me he might be shitting me same as I was shitting him.

Christ, it gets to where you been saying you're doing it so long, when you're not doing it, you get freaked it's never going to happen. You're jerking off twenty times a day and alls you can think about is I got to get it or I'll bust. You can't concentrate. Sit in shop class and just putting a nut in a bolt's enough to give you a boner. You get where you think maybe you'll go crazy, end up in the state hospital. "What you in for?" they ask you. "Incurable hard-on." "You abusing any substances?" "Yeah. My right hand."

I was thinking Lydia might be the one. I mean, the girl didn't have to be no Miss America. Only once you got this reputation that you know what you're doing, you got to live up to it. Truth is, I wasn't sure where to start. Do I kiss her or go straight for the tits? What if I get so freaked I can't get it up? What if I come all over the place before she wants it? And then you wonder what you're supposed to do after. Do you lie there on top of her or what? Are you supposed to kiss her, hand her her bra or something? Then next time she sees you do you just act like you never fucked or do you grab her ass and jump her again? Man, once you start asking questions it can drive you crazy.

That's where I was at the night Mrs. Maretto showed me her tattoo. When it happened I was thinking maybe this is my brain going soft from wanting it so bad. Maybe I'm having these hallucinations like what happens to my uncle when he gets drunk. But then I thought, well if I'm dreaming, at least I'm going to make it a good dream. That's when I unzipped my pants and nailed her.

Christ, all the times I thought about what it would be like, but it was better. Her skin's so soft. Her hair fans out on the sand like she's in a shampoo commercial. I put my tongue in her mouth, and I can taste the Tic Tac she was sucking on. We're so connected, I taste her Tic Tac.

That first time, alls I wanted was to get inside her. I don't have time to look at her tits. She's so warm and tight all around me, it's like I'm in this underground tunnel, and there's diamonds sparkling all around, and, I don't know, waterfalls, stars. I'm pumping her, and she's digging her fingers into my back, and I guess most likely there's noise from over at the boardwalk and the bars and that, but I don't hear none of it, I'm in this other world that just has two people, her and me. Partly I'm afraid I'm going to hurt her, I'm pounding so hard, and she's so little and delicate, but I can't stop, I just got to do it. Then all of a sudden I know it's about to happen and for a second I think, What if I'm not supposed to do it now? but it's too late, I can't hold back. Man, I just explode all over the place, like someone pulled the pin on a goddam grenade. I black out, see this white light, the works. And then I just fall on top of her. Can't move.

I guess it's different with girls. When it's over, she wants me to get off her, and I'm just wishing I could climb back on top of her and do it again. But her, she's wired. Hopping up, pulling up her pants, hooking her bra, checking she's got both her earrings.

"Mrs. Maretto—" I say. It's funny. I just finished fucking her, and she's still Mrs. Maretto to me. I don't even know what I want to say after that, I just got to tell her something that's big enough for the way I'm feeling. Now I get it why people say "I love you" and "Will you marry me." Maybe there's words in the dictionary to go with how you feel at a moment like that, but I sure as hell don't know them.

But she always knows what to say. She's still buttoning up her blouse and she's telling me these, like she calls it, rules. Number one being, I can't tell anyone. Or it's over.

This makes me happy, because what that means

is, long as I don't tell we get to do it again. "Sure,"
I say. "You got it. Absolutely. You think I'm
crazy?" Of course in the end I did tell Russell, but
like I said, when you've just finished doing it you'll
say anything. You don't know what you're doing.
It was just later that I lost it there and had to blab.

The next rule is, don't ever call her up. No problem I say. I don't have no phone anyways.

She says her husband is a big problem. She don't
know what she's going to do about him. He could
be a very violent guy she says, and he's Italian. You
know how they are. I say don't worry, I can take
care of myself. Her too. She don't have to worry.
Whatever she says, I'm ready.

The last rule was you got to take a shower every
morning, and use deodorant and mouthwash. A
person should brush their teeth after every meal
and have a clean shave every day.

I only have to shave like, every three or four
days, but I don't tell her that. I just say you got it.
Then we get up and walk back to her car. I want
to have my hands all over her, just touch her hair.
But she walks in front.

Russell Hines

We're outside having a smoke as usual, and Jimmy's not saying nothing. Along comes Susie Q in her Datsun, with this look on her face like she never shits, and only pisses perfume.

"Think she ever spreads her legs?" I say. Tight bitch like that. Freeze your dick off if you try sticking it in that one.

Jimmy don't say nothing. "I've had enough of this TV shit," I tell him. I mean, it seemed like we might have some fun with old Lydia there, but why bother, you know? It didn't seem worth the trouble no more.

Jimmy still don't say nothing. So I say, let's just bug off her old project there. Just blow this place.

He says no. He don't want to blow. He wants to finish the video. He's into it.

"You've got to be shitting me, man," I tell him. "What've you been smoking? You turning into some altar boy on me?"

"It's not like that," he says. "I just like her. I don't think we should let her down." Can you believe it?

"Man," I say. "Am I losing my mind? Is this Jimmy Emmet I'm talking to or did I walk into the national honor society by mistake?"

"It's not like you think," he says. That's when

he tells me he balled her the night before. "You don't know what it's like," he tells me. "I feel like I got let into heaven." I kid you not. Like they let him into heaven.

At first I thought he was fucking with my mind or something. "Yeah, right," I say. "And I was balling Paula Abdul."

"No," he says. "I mean it. She wanted me to take her to Little Paradise and we had our picture took and she got a tattoo and then she balled me. You don't know what it was like. This isn't some cunt you jerk off with. This is like a movie star or a ballerina. Married and everything." And she chooses him.

All I can think is, it's got to be a trick. They're trying to nail him for something. But that don't make no sense neither.

"So," I says. "You going to do it again?"

"I got to," he says. "Now I just got to have her." He's going crazy.

This is when she gets out of her car and walks in the school, right past us like she done all the other times. Nothing unusual. Only Jimmy there, you think he might just have a terminal hard-on. "Hey," he calls out to her. "We getting together after school or what?"

"Gee," she says, "I guess not. I'm interviewing the guidance counselor today." Cool as a goddam iceberg. Jimmy, he's standing there dying. She wiggles that butt of hers and pushes open the door.

"Wait a second," he calls to her. "There's something I need to talk to you about."

"You look so serious," she says to him. "Did somebody die?" Then she laughs this laugh of hers, where she kind of throws her hair to one side and, I don't know, bites her lip or something. Alls I know is, right then the cunt looks like she's sixteen years old. Cock tease is the name for it.

"I was thinking," he says. Then he just stops, like he don't know what to say next.

"Oh yes?" she says. "Well, we'd just better send out a news flash to all three networks, hadn't we?"

"No," he says. "I mean, I had some things I need to talk to you about. About the video and stuff."

"Well OK," she says. "Stop by my place tonight." Then she's gone, and it's like he's melted into a puddle on the ground. You ever seen a dog sniffing after a bitch in heat? That was Jimmy.

"So," I say to him. "Was she good?"

Jimmy looks at me, and I swear the boy has tears in his eyes. "You wouldn't understand," he tells me. "This isn't just about sex. I'm in love with her. She cares about me. In my whole life, she's the first good thing that ever happened."

Mary Emmet

After Jimmy started working on this video with Mrs. Maretto, I got to admit I was happy for him. I should've known it was bound to lead to trouble, but he just seemed so excited all of a sudden. He was taking all these showers, shaving, buying hair gel, so I figured a girl was involved, but I thought it was Lydia, the heavyset one. I even waited up for him one night and sat him down. I had this speech all planned about birth control. "Take it from me," I said. "You don't want to go having a kid when you're sixteen." Right after I said that I felt bad, because of course the kid I had when I was sixteen was him, but he didn't even seem to notice to take offense. He just said, "Don't worry, Ma, nothing's going to happen."

"Famous last words," I told him. "Young girls think they've got some magic out there protecting them. They don't know anything."

"You don't have to worry about anybody getting knocked up, Ma," he told me. And of course he was right about that. But don't I wish all I had to worry about now was some girl making me a grandmother.

Jimmy Emmet

After we did it that time it was like I was on drugs. I had to have it. I thought about her every minute. They could make one of those fucking TV ads about me. This is your brain. This is your brain after you've had sex.

I'd wake up with a boner, same as always, only instead of stopping there, it kept happening all day long.

I'd be combing my hair and I'd remember how it felt, her fingers in my hair, and I'd start shaking. I'd hear "Home Sweet Home" on the radio, that was playing when she gave me a ride in her car, and all of a sudden I'd be sweating like a pig. I'd pick up the phone to dial her number, hang up, pick up the phone again, start to dial. Hang up. I knew I wasn't supposed to do that, but it was like my dick was on fire and the only thing that would give me any relief was hearing her voice. Just walking down the street I'd think, man, everybody must know what's on my mind. I read someplace there's this disease where you have a hard-on that never stops. That was me.

I still don't get it, how there can be this feeling that's so good that when you don't have it, it feels worse than anything you ever felt before. My balls ached. I felt like I was going to throw up. I'd open my mouth to say something, and my voice would crack like some fucking seventh grader.

All day long I'd wait for the moment when I'd get to see her. But when I got to see her, that was even worse. Seeing her and not getting in her pants, you know? Seeing those perfect smooth hands of hers, with those red fingernails, and remembering how they'd dug into my back. I'd remember seeing them pressed into my skin. I could never understand how she did it, acting so calm and cool when I saw her at her condo or Pizza Hut, knowing what she was like in the backseat of her car when it was just her and me fucking. Hearing her clear her throat, that way she always did, and remembering how she'd scream when I was on top of her. Her hair pulled back in that little ponytail, and it used to be hanging all loose over my chest. Her bra straps just barely showing through her blouse. Her nipples making these two little stick-out places when she wore a certain kind of shirt. How could people keep acting normal around that kind of thing? Didn't everybody see? Was it just me?

Sometimes I'd wait for her out by her car. Lean on her hood, light up a stink butt, then another. There'd be a whole pile of them on the ground all around me by the time she showed up. I'd try and act casual, like I just happened to drop by, but my leg would be shaking.

"So," I'd say. "You got any plans? You want to take a drive?"

Meaning in her car, of course. The whole thing being out of my control. Her car. Her house. It was like I was her puppet. It was all up to her, and whatever she said went.

She'd laugh. She always laughed, this way she

had, where the sound of laughing came out, without her face looking she was laughing. "What am I going to do with you, Jimmy?" she'd say.

What did she think? "Fuck me, I hope," I wanted to scream at her. "Put me out of my misery, like some dog that's got rabies." Which was about as messed up as I felt most of the time.

Then she'd reach up—she was so small and delicate, she only came up to my nose, maybe—and brush my hair out of my eyes, like something a mother might do, only not my mother. "You are such a silly boy," she'd say. Alls I could do was stand there.

She always had a million places to go. "Hmm . . ." she'd say. "I haven't been to aerobics in two days. I'm getting so fat it's disgusting."

I told her I'd wait for her if she wanted. I didn't have plans at the moment. Or any other moment, if you want to know the truth.

"But . . ." she'd say. "We don't have a thing for dinner back home. I really should go to the store. Larry'll kill me if I ask him to bring home pizza again. God, what'll I make?"

What was I supposed to say to that one? I know some great recipes?

"I was thinking maybe we could drive out Langley Road," I said. "Out past the trailer park."

Then she'd laugh again. "Now why would I do a thing like that?" she'd say. And then just when I thought I'd have to beat my head against the side of her car, she'd open her door and tell me to get in the other side. Then she'd gun the motor and turn on the radio, not even looking at me. Look at her hair in the mirror. Check this list she kept on the dashboard that told her all the errands she needed to do. Pick up his shirts at the cleaners and shit. "I have thirty-five minutes," she'd say. She had a little timer on her watch that set off a beep when the time was up.

But thirty-five minutes was enough for me. I was always ready. Only problem I had was holding it in that long. And then knowing once it was over I'd have to wait a whole day or maybe two before I got it again. Because the minute she dropped me off at the Sunoco station back in town, even before her car disappeared at the stoplight, I could feel it starting again. That same feeling of needing it. The more you had the more you needed. Whatever you got it was never enough.

Suzanne Maretto

A Lhasa apso is a very sensitive kind of dog, very high-strung. And Walter is even more sensitive than average, so you can imagine. Which I could relate to, being a sensitive person myself.

I'll give you an example. It's kind of intimate, but this is the best way I can think of to convey to you the kind of feelings inside this little puppy of mine. And how easily hurt he can be.

Larry and I were in our bedroom one morning, and he wanted to, you know, make love. Mornings weren't a usual time for us, due to our busy schedules, but I guess he'd gotten a little carried away on this particular occasion.

The thing was, Walter slept downstairs in this bed we had for him in the kitchen, but he always liked to come into our room in the morning, as soon as he woke up. He'd jump up on the bed—just getting up there, mind you, wasn't easy, but he would jump his little heart out, trying, until he finally made it. And then he'd come over and lick my face and curl up on the pillow next to us. Truthfully, I'd have to say he always preferred me. I think he was a little jealous of Larry getting to sleep with me, while he had to stay in the kitchen, you know.

So anyway, this particular morning, we were having sex, and we didn't hear Walter coming in.

But looking back on it, I have to guess that the sounds we were making must've scared him—I'm not saying we were like some X-rated movie or anything, but you know how it goes. I suppose he thought Larry was hurting me. And being the brave little dog he is, with no sense of his own limitations, he jumped right up on the bed without our seeing him until the moment when Larry let out this yell of pain. It turned out Walter bit him. Right on the behind, if you want to know the truth.

I thought it was kind of funny myself. I mean, he wasn't badly hurt or anything—mostly just surprised. I took Walter in my arms and comforted him, but how do you explain to a dog about something like that? All you can do is reassure them that you love them and you're there for them.

Larry, on the other hand, didn't seem to show much patience in this regard. Not everybody can understand the way dogs think, I guess. I just happen to be one of those people with a kind of sixth sense, that can identify with them. But before he even had a chance to think, Larry had picked Walter up by the scruff of his neck and tossed him on the floor, like he was an old towel. "Sometimes I wonder if maybe this dog's plotting to do me in," he said. "So he could have you all to himself."

We laughed about that. Because of course, Walter would never do such a thing. He was just following his natural animal instincts, I told Larry. Just like we all do.

Jimmy Emmet

Her old man was going to be away at some pizza-making convention in Las Vegas. So I figured we'd be fucking seven days nonstop. Only she kept putting me off. One night she's got to go to her mother's. Then she says she's got to do something to her hair, don't ask me what. It looked fine to me. There she was, rid of him, we could've been balling all night. And she's getting her hair done.

Wednesday, Thursday maybe, I can't stand it no more. I show up at her work, where she always told me never to go, and I walk in her office and I don't care who hears me. "I got to see you," I say. "I can't take it."

"Be quiet," she says. But when she sees I'm not going to shut up this time, she says, "OK, come on out to the parking lot where we can talk."

I told her I felt like she was dragging me along on a string and it's tied to my balls. I told her I feel like I'm going to bust if there's one more day like this. It's like I'm a goddam drug addict.

"Wait a second," she says. Then she touches me in this way she has, on this place on my neck that when she does it I just can't hardly breathe and she knows it. She puts her hand down my shirt and pets me right where I got my tattoo.

"Didn't you ever hear the expression good things

are worth waiting for?" she says to me. "Why're you in such a hurry? We got all the time in the world."

I tell her it don't seem like that. It seems like when I was a little kid, waiting for Santa. Don't ask me why, he never brung what I wanted anyways. But still, you couldn't sleep, just thinking about it.

It's just she's got a lot on her mind, she says. She's trying to get our video all finished up. She's getting ready to go talk to her boss about expanding the weather broadcast. And then she got to attend to her roots, she says. Guys just don't understand, she says, and she's laughing. And it kind of feels like she's laughing at me.

"OK, little boy," she says to me. "You can come over to my house and play tonight. In fact, you can even come for a sleepover."

It's a long walk over to the condo development, but I don't want Russell or nobody driving me over and giving me a hard time. This is personal like. I don't want to talk about it or nothing. I want to concentrate.

So it's nine-thirty, ten o'clock when I get there. TV's on. She's watching some Barbara Walters special, eating pizza. They got Sylvester Stallone on. Barbara Walters is asking him why he keeps changing girlfriends. Why he don't settle down and marry one of them or some shit like that. "Well, Barbara," he's saying, "there's a lot of great girls out there. It's kind of like picking an ice cream flavor. You have a hard time narrowing it down to one."

I tell Mrs. Maretto that's not where I'm at. She's all I need. All I want. All I'm ever going to want.

I could look at her forever and never get tired of her. I don't need to fuck nobody else, now I'm fucking her.

"When was the last time you took a shower, James?" she asks me.

Yesterday, I tell her. It was probably more likely the day before though. And I don't want to be worrying the whole time that I might smell bad or something. So I say, "You want me to jump in the shower?"

"Good idea," she says. "Then I can see the Tom Selleck interview."

I never was in a place like that. You walk into the room it's like you're in a flower garden, there's all this perfume smell. Carpet on the floor instead of linoleum and shit. There's this light that when you turn it on, it's red. Turns out when you stand under the light bulb dripping wet and bare-ass naked, it makes you so you don't get cold.

There's two sinks—one for him, one for her. Next to the one I figure is his, there's this aftershave and hair gel or what have you. Deodorant—after my shower, I squirt on some of that. The after-shave too.

Of course hers is the one with all the makeup and shit. All these little bottles and brushes and tubes, I never would've believed a chick could put so much stuff on her face. She's got these hot roller things and a blow dryer and perfume for her too, naturally. Even her razor looks so pretty and fancy. Pink.

I take off my jeans and shirt. Step into the shower, lather up. I'm so excited I can hardly stand it, washing my cock, thinking where it's going to be, who's going to be touching it.

Then I get out, stand under the red light bulb

like I said, squirt on some good-smelling stuff, put a little toothpaste in my mouth. There's this real soft bathrobe, made out of towel material, hanging on a hook. I put it on, step in the hall to see if she's there. But I can still hear the TV. OK, I think. I'll just wait up here. On her bed.

I lie there. There's a *Sports Illustrated* on the bureau, and I pick it up but I can't concentrate. I walk over to the closet, look at her dresses. Everything's real neat, all the shoes lined up in this little rack she's got. Belts hanging from special hooks. His ties. I see this one shirt she wore the first time we made it, over at the beach. Smell it.

There's pictures all over the place. Mostly of her, but some of him too, or the two of them together. Him and her in front of this castle at Disney World, holding these stuffed dogs. Her when she was a real little girl in this little ballerina dress, sparkles all over her skirt.

I lay down on the bed. Downstairs I can hear the TV go off. Then I hear her talking. Must be she's on the phone with her sister or one of her girlfriends. I can't hear what she says or nothing. Just laughing now and then. And then she's finally done. Must be she's turning out the lights. Then I hear her coming up the stairs. I can't hardly stand it.

But she don't come in the room yet. I hear her in the bathroom. Water running. She's brushing her teeth, taking a shower. She's in there a long time.

Just when I'm thinking is she ever going to come in here, she does. She's got this robe on that's got flowers all over it—long, but it's not fastened too tight, so you can see her legs. She just stands there a second. Giggles. "Look at you," she says. I wish she'd leave the light on so I could keep on seeing her the whole time, but she turns it off. Sets the robe down next to the bed. Lays down next to me.

I put my hand on her tit. I'm shaking. Then I'm kissing her on the mouth, kissing her on the neck. My dick's so hard I feel like it could drill through concrete, but I don't want to rush. I don't want it to be over.

Only she's ready too. She spreads her legs apart and guides me over to where I'm on top of her. I go inside her. "This's got to be what heaven's like," I say. She laughs that laugh of hers again.

I said a lot of other stuff too, I don't remember half of it. Only I know I said I love her and I want us to be together always. She's the most beautiful girl in the world.

She don't say nothing herself. She's not the type that talks when they're fucking. When I can tell I'm just about to come I say, "I can't help it. I got to come now. Is that OK?"

She says yes. And then I do, and it's over. And I just lay there thinking I'm the happiest guy in the world.

I'm almost asleep when she kind of shakes me to wake up. "You can't sleep here in this bed," she tells me. "You got to go in the guest room."

What's she mean, guest room? I'm halfway asleep so I don't hardly know what's going on. But she's pulling on me, she's getting up, walking me down the hall to this other bed that's like a couch. She hands me a towel and a blanket.

"I got to be out of here by seven for my aerobics class," she says. "So don't sleep late." She says, "Sweet dreams."

"Of course they'll be sweet," I tell her. "I'll dream about you."

Suzanne Maretto

Whenever Larry would go out of town, I'd get scared at night. You never know what kind of people there might be hanging around that could break into your condo. And of course, I was right to be concerned, because in the end that's exactly what happened.

So I suggested to the kids in my video project that we could all get together at my house, have a pizza and work on tying up the loose ends of my video. I was very pleased with my work on this project. I felt sure that once I got the whole thing edited and my station manager saw my work he'd put it on the air. Mostly all that was left at this point were things like reaction shots and rerecording a couple of voiceovers.

But for some reason, James was the only one who showed up. I mean it didn't surprise me that Russell would skip our meeting. He was a total loser. But as for why Lydia didn't come, I don't know. Except that I think she was coming to resent the interest James showed in me. Which was all one-sided of course. But anyone could see that Lydia had developed a crush on James. And I think that made her very jealous of me.

Of course if I'd known that it would end up being just me and James I would have made other plans for the evening, maybe invited my sister over. But there I was, thinking we'd be getting some work done, and then nobody shows up besides him.

So I tried to make the best of the situation. I invited him to have some pizza with me. I tried to get him to do a little work on the video, but it was obvious he had his mind on other things, if you know what I mean. I mean, he'd say things like how my hair smelled pretty, and did I wear a one-piece bathing suit or a bikini? He said he hoped bikini, because he could tell I had the figure for it. You could see the way he was headed.

There was a Barbara Walters special on. She's an idol of mine. I mean, she may be getting up there, but she really knows her craft. So I suggested that we watch it. See how a real pro handles herself in an interview situation.

I sat in Larry's chair, on purpose, so James wouldn't even have the option of sitting next to me. He sat sprawled out on the couch.

Barbara was interviewing Sylvester Stallone as I recall. Stallone was talking about his history of relationships. James made some kind of inappropriate remark about what kind of a relationship he'd like to have with me. Tom Selleck was coming on next, and James said he really wanted to see that interview, but at this point I'd had enough, so I told him it was time to go home. He made up some story about how he couldn't go back there tonight, his mother's boyfriend was drunk and he knew if he went home now he'd get beat up.

Knowing his family background, I was prepared to believe this was true. So I said, "All right, you may stay over in my guest room, but I have to be up and out of here by seven, so don't sleep late." I said something like, "Sweet dreams." He said something silly like, "Of course they'll be sweet. I'll dream about you."

Lydia Mertz

She called me up this one time. She said Larry was going to be out of town, and Jimmy was coming over again. He'd been staying there quite a bit by this time, and she was starting to worry people might get the wrong impression. So she wanted to know if I'd sleep over too. The idea was, if Larry asked any questions, she could say, "Yeah, Lydia and Jimmy were over working on the video, and it got so late I let them camp out on the couch." Only of course it was really just going to be me on the couch. Her and him were so much in love by this time.

We got a pizza as usual, and rented some videos. A Motley Crüe concert video, that was one. Also this Tom Cruise movie where he's a bartender. We both thought he was so cute. And then we got this other movie that had the girl in it from "Twin Peaks." Only the stuff in this movie they never would've shown on TV.

It felt weird sitting there with the two of them, watching this movie. I mean the girl's basically naked, except for a garter belt, and she does all this stuff. With her mouth if you know what I mean. Watching it made me think about back when Chester was still around. Here I'd eaten all this pizza, and now I thought I was going to throw up. So I

told Suzanne and Jimmy I was going to go outside
for a minute. I took Walter on his leash and walked
him around the cul de sac where her condo was,
out to the dumpster where they brought their
trash. I threw a couple balls for Walter. You tried
to think about nice stuff, you know. Happy stuff.
Just don't think about that other part, I'd tell myself. But you know what happens when you tell
yourself, Don't think about such-and-such. Before
you know it, that's the one thing you can't stop
thinking about. No matter what, you can't get it
out of your head.

Walking around in the fresh air like that, though,
I started feeling better. Just seeing the stars and
stuff, the tricycles of all the little kids lying around
in front of the condos. Looking at the lights in the
windows, picturing the families inside, tucking
their kids in, the husbands and wives sitting down
on the couch side by side, watching TV, and talking about their day. You tried to think about nice
stuff, you know. Happy stuff. After a while, when
I stopped feeling like I was going to barf, I went
back to Suzanne's condo. Only when I went back
the TV was off and the living room was empty. I
called out to Suzanne and Jimmy, but no answer,
and they weren't in the kitchen either.

Sitting there with Walter, I heard these sounds
coming from upstairs. OK, I said. Just pretend like
nothing's happening. It'll be over soon. So I picked
up one of Suzanne's magazines and started reading
it. I couldn't concentrate on the words, so I just
stared at this one page of fashion dos and don'ts. I
turned on the TV and watched the shopping channel for a while. They had a guy on talking about
this product called QRB that removed all this
caked-up paint and dirt off wood furniture without

having to sand it. I was trying so hard not to think about what was going on upstairs I even wrote down the 800 number of this wood stripper, to tell my mother about it. Knowing I wouldn't ever really keep the number, and my mother wouldn't care anyways. I just wanted to keep my brain occupied, so I wouldn't start thinking about the two of them. Suzanne and Jimmy. Doing it.

After a while I needed to go to the bathroom. Which was upstairs, right next to Suzanne's room. They've got to be done pretty soon, I kept telling myself. Any minute now they're going to come downstairs again and we can make a big bowl of microwave popcorn, maybe watch the Motley Crüe video we still hadn't got around to. Only they didn't come out.

Finally it was quiet up there. And I couldn't hold it in anymore. OK, I think. I guess they've just gone to sleep, so what's to keep me from tiptoeing up the stairs and sneaking in the bathroom? I wasn't even going to flush.

By the time I got to the top of the stairs I realized they weren't asleep after all, but by then it was too late to turn around, plus I was desperate. Her door wasn't even shut. So I couldn't help seeing.

He was laying on the bed, stretched out on the pillows. I never saw a guy like that before.

Suzanne had the garter belt on that we bought at Victoria's Secret. And one of those see-through type bras. No underpants. She was standing at the foot of the bed with her hands over her head.

It took me a minute to understand what she was doing. She was doing a cheerleading routine. She was saying, "Give me and E, give me an L," like that. And Jimmy, he had this look on his face like it wouldn't have mattered if the whole condo development was on fire. He'd just stay laying there. A person could come up to him and say, "Get off this bed or I'll blow your brains out," and he wouldn't have moved, that's what he looked like. Like he didn't care if he was dead or alive, so long as he could see the rest of her cheer.

The two of them were so into each other right then I could've walked right through the room and I doubt they would've noticed. It was like they were the only two people on earth. Like I didn't exist. So I just sneaked into the bathroom and took a leak.

When I went downstairs I finished off the rest of the pizza. Then I lay down on the couch and went to sleep. And when we got up in the morning, nobody said a word. Suzanne's running around in a sweatsuit, getting ready to go to her aerobics class and making an appointment to have her hair done. I hear her on the phone with Larry's mother, saying something about getting together for dinner that night. "Jeez," she says to me when she gets off the phone. "Have you ever seen anything as gross as these split ends?"

But Jimmy, it's like he's possessed. He just sits there at her dinette table staring at her, practically licking her hand. Suzanne even had a joke about it. She used to say the only difference between him and Walter was Walter wore a collar. And Walter didn't have fleas.

Russell Hines

The way she did this TV show of hers was, she'd get us sitting around in her living room, set out a plate of Oreos and maybe some Coke, and then she'd ask us to talk about a particular topic. One time it might be dating—like we really know a lot about that—or maybe parents. Sometimes she'd bring up some big idea she had, like Who Are Your Heroes? or What Do You Do If You're at a Party and Someone's Drunk and They Say They're Going to Drive Home? You get my drift.

The whole thing was a total crock, mind you. I mean, last time I was invited to a party was back when I was seven or eight and my old man was doing time at the county farm for assault. They had this Christmas party for all the families. Santa Claus and the whole bit. I still remember the present he gave me out of his sack. A bottle of bubble solution.

Same thing applies to dating as parties. You ball chicks, but you don't exactly buy them no corsage, you know? It was like that with all her questions. They weren't really about my life at all. She should've called her show "Nerd Life" or "Secrets of the Dorks." It sure wasn't about me.

And the truth is, I never planned on being part of this shit. I only signed Jimmy up to piss him off.

But then the guidance counselor over at school got wind of it and said, "Listen, you cooperate with this, we'll forget about that two months of detention for defacing the boys' locker room." Just because I write the principal's a fag on the outside of the trophy case, they want to keep me after school scrubbing toilets or something all fall. So I figure, OK, she'll never use what I say anyways. I'll just be sure I've got my hand on my dick the whole time I'm talking, so they can't put it on TV.

That was Jimmy's plan too. But then I don't know what got into the boy. Come to think of it, it was what he got into that screwed up his head. Pussy. The fucker got hold of her tail and lost his head.

So there he is, sitting on that couch of hers, while she's sticking the camera in his face, and he's answering her questions like this was a goddam congressional investigation. "Well," he says. "Like I always said, if you got a friend that's drunk and they say they're going to drive someplace, it's your responsibility as their friend to stop them, whatever it takes. I'm not saying I never get loaded myself. But if I do, at least I got the sense to stay off the highway." Yeah. Right.

This one time she gets us over there. You knew it was going to be major on account of instead of Oreo cookies she's got pizza waiting for us. "This time, I thought we'd tackle adolescent attitudes to sexually transmitted disease," she says. Maybe I got my attitudes, maybe I don't, I want to say to her. One thing's for sure, you'll never hear about it.

"All right, let's put our cards on the table," she says. Like you know she's been studying tapes of

"60 Minutes" or some shit like that. "What do you think of when I say the word *AIDS?*"

"Homos," I say. "Queers. Perverts. Ass fuckers." You knew they weren't going to use that. Keep those four-letter words coming, is my motto.

"How about you, Lydia?" she says. "Supposing you were in a sexual relationship with a fellow student"—we've clearly entered the world of fantasy here—"Would you expect that person to wear a condom?"

She is a little on the dim side, that one. "It would depend," says Lydia, "on how well I knew them. And what kind of a person they were. I don't think I'd get involved with someone that was untrustworthy." Mrs. Maretto there always shoots old Lydia from the side, so her cross eyes won't show so bad.

"How about you, Jimmy?" says Mrs. Maretto. "Are you concerned about AIDS? Personally, I mean."

I love this part. He gives her a look like you know he's thinking about what she looks like bare-ass naked. "In my present situation, in the relationship I got going, I don't think I need to worry," he says. "She's not that type of person, if you know what I mean. She's real clean."

Right around there Mrs. Maretto says maybe we want to take a break for some pizza. When we get back to it, she's on to a new subject. Should they put warning labels on rock music. You knew she wasn't going to touch the sex part again. Not on camera, anyways.

Jimmy Emmet

We were laying on her bed this one time, Mrs. Maretto and me. Most times after we did it she'd want to get right up and take a shower, but this time was different. She lets me just lay there, leaned up on the pillows, and she's laying next to me, bare naked. Don't ask me why, with a body like she got, but after that one time she did her cheerleading for me, she was shy about me seeing her. "What are you looking at?" she'd say. Then she'd turn off the lights or pull up the covers or something. But this time she didn't seem to mind. I didn't want to stare, but it was the first time I ever got to see a girl like that, all the parts together at once, and not in a magazine but for real. She was just so pretty. I was scared if I reached out to touch her she might remember she didn't have nothing on and cover up. So I just lay there, trying not to look too hard. Thinking, This is all I ask for. If she'll just stay with me, I won't need nobody else.

She's petting me, kind of like she used to pet Walter. Real gentle. She rubs her hands over my chest. I'm wishing I had hair there. Figuring Larry probably does, him being Italian, and old. But she's with me, not with him, right? So I guessed it was OK I didn't.

She musses up my hair, kind of like those moms

on TV shows that muss up their kid's hair when they're running out the door to play baseball or catch the school bus. Come back here and have something to eat. Then they hand the kid a Pop Tart. Those moms that shake their head, only you know they aren't really mad at their kid. Really, they love him. Mrs. Maretto was like that. "You silly boy," she'd say. "You idiot." But you knew she liked you.

I get up from the bed and put on the tape that was playing when we were making love. Motley Crüe, *Theater of Pain*. Then I get back in bed next to her, put my arms around her and stuff. She was facing the wall, curled up like. Even though she was married, with a car and everything, I always had this feeling like I've got to take care of her. She was so delicate and sensitive.

When she turned around there was a tear on her cheek. "What is it?" I say. "What did I do?"

"Nothing," she says. "You don't understand. You never could. If I didn't love you so much I wouldn't be crying this way."

"What then? What's the matter? You gotta tell me."

"I can't go on this way," she says. "I can't keep living a lie. Loving you and then seeing him walk in the door, wanting to kiss me and everything. I feel like I'm a split personality. I feel like I'm going to lose my mind."

"You think it's easy for me, going home and leaving you here, knowing he gets to sleep with you?" I say. "Just thinking about him touching you, kissing you, I go nuts."

"If all he wanted to do was make love that would be bad enough," she says. "But that's not all. When he drinks he gets violent. He can tell I don't love him anymore. And instead of accepting it, he won't leave me alone."

"You got to divorce this guy," I say. "You got to get away from him."

"You don't understand," she says. "He's violent as it is. If he knew there was someone else, if he knew he couldn't have me, he'd never leave me alone. And then there's Walter. I know Larry. He'd take Walter. And I'd have nothing."

That's when I told her I wanted to marry her. I wanted to spend the rest of my life with her. She was all I ever needed. "Look," I said. "I may be young and I may not be some hotshit restaurant owner, but I swear to you, I'll always take care of you. I'll never let you down. I'd do anything to make you happy."

For some reason this just makes her cry more. Now she's got her face buried in the pillow and her whole body's shaking. I put my hand on her shoulder, I lay down on top of her just to stop the shaking. "Suzanne," I say. "Suzanne. Suzanne." It's the first time I ever called her that. I just kept saying it.

"I can't see you anymore," she says. "I can't see you ever again."

For a minute there—Jesus, I don't know how long—I couldn't even talk. I couldn't hardly breathe. Everything I ever heard about that people sing about, having their heart broke, that was me. The room's spinning. It's like someone punched me in the gut. It's like—what can I say?—it was like nothing would ever be OK again in my whole life.

"No," I say. "There's got to be another way. I love you too much to ever let you go."

"And I love you too," she says.

"I'd do anything," I say. "I'd die for you."

"Larry would never leave us alone," she says. "He'd be like that woman in *Fatal Attraction*. He'd never give me any peace."

All I could do was keep saying it. I love you. I love you.

"He used to say if he couldn't have me, he'd want to be dead," she said. "And I believe it. He'd lose his mind."

I said I saw a show one time where that happened. Guy went mental, ended up in the state hospital, drooling and banging his head against the wall.

"Larry wouldn't want to live if he knew I'd stopped loving him," she says.

"I know how he feels," I say. "But me, I could never lay a finger on you, to hurt you. A guy does that to someone like you, he doesn't deserve to live."

And that's when she says it. "Well," she says. "I did have this one idea."

Lydia Mertz

I know you could think Suzanne was some cold-hearted person. Like she didn't have any feelings. But you don't know her the way I did. All the hours we spent, pouring our hearts out and stuff. You can't understand.

For instance, how hard it is for a person that wants to get into television. A person like Suzanne that has a dream. A person like that's not like the rest of us. The only way you can reach your goal is if you just keep your focus and never let anything get in the way. It's not like you're selfish or anything. That's just the only way a person like that has to be if they're going to get ahead in this world.

She had to make a lot of sacrifices, and that was hard for her. Kids for instance. I know Suzanne would've liked to have a couple of kids. Somebody like her, married to a nice-looking guy like him, you know they would've had the cutest kids. Sometimes we'd be out shopping and she'd see these little smocked dresses or these little tiny shoes or something, and we'd both say, "Oooh" and stuff, thinking about how neat it would be. But she told me she wasn't going to have any kids, on account of she had to focus on her career. And I happen to know that hurt her. But you can't have everything.

Another thing people don't know about her is how generous she was. One time when we are at the mall she took me into The Gap and bought me a whole entire outfit. Shirt, skirt, pants. They were size 9/10 so I couldn't try them on, me being a 13/14. She said I should put them in the very front of my closet, to be motivation for my diet. I finally gave them away, it got so depressing looking at them all the time. But that was Suzanne for you. She just can't understand a person like me that doesn't have willpower, because she's got so much of it herself. Whatever she wants, you know she'll be able to pull it off.

The ankle bracelet she bought me though. I wear that all the time. Suzanne said it's the little things like that people notice. Things like having a real leather watchband and not plastic. She taught me it's better to have one pair of gold earrings than a whole pile of plastic ones. Look, the chain is small. But it's real gold. Suzanne said it would draw attention to my feet, and how petite they are. We're the same size actually. Same shoe size I mean. Don't I wish we were the same jeans size.

Larry didn't understand her. Her career and everything. And how a person's got to follow their dream. She said he used to be this wild musician, like Tommy Lee, but then he sold out and now he wanted her to do the same. He acted like a nice guy and everything, when I saw him at their condo, but Suzanne said I wouldn't believe what he was like, when no one was around. She didn't like to talk about it, but once we got to know each other real well she admitted to me how he'd drink, and then he'd hit her. He even forced her to have sex. It was like he wanted this slave, she said. Someone to just stay at home and cook meals for him, and

never have any life of her own. If she didn't have
her career, and me and Jimmy and her dog Walter,
she told me she would probably have lost her mind
by now.

You've never seen someone care about an animal
the way she cared about that dog. It was like he
was her baby. She'd cook him a hamburger—
ground round, not chuck—just like he was a person. Gave him baths all the time. She was always
buying him some little chew toy. You know how
some people carry around pictures of their kids in
their wallet? Suzanne carried around pictures of
Walter. Not just one, but a whole bunch.

In fact, it was her loving that dog like she did
that was the reason she couldn't just divorce Larry.
Because Larry was crazy about the dog too, and she
told me she knew if they ever got a divorce he'd
fight her for custody of the dog, and most likely
he'd win since it was him that bought the dog in
the first place. Which wouldn't be fair of course,
on account of Walter was actually a present to Suzanne. But you knew she was right, on account of
how it was Larry's name on the bill of sale from
the kennel. She'd lose the dog. And that would've
killed her.

And then of course there was their condo, that
she'd worked so hard on decorating. She had a real
touch. It was just like in a magazine. She had all
these neat ideas, like this lamp she had that was
made out of one of those plastic geese people put
in their lawn, and this mirror that had the words
Time Magazine Person of the Year, so when you
looked in it there you'd be, on the cover of the
magazine. She had this vase on the dining-room
table, but instead of having flowers in it like every-

body else would do, she had these peacock feathers. She always came up with ideas like that.

If they got a divorce, he'd get the condo, since he was the one that had come up with the down payment. While she was just a struggling television journalist.

"I'd be like one of those homeless people," she told me. "If I leave Larry, I'll end up with nothing but the clothes on my back." There were her parents of course, but she said they'd side with Larry, and they'd just figure she was crazy, especially after they spent so much on the wedding and the reception. As for Larry's parents, them being Italian and everything, they had connections everywhere. There was no telling what they'd do to ruin her reputation, her career, everything she'd worked so hard for.

I told her I could ask my mom if she could stay with us, but she said no thanks, she had to take care of herself. I'd be embarrassed to have her see where we lived anyways. It's not like Russell's family, but my mother just doesn't understand about things like decorating.

So one time—I think it was the day we bought me the ankle bracelet—we're driving home from the mall and she gets to talking. "You'll think I'm terrible if I told you what I was just thinking about, Liddy," she says to me. That's what she called me. "You wouldn't even want to be my friend anymore. And then I'd have no one."

I told her I could never hate her. No matter what. I told her I was her friend for life. Just like that song, "Just call my name and I'll be there." You know the one I mean? They play it a lot on the oldies station. I'd do anything for her.

"You don't know what I'm really like," she said.

"You just think I'm so nice. Sometimes these ideas come to me, and I hate my own self for having them, but I can't help it. I can't get these thoughts out of my head."

"I know what you mean," I said. "Sometimes I used to think about Chester and wish he'd get hit by a car. I'd have these dreams he got cancer. One time I even dreamed I killed him with my bare hands."

When I said that her head snapped around like she got an electric shock. "What are you saying?" she said. "What did you mean by that?"

See, I think it was me that put the idea in her head in the first place, saying what I did. It wasn't her at all that started the whole thing, it was me. And now it's me that told on her and got her in trouble. It's me that deserves to rot in jail. No wonder everyone hates me. Sometimes I make my own self sick.

I should've just killed myself. It would've been the only smart move I made in my whole life.

She said she sometimes wished Larry would just die. Then they'd all be better off, including him. Because even though she didn't love him anymore, she knew he loved her and she didn't want to break his heart. If someone just killed him it would almost be like they were doing him a favor.

If he was dead, she said, then she could just start out fresh. Go to California. Take this new broadcasting workshop that she'd heard about at the conference in the city, only Larry said it cost too much money, and they were just taking advantage of people. Which just went to show you how he didn't understand. Didn't support her dream stuff.

"I know you're going to make it on television someday," I told her. "I just know it. And then I'll be able to tell everyone we're friends. Every night I'll turn on the news and watch you and say, 'See her? I know her.' "

"But now it looks like it can never happen," she said. "Larry doesn't even want me being friends with you anymore, because it takes up too much of my time, he says."

"I couldn't stand it if I didn't get to see you anymore," I told her. Which was true. Once I was friends with Suzanne, I'd look back on my old life, before, and wonder how I ever stood it. Before I knew Suzanne, there wasn't anything to live for. "I'll help you," I said. "I'd do anything for you. I know Jimmy would too."

It was like a movie or a soap opera. Nothing like this ever happened to me personally—I mean knowing someone that had something that big going on in their life. The kind of thing you only hear about in songs, it's that intense.

"You're the best friend a person could have," she said. She said she'd been thinking, when she got on a talk show or something, she'd need a secretary. To answer her fan mail and so on. She wanted it to be me.

Right around then we got to my house, and she dropped me off out front like always, on account of I never liked her to see my mom, I was too embarrassed of her. So I just jumped out of the car and grabbed my books.

"You know what?" she said to me. "I think you're looking slimmer these days. That diet's paying off."

Valerie Mertz

First time I saw that Mrs. Whatever-her-name-is I said Erica. From "All My Children"? That's who she reminds me of. If you put a brown hair wig on her. She's got that same evil look in her eye. That same kind of attitude like all she has to do is wiggle her rear and the whole world will kiss it. She's trouble, I said. You watch soaps as long as me, you get so you can spot the type.

Then when she started getting all pally with Lydia there. Well you tell me—what's a credit-card bitch like that want with my daughter? You think she picks Lydia so they can trade recipes?

And Lydia. She's what you might call bewitched. I heard about this on "Geraldo." It's not like the only way a person does it is hang a gold watch in front of your face and swing it back and forth. There's other techniques. Mind control and such. You know where she lived, at that condo complex of hers? Number 6. Satan's number. I could give you more examples. Plenty.

So my daughter comes home from school one day like she's on drugs, she's so excited. Talking about how she's working on making this television show with this news reporter named Mrs. Maretto that said, "I can tell you got a knack for the communications field." And how someday she's going to be

Mrs. Maretto's personal assistant on her talk show. Is that a crock or what?

Now that we know what's what, I've done some research. They had this show on one night, the Christian channel. All about how they sneak these messages in between the words of those rock songs there. Right before your eyes, they showed these videos of certain groups the kids all listen to, and then they played them real slow, backwards. I didn't want to listen, on account of they could be doing it to me, right then and there, sneaking those messages in my brain, but Derek, the host, said, "Don't worry, as long as you keep Jesus in your mind, Satan can't ever get to you." So I just did that.

And you know what you heard, when they played those tapes backwards? One of them, this group where all the guys look like they just swallowed Drano, they're saying "Satan I love," over and over. On this other one it's "Kill the lord." Can you beat that? And this is what our kids are listening to day and night? The very group this Mrs. Maretto person is evidently such a fan of. I mean, you don't have to be Dr. Joyce Brothers to see the writing on the wall.

I know what you're thinking. How does a mother let something like this happen to her child? And don't think I haven't asked myself that question. All I can say is, I had enough other worries on my mind I just didn't face what was going on. I'm not well. Diabetes, if you want to know. They were telling me I might lose the leg. And look at me. I can't keep the weight on. Then Chester up and left, and disability says unless I got a letter proving I don't have a husband to support me they can't send the checks, but how am I supposed to have a letter like that when the whole reason I need the check is I can't find him, he's gone? It's a crazy world.

You see what you want to see. It's like on "As Long as We Love," where Jennifer won't admit to herself her husband's gay, even though she finds this picture in his drawer of Roger. And her mother said she saw them together at Le Café. I mean, the writing's on the wall, but she won't let herself see. That was me. I just had too much heartache already to deal with any more.

So when Lydia starts coming home with these expensive clothes from the mall, and jewelry, I just swallow my doubts. You should be happy, Valerie, I tell myself. Knowing you don't have the strength yourself to take her places and buy her nice clothes, be glad someone else does.

She puts this picture of herself that Chester took one time, her and me in our shorts, up on the refrigerator, along with this diet the teacher cut out of a magazine. You should've seen the stuff the teacher wanted her to live on. Breakfast, one rice cake, whatever that is. Lunch was this milkshake kind of thing with fifty million ingredients you never heard of from some health-food store. They talked about potions on "Geraldo" too, incidentally. You wouldn't believe what's going on out there. People sacrificing their pets. Babies even. You don't want to know.

She doesn't tell me about none of it, unless I ask her. It's like I wouldn't understand, like I'm this vegetable sitting here. She just comes home, fixes these carrot sticks of hers and goes to her room. I try talking to her. "You'll never guess what they had on 'Oprah' today," I say. Thinking we'll have a mother-daughter talk. Maybe she'll open up. Kids that come from these broken homes, which I guess is what we have here now Chester's gone, they need to get it off their chest. They were just talking about that on "Sally Jessy Raphael."

But she doesn't answer me. "I probably wouldn't," she says. Can you beat that? It's like this man I stopped in the drugstore one time and I asked him, "Do you have the time?" "Yes," he says. That's it. Yes. I mean, people treat each other like dirt.

I know she was hurting, and it was breaking my heart. Sometimes this boy, Jimmy, would come over and they'd sit out on the front step. They always pretended like they just had to work on this TV business, but really you could tell it was more than that. She was nuts about him, you didn't have to be Kreskin to see that. Only one who didn't get it was him, that all he could do was go all moony-eyed over the teacher.

It gets to be every day my daughter goes off for the afternoon with this Mrs. Maretto. Then round about supper time, which Lydia isn't eating anymore of course, the boy, Jimmy, stops by to find out what they talked about, and was it him? If she had my daughter hypnotized, that was nothing compared to what she did to him. You had to wonder how the kid got dressed in the morning, he was going around like he was a zombie. She could've told him to go jump in the lake and he'd of done it.

Jimmy Emmet

I'm walking down to the beach. No place special to go. Just hanging around, looking for something to happen. Then she pulls up alongside me in her Datsun and rolls down the window. "Want to go for a ride?" she says.

I get in, no questions. Wherever she's going it's better than anyplace I had in mind.

"You shouldn't be so trusting," she says. "How do you know I'm not kidnapping you?"

"So what if you are," I say. "Only if you are, you'd better not be looking for no ransom. My ma would be glad to get me out of her hair."

She's got her music blasting, same as always. "I had a boyfriend in the rock-and-roll business one time," she says.

This isn't what I want to be doing. What I want is to be kissing her. I want to be rubbing my face in her hair.

"He was a sound man for all these rock shows," she says. "He got us backstage passes to see Aerosmith one time. I even met Steven Tyler."

This was all pretty weird to me. Last time I seen her I was laying on top of her, fucking her brains out. Now we're just shooting the breeze. You act like everything's normal, when you both know it's a fucking lie.

Seems to me it should work like this. Once you fuck someone, then everytime you see them after that, you just go right over to them and jump them. Go up to them, take off their shirt or whatever. None of this "nice weather we're having" crap. Who's she kidding?

Everyone tries to pretend fucking never happens. First your parents. You know they done it. Only once they've had you, they spend the rest of their life acting so fucking shocked any time you give them any idea you might be interested in a little nookie yourself. Like what kind of animal are you? When if it wasn't for them fucking you wouldn't even be there?

Mrs. Maretto, she was the same way. We'd screw our brains out one afternoon over at the clam flats and then next time I run into her it's "Did you know we're scheduled to do some taping next Tuesday?"

I'm going crazy from being this close and wanting to kiss her so bad. I'm too desperate to be like some movie star type, all cool and smooth. So I say, "We fucking today?"

She laughs. "Watch your language, James," she says to me.

"OK," I say. "We having intercourse?"

She don't say nothing. Just keeps driving. We're way out of town by now. No houses or nothing anyplace nearby. I can't keep my hands off her one more minute. "Please," I say. But no sound comes out of my mouth.

She pulls over by the side of the road. Opens her trunk, that has one of them aerobics mats inside. It's blue, with pictures of all these exercises printed on it, in case you forget I guess.

She hands me the mat. She's walking a little

ways in front of me, so I follow her. I know what's coming, naturally, so I'm getting pretty hot. I mean, it got to where basically the minute I laid eyes on her I'd get a boner.

"Here," she says. She's pointing to a spot on the ground with plenty of bushes around, so nobody could see us or nothing. Then she lays down and pulls up her skirt. For the first time it hit me that she never looked so excited about doing it as me. I mean, to look at her that afternoon you'd almost think she was doing her job. Not that I cared at that point, I was wanting to get in her pants so bad.

So we fucked. Whole thing was probably over in four, five minutes max. I just couldn't wait, and that didn't seem to matter to her.

When it was over, I was just laying there same as before, wishing we could do it again and knowing she was going to jump up in a second and say we had to get going. Only this time, she sits up but she don't seem in her same rush.

"So," she says, "we can't keep putting off taking care of Larry. I'm getting all stressed out."

"I don't know if it's such a good idea after all," I say. "I been thinking about that. Maybe you two should just get a divorce." I mean, up till this point, I don't think I really believed she was serious. I thought it was kind of like a game, talking about killing Larry. I didn't think it would ever really happen.

"I thought you understood," she says. "But I was wrong about you. You don't really love me like you said."

"I love you more than anything," I tell her. I wished I was better in English, so I could think of how to tell her. I just didn't know the words for it. "Only I just don't think I could kill anybody is all."

"Right," she says. She's real quiet and cold all of a sudden. "I should've realized it was too much to ask. Forget it. Let's just forget the whole thing. Forget we ever met."

"Please," I say. "You don't understand. I want to be with you. I just don't want to kill nobody."

"Well grow up, little boy," she says. "You can't have the one without the other. You can't ever be with me again so long as Larry's around."

I'm frozen there, just looking at her. That perfect face. Her golden hair. Her hands, with those delicate fingers of hers, that used to touch me all over. "It's just that I never did something like this before," I say. "It's different from ripping off a cassette or something."

"Well you never made it with a twenty-five-year-old married woman before either," she says. "That's unusual too.

"It would be better for everyone, you know," she says. "Even him."

I forgot how she figured that, but if I asked her to remind me she might think I was dumb. So I just said, "Right."

"It would look like an ordinary robbery," she says. "Nobody would ever know."

"Yup," I say. It's like I'm hypnotized. She could've told me to stick a fishing knife in my own hand right then and I'd of done it.

"And then afterward of course, there wouldn't be anything getting in the way of you seeing me anymore. We could get together as much as you wanted then. You could sleep over and everything."

That gets my boner going again. I'm dripping

with sweat. I say that sounds good. I can barely talk at this point but she's back to that voice she uses on TV.

"I mean, I'd want to keep a low profile for a while. And naturally I wouldn't want to broadcast it at work or anything. But eventually I'll be finding a position someplace else. It's just a matter of time."

Now I look back on it, naturally, I can see all the problems that would've come up. Now I know it wasn't ever going to work. She wasn't ever going to be mine. But at the time alls I heard was how we could make love whenever we wanted to. That's the way it was for me. It wasn't just about fucking anymore, although that was incredible. It was about love.

So I said yeah. We were on. I'd talk to Russell. But I was pretty sure he wouldn't give us no trouble. He was always up for anything.

Russell Hines

Yeah, he asked me if I'd help off her old man. You're fucking right I said yes. Not because of this shit about how tough her life is. Money, man. She was going to pay me a thousand bucks.

You could tell Jimmy was pussy whipped all right. I mean, he'd of jumped off a cliff, sniffing after that tight little crotch of hers. The boy was gone. I just needed new wheels.

The plan was we'd get these gloves so we wouldn't leave no fingerprints. My car made too much fucking noise, so she was going to lend us hers. She'd leave it with the keys inside at the parking lot over at the mall, and then while she was in there shopping we'd take the Datsun over to her place, get in the back door that she'd leave open, only make it look like we broke the locks. We'd trash the house and shit, then wait for him to come home from work. I'd tackle him, Jimmy'd shoot, on account of it was him that was getting the pussy and all I was getting was cash. Then we'd take off in the car, back to the mall. Leave her car where we found it and cut out of there. No sweat. She'd come out with all her bags—and I mean, you knew she'd make sure plenty of people noticed her in stores, which wouldn't be a problem.

Then she'd drive home, open the door, and freak out naturally. The grieving wife.

She even made this list on her computer of shit to remember for chrissake. Like he's got this exercise bike sitting in the kitchen right by the door so don't bump into it or you'll get real bruised, and be sure when we're trashing the place not to wreck her stereo because it's a real bitch to reconnect all the components. Just mess around in her jewelry drawer and stuff. And could we try and make sure when we shot him not to do it where he'd drip on her carpet she just installed? She tells us to throw the gloves in the harbor and dust the gun off to make sure there's no prints on it before we get it back to Lydia. And one more thing: The dog's got to be shut in the bathroom. Seeing something like that, Larry getting shot and all, could really traumatize him.

I think I'm pretty cool, but this chick is strictly Eskimo material. She tells me it should take six, eight weeks to get the insurance money. In the meantime she'll give me this gold chain her husband had in ten days or so. Once things quiet down.

Jimmy's sweating like a pig, not really listening to any of this, you can tell. He keeps trying to make out with her, kiss her neck. Her, she flicks him off like he's a bug landed on a piece of meat. The cunt, Lydia, she keeps giggling like she's been sniffing glue or something. Can't quit laughing. I can tell it's up to me—the Maretto chick and me anyways— to pull this thing off right. Jimmy won't be good for shit.

The plan is to do it Valentine's Day. Not for any message or nothing, that was just the day it worked out to be. We get our clothes all set, the gloves and all. Her and Lydia are all set to go shopping. "I could use a new bathing suit," she says. "It's always good to have a girlfriend along when you're swimsuit shopping, to give you their opinion." She wasn't kidding neither.

That afternoon, Lydia gets her old lady's gun, and we buy the bullets. Jimmy and me take a few practice shots down at the clam flats, just assassinating sea gulls. Gun works fine. We smoke a little weed, get to the parking lot at seven-thirty, right on schedule. He's nervous, you can tell, but he's really got hisself psyched too. "After tonight she's all mine," he says. "Then I'm going to fuck her till it drops off."

Sure, I think to myself. Right. But it ain't none of my business.

I drive. She's got this tape in the cassette, starts playing right when I turn the key. I mean it didn't mean nothing, only it kind of made you jump, hearing this music come blasting out of nowhere when you wasn't expecting it.

So we drive over her place. No trouble finding it. She'd told us how we should pull in round the back, where nobody'd spot the car or nothing. Door was open, just like she said. I step inside.

That's when the dog starts going crazy. I mean, you'd think there was a whole pack of dogs in there, instead of one little mutt, from the sound of it. He's howling and jumping up and stuff. I reach for the gun in Jimmy's hand, thinking I'll just blast him too. Jimmy stops me.

"Fuck man," he says. "She loves that dog. She'd go apeshit if you killed it."

"What the fuck am I supposed to do?" I say to him. "Turn on the lights and invite the whole fucking neighborhood over?"

"It's no good," Jimmy says. "We got to split. We can't do it tonight."

I don't even try arguing with him. You can tell the guy means it. He's done for the night.

"Christ, man," I say, once we're back in her car heading to the mall. "You think I got nothing better to do than drive around town checking out animal life? Now we got to return the gun and everything. I could've been down by the beach balling some chick myself."

Jimmy wants to go in the mall and explain it to her, how come we couldn't finish the job. You can tell he's relieved, but he's scared too, that she'll be mad. "Forget it, man," I tell him. "It wouldn't look good, later, if someone saw us tonight." I mean we don't exactly look like the type that would be wandering around the bathing suit section of some fancy store. Looking for a chick like her.

So we leave a note in the car, on the back of a gum wrapper. "Dog barked. Better luck next time." Then we cut out.

When Mrs. Maretto found out, man, was she pissed. You should've heard her lay into Jimmy. I tell you, if things had worked out for them, he would've got a different kind of punishment. Endless pussy whipping. But try and tell him that.

Lydia Mertz

All that winter we used to drive around in her car, me and Suzanne and Jimmy, drinking Southern Comfort and listening to tapes. Not Russell. She never liked him so much, and to tell you the truth, I don't think she was his type either. But the three of us, we were just like that. We did everything together. Well, not everything of course.

I didn't have my license yet but Suzanne let me drive so her and Jimmy could make out. She was a different person, when it was the three of us together like that, from how she was when we were making our video, and giving her weather reports on TV. She'd take her hair out of the ponytail she wore. Then she'd sit on his lap, stick her hand down his pants and stuff. At first I'd be embarrassed, but you got used to it. They said if it wasn't for me, they never could've been together. If it wasn't for me being with them, everybody'd be suspicious, instead of just figuring we were working on the video. She said I was kind of like that nurse in the *Romeo and Juliet* movie, that believes in their love and tries to help them be together, when the whole rest of the world is against them. Without her, they never could've got together. And that's how it was, with them and me.

We did dumb stuff. We'd buy pizza and have

food fights. Go to malls and look at tapes. Go down to the boardwalk and get cotton candy. One time we went to this car dealership to test-drive a convertible. I mean if it was just Jimmy and me of course no one would take us seriously. But her being the way she was, the salesman was happy to let us take the car.

But mostly we'd just drive around. Suzanne was always saying how much she missed just hanging out and being crazy like that. She said Larry used to be like that, but then he got all serious, and now he wasn't any fun anymore. "It's like he's dead already," she said.

I always hated it when she wanted to talk about the plan. I don't think it was exactly Jimmy's favorite thing to do either, but Suzanne said it was important to get all the details worked out so nothing went wrong. And of course we knew she was right.

So we'd be driving along, blasting the music or sticking her bra out the window, tied to the antenna or something, and then she'd get that other way all of a sudden, like she was on the news, only it wasn't the weather she'd want to talk about, it was stuff like "Where are you going to put the gloves after it's over?" or "How do you think I should act when I find the body?"

The plan was, Jimmy and Russell were going to make it look like somebody just broke into the condo to steal the TV and stuff. They'd hide in the living room closet, and then when he came home they'd shoot him. Jimmy said Russell wanted to use a knife, on account of then they wouldn't have to come up with a gun, but Suzanne had these brand-new white couches, and anyways, she was afraid if she saw all that blood she might just faint or something. My mom had this gun she bought after Chester left and she started hearing about all these sex killers on the loose. I said I figured they could use it, so long as they got it back without her knowing.

Jimmy and me were helping her just because we were all friends, naturally. But you knew Russell had to get something out of it. Suzanne said to tell Russell he could take Larry's gold chain that he always wore, and some CDs. They had this portable color TV she thought he'd like. And later, when the insurance money came through, she'd pay him a thousand dollars. He was going to buy a car.

In the summer, when it was all over, Jimmy and Suzanne and me were going to take off in her car, and drive to Orlando. She was going to take us to Disney World. She was always telling us how great it was there—the rides and everything, and Epcot Center, where you could walk around for a day and feel like you'd seen the whole entire world, you never had to go any farther. She said they had these horses pulling carriages that take you all around. And everything's so clean there, the minute a horse starts to drop a turd on the street, there's some guy jumping up with a broom and dustpan to clean it up before it even hits the ground. That's how perfect it is.

Danny Ricardo

I met him at his family's restaurant. I was sitting at the bar. We got to talking. It was a slow night. He pulled up a stool, fixed himself a sandwich, and sat down next to me.

You had to like this guy. And something else, you got the feeling he was really looking to talk to someone. Search me why it would be me, but I figured, no sweat. Which is how I happened to be the one. That he was having dinner with that night, I mean. The night he got killed.

Of course now, knowing what happened, you think back over that night, trying to remember any clue something could've been wrong. Maybe I missed something, but it sounded like the guy had it made. Somewhere along the line he even took out a picture of his wife to show me. "No kids yet," he says. "But we're working on it." Big grin.

She was pretty, I remember that. Looked like a girl I used to go to school with, not that I dated her. Homecoming queen.

He said he went off-roading on weekends, and maybe I'd like to join him sometime. Sounded good to me. As long as it was OK with the wife.

One thing I do remember about that part. "My wife's always tied up with these workshops and special projects, weekends," he says to me. "That and shopping. I'm lucky if I'm still awake when she gets back from the mall." He said he guessed that would change, once they had kids. "But she's not your stay-at home type," he said. "She's a career girl."

I told him my wife sells Mary Kay. It works out nice—she can be home with the kids, and still bring in a little something extra, get out of the house, have some excitement.

"Yeah, I know what you mean," he said. "If my wife had to be home all day, she'd go nuts." Still, he knew she'd develop her maternal instinct or what have you, once the babies started coming. You could tell from the way she looked after their puppy. And there were these high school kids she'd befriended too, he said. Bunch of sick puppies, themselves. She'd really taken those kids under her wing. She really knew how to give of herself.

Funny to think, I guess I was the last one that saw him alive. Besides, you know, the ones who did him in.

Lydia Mertz

She said I reminded her of Winona Ryder. Or I would once I got the extra weight off. She said I had porcelain skin, if I just wouldn't go out in the sun and freckle it. Suzanne told me my skin is one of my most positive assets. What she did actually was help me make these two lists: one list of my beauty flaws, the other one with my assets. Every time I listed a flaw I had to think of one asset to cancel it out. Then she showed me all you had to do was learn how to accentuate your positive traits and conceal the negative.

Like for example my eyes. She said saving up for contact lenses was a beauty must. In the meantime I just shouldn't wear my glasses unless I absolutely had to, like if I was walking down the street and somebody asked me what some sign said three blocks away, or it looked like I won the lottery and I had to read the fine print on my ticket. And I should keep doing my eye exercises, naturally.

My weight was a negative of course. But she said until I lost the weight I could just learn how to conceal my figure flaws. Padded shoulders for instance. Those make your waistline look smaller. She'd take me to the mall and we'd go window shopping sometimes for hours. Trying out different shades of blush. Her telling me what styles were good. Which colors went with my skin.

Sure I felt weird, getting my mother's gun. It's awesome if you stop and think about it, how you're holding something in your hand that has the power to just bam, end a person's life. One minute they're walking into their house, just wondering what they're going to fix for a snack or if there's a good show on TV. The next minute, they're just this lump on the floor, and you know they'll never go shopping or celebrate Christmas or drink a Coke ever again.

But the other way of looking at it that Suzanne told me is everything that happens is just meant to happen. Like she was just meant to get the job at WGSL where we'd get to be friends. And then Jimmy was just meant to fall in love with her. She said that kind of thing was always happening to her. Like one time she went to this Aerosmith concert and Steven Tyler looked right at her, even though she wasn't sitting in the front row or anything. And that was just when he started playing her all-time favorite song, "Dream On." I mean, you could say it was just a coincidence, but you've got to wonder.

That night at the mall together was weird naturally. I mean, we knew what Jimmy and Russell were doing of course. She'd be taking a pair of pants down off the rack and holding them up to see what they'd look like with her vest, and I'd be thinking, This could be the very second it's happening. This could be his last moment on earth.

We went into Essence and tried on perfumes. Just for fun. We weren't actually buying any. We just kept squirting each other, like we were little kids. I mean, I had one smell on my wrist and one on my elbow and one behind my ear. You got so you couldn't tell them apart. It must've been all those perfumes at once, all mixed together that did it, because all of a sudden I started feeling like I was going to throw up. I told Suzanne I had to go to the ladies' room. I just stood over the toilet bowl for the longest time, but nothing happened. So then we went to get a milkshake, to calm me down.

We were sitting there drinking our shakes. And then I just felt this crazy feeling like, We've got to stop it right now. We've got to call them up or something, or borrow a car. One way or another, we just had to get back to Suzanne's house before it was too late. I think it was on account of I was watching this little boy and his mom having an ice cream cone together. I started to think that Larry used to be a little boy like that, and he had a mother someplace that probably loved him a lot. I thought about Patrick Swayze getting shot in *Ghost*, and how I bawled my head off. And for a second there I got to wondering if Larry really did hit Suzanne or if that was just something she said to make me feel better about the whole thing. He always looked like kind of an easygoing guy to me. I thought about their wedding picture that I used to see on Suzanne's desk at school and how proud and happy he looked that day, with his hand stroking her cheek like he could hardly believe she was real.

I told Suzanne I thought we'd made a big mistake and we had to do something. She said, "Don't worry, everything will be OK, you'll see. It's too late by now anyways."

"We could try," I said, and then I started bawling.

"Shut up," she said. It surprised me, her saying that. So I started crying even harder than ever. She said she was sorry, but I just had to understand that we were doing the only thing we could, and we couldn't change now. "It's not even so important what you do in life, Liddy," she said to me. "The important thing is following through with what you started. Sticking by your commitment."

Then we went into Victoria's Secret. She loved that place, but to tell you the truth I was always kind of embarrassed going in there, and especially that day. Looking at bras and panties, knowing what was going on back at the condo. It had me weirded out. "When you wear really beautiful, good-quality lingerie," she told me, "even though nobody can see it, you just get this feeling of being beautiful, and it shows in how you act." She said the first time she ever goes for a tryout for some TV job, she's coming to Victoria's Secret first to buy a matching bra and panties set. Real silk.

Then the mall was closing, so we went out to the parking lot. I've got this sick feeling, not from the shake, but she's acting like this was just another shopping trip, no big deal. She says it's her broadcasting training that does it. She knows how to stay cool under pressure.

We get to the car. I don't know what I expected to see, blood spattered all over the seat maybe. But everything's just the same. Just like when we pulled in the parking lot. Then she spots the note Jimmy and Russell left on the dashboard. About how they didn't do it after all.

I'm so relieved I just about wet my pants. I start giggling all over the place. I just laugh and laugh.

Suzanne, she just buckles her seat belt and turns on the tape player. "We'll try again in a couple of weeks," she says. Then she says how she's got to get this whole mess over with before summer vacation. So she'll have a chance to go down to Florida. And take Jimmy and me with her.

That made it easier to think about what we were doing. With Larry and all, I mean. Just knowing I'd get to Orlando. I always dreamed I'd get there someday.

Russell Hines

We were going to try again that Thursday night. She had a job interview in the city. She told us the husband would be working over at the restaurant till eight-thirty, nine o'clock. She got all signed up to send the dog to a kennel overnight to have his hair brushed and shit. Lydia gets the gun again. Me and Jimmy, we take out them black suits and gloves. It's like what they say, dèjá vu all over again.

And this time everything goes smooth. Door's open. We disconnect the TV and VCR, scatter her jewelry around a little. Open some drawers. Then alls we got to do is stand there waiting for the sound of him pulling his truck in the driveway. After a while we hear it.

You can hear Jimmy breathing deep then and shaking. Me, I could be squirrel hunting. I'm just thinking about the thousand dollars. And how once she's got her insurance money I'm going to tell her I want five. Which is still a bargain.

Door opens. He sets down his briefcase. "Honey?" he says. Must've forgot she was going to be at the meeting. He's just reaching for the light switch when I grab him around the neck.

"What the hell?" he says. "What—"

"Don't move," I say.

"What do you want?" he says. "Why don't you just take what you want and get out of here?"

This is already more chatter than I was planning on. The guy should of been history by now. Only Jimmy's froze. He's just standing there with the gun. Not moving.

"Jimmy," I say. "Now." He's still just standing there.

"Wait—" says the guy. You can tell now he's had enough time he's beginning to figure out this ain't no ordinary burglary. I mean he was scared the minute I grabbed him, but now he's about to shit in his pants. He's like some fish flopping around on the pier that's going to stop breathing in about ten seconds if he don't get back in the water and he knows it too. He's desperate. Gives me his gold chain. His watch. But when I tell him to take off his ring he says no. "I can't do that, man," he says. "My wife would kill me." Poor dumb asshole, I'm thinking. If he only knew.

Up to now the guy doesn't see Jimmy's face on account of how I've got him by the neck. But now he kind of jerks around to where he's looking right at Jimmy. Which if he ever had a chance of getting off is like, curtains for him. I get the feeling he knows that now too. He's not even fighting me so much anymore. He's gone limp all of a sudden. That's when he turns to me and says, "You know my wife?"

Bam bam. Jimmy does his thing. Hubby there, he flops down on the rug. So much for not getting no blood on her fucking carpet.

We're out of there.

Lydia Mertz

The day they rescheduled, Suzanne was going to be out of town, auditioning for this arts and entertainment job at a TV station in the city. They picked that night because they knew Larry'd be working at the restaurant till eight-thirty, nine o'clock. Which gave the boys enough time to get their stuff together, pick up the gun over at my house, drive over to the condo, and get everything set up inside before he got back.

Suzanne was cool as a cucumber that day. She stopped by school just when they were letting us out, to show me the outfit she was wearing to her audition. It was a pantsuit, peach colored. She had this matching peach-colored bag, and mauve shoes, mauve scarf, mauve and peach earrings. I said, "Aren't you a nervous wreck?"

"Why should I be?" she said. "I always feel relaxed on camera. All I have to do is be myself."

"I mean about tonight," I said. "You know. The job. At the condo."

"Oh that," she says. "Why should I be? It's not my problem. Or yours either."

"I know," I said. "But I can't help it. I can't help thinking about it, wondering if we're doing the right thing."

"Blah, blah, blah," she says. "We've talked this

thing to death. Who's to say what's right and what's wrong? Am I God or something? How are we supposed to know anything for sure? All I know is, you can talk a thing to death. You can go back and forth forever: Should I? Shouldn't I? And then you know what happens? You've wasted your whole time talking, and never accomplished anything. Sometimes a person just has to take action."

"I know," I said. But at night when I lay in my bed, I keep seeing his face. I keep remembering that time he dressed up as Cupid, in this big diaper, for Valentine's Day, and came by her office at the TV station with a giant bunch of balloons. I keep thinking about the way he set the timer on their VCR so even if he wasn't home he'd always get to look at her weather reports. And then I looked in the car, and there was this present he gave her one time, of these two little dolls, a boy and a girl, with wobbly heads on a spring. He put them in the back window of her car so when you drove along, they kissed.

"I keep asking myself if maybe the two of you should just go to a marriage counselor," I said. "Maybe have a trial separation."

"I explained that already," she said. She was starting to sound mad at me, which was the worst. I guess I started to cry.

So she slapped me. On the cheek. Not hard, just enough to kind of shock me. I mean sometimes it's the best thing a person can do for another person if they're falling apart, knock some sense in them. "Get a grip!" she says to me. "If you keep this up you'll ruin everything."

"Right," I said. That got me calmed down. "I don't know what's the matter with me. I wish I could be like you."

"It's probably just that time of the month," she said. And as a matter of fact, it was. That hadn't even occurred to me.

"Look," she said. "Here's twenty dollars. Go to the mall, get yourself a cute top. Treat yourself to a frozen yogurt—but make it the low-cal kind, OK? Then go home, tuck yourself in bed early. Everything will look different in the morning. It's the waiting that's hardest. Remember how it used to be, when you were a little kid, Christmas Eve? Listening for the sleigh bells and stuff?"

I didn't tell her it wasn't exactly like that at our house. "You shouldn't be giving me this money," I said.

"Forget it," she said. "I want to."

So that's what I did. Went to Casual Corner, found this Bart Simpson Underachiever shirt, extra large for the baggy look. Got a piña colada frozen yogurt sundae. Went home, watched "MacGyver." My mom had been giving me a real hard time lately, but for some reason that night she lay off me. At nine o'clock, when I told her I was going to bed, she turned off the TV herself, without even staying up for "Love Connection." "I guess I'll call it a night myself," she said.

So then I just lay in my bed, wondering what was happening, over on Butternut Drive. Think about kittens, I'd tell my brain. Pretend you're on a date with Bon Jovi. Imagine you could eat all the candy in the world, and none of it had any calories. But none of my usual stuff worked. I kept ending up with this same picture of Larry, opening the door to the condo, and Jimmy standing there, waiting for him, with my uncle's gun.

When I woke up next morning, my nightgown was covered with blood. There was even blood on my hands, on my face, don't ask me how. I remembered what happened the night before and I let out this scream. Then I realized, all that happened was I forgot to put in a fresh Tampax before I went to sleep. I was in the bathroom, washing myself off, when I heard the news on the radio. Larry was dead.

Jimmy Emmet

I try not to think about stuff that much. It's like what happens if a guy's taking a foul shot in a basketball game and just before he shoots someone on the bleachers yells, "Miss it, dipshit." Or you're fucking and you're just about to come and all of a sudden you picture your mother standing there or a priest or something. Messes up your mind. You try to keep your brain blank.

Which is what I was trying to do the night we did the job. Over at her condo there. Putting on those black pants, sticking the gloves in my pocket. Heading out the highway with Russell—the whole time I was just trying to not think about nothing. It's like I'm playing Nintendo. I just concentrate on getting Super Mario where I want him on the screen without him getting zapped. I don't look around the room or listen to the stuff people are saying or nothing. It's like the whole world is on that screen. Those are the times you get to the highest level.

It was working too. Parking the car. Opening her back door. Sneaking in the kitchen, stepping past that exercise bike, it's like I'm Super Mario just blipping across the screen. Disconnect speakers, Blip. Throw the jewelry on the rug. Blip. Empty drawers. Blip.

Then we're just standing there waiting for him. It's dark. And you don't hear a sound except the TV set of the people next door.

And I think maybe it's because I don't have nothing to be doing no more, my brain starts to do tricks on me. I see the face of Freddy Kreuger in the shadows, holding one of them knives like you use for shucking clams. I see this teacher I had in third grade that liked me, don't ask me why. Then I see one of them sea gulls we nailed down at the beach earlier that day, with his beak open and his eyes staring and a little trickle of blood seeping onto his feathers.

I try to block it out. I try to think up different pictures to put in instead. Like this girl from the December *Penthouse*. She didn't have the biggest tits but she had this look on her face like she just said something to you, and it was something nice. She's got one hand behind her head like they do. But the other hand's touching herself down below, you know. And there's this little piece of hair kind of curled around her finger, like it just happened by accident. I tried to picture my hand was right there, tangled up in her hair. Instead of holding on to the fucking gun.

It was working too. I almost didn't even notice when the door starts to open. Then I hear his voice. "Honey," he says. He sets down his gym bag. Reaches for the light switch. That's when Russell gets him by the neck.

"What the hell?" he says. And Russell tells him not to move.

He seems like the type that doesn't want to make trouble. He tells us we should just take what we want and get out of here. He don't know what we want is him.

Now I know what Russell wants me to do. Now's
when I'm supposed to put the gun up to his head
and blow him away. There's no point having a big
discussion. Only I can't move. It's like someone
pulled the plug on me, and I can't do nothing but
stand there looking at him.

I guess I never really thought about him before.
Or if I did I pictured him more like someone's dad.
Some guy in a suit. But basically, this guy looked
like he could go to my school. He wouldn't be the
type to hang around with me or nothing. He'd be
one of the guys that plays on a team and dates the
prettiest girls. But you knew he was an OK guy.
Just because you lived over by the clam flats, that
didn't mean he wouldn't ask you how's it going
when he bumped into you in the hall. He's the type
that's friends with everyone.

Now Russell's getting antsy. He says my name.
"Now," he says. And when he says that, you knew
the guy understood what he was talking about. So
I figure, right. Now's the time. Here I go. Just like
I'm on the basketball court you know. And I'm
about to take that foul shot. Just like I'm playing
Super Mario Brothers 3, and in one-tenth of a sec-
ond is the time I'm supposed to push my zapper.

"Wait," he says. That's enough to where I miss
my opening. I'm off center again, you know. I got
to build myself up again.

Russell there, he's pissed. You knew he'd grab
the gun and do it himself, only he's got to hold the
guy down. But he's giving me this look.

OK, I think. I make myself picture Mrs. Maretto
again, and the December *Penthouse* Pet. I'm getting
back on the track. I put the gun up against his hair.
Russell tells him to hand over his gold chain and
his watch. "Now the ring," says Russ.

"Not my ring," says Larry. "My wife would kill me."

Well that shook me. Even Russell, you could tell he wasn't prepared for the guy to say something like that. Neither one of us can think what to do next, so we just stand there, holding him down. Larry's on his knees at this point, with his hands in front of him, like he's praying.

"Hold on," he says. Man, he's desperate now, you can smell it. "Just wait a second," he says. "Don't do anything."

Russell says "Now, Jim." Another minute and I figure he's going to blow us both away—Larry, and me too. And I'm practically thinking that would be OK. For a second there, I can't even remember why we're even doing this.

Larry turns to Russell and looks him right in the eye. "You know my wife?" he says. That's when it's like I got a new energy pack. I wake up. All the static goes away. I'm clear again. It's like I'm just playing Nintendo again, and alls I got to do is push the buttons, nothing else matters. I pull the trigger.

He goes limp. Blood everywhere. But what I seen was his mouth, just hanging open like one of them sea gulls. Or like a guy that just finished fucking, came all over the place, and fell asleep. I mean, if you saw a dead person like I did you'd know it too: dying and coming look about the same. Only when you die you don't wake up again naturally. And there's the blood.

Russell Hines

I never saw nobody dead before. I killed a cat one time, back when I was a kid and you did dumb stuff for no particular reason—nobody paid me or nothing. I seen my grandmother's stump, from where they cut off her foot after she stepped on a clam shell and it got infected. I even seen this guy that didn't have no eyeball, took out his glass eye and put an olive in the hole, at this club over at Little Paradise. He was plastered at the time but I mean, the rest of us wasn't exactly ready to walk on no tightrope neither. I never seen no dead person before though.

They don't look the same as alive people, I'll tell you that right now. I mean, not just because half the top of his head got blowed off. That's the obvious part. And not just because there's blood all over the place, and he's not moving, except for a second there, when his leg keeps twitching like it hasn't got the news.

Usually when a person's mouth is open it's on account of they're saying something. That or they're eating. Him, his mouth was open but he wasn't making a sound. "You know my wife?" That's the last thing he said. And then his lips just stayed in that position where they left off, and you kind of wondered what he'd be saying now, if he knew.

If he knew, he'd be saying what a cunt she was. If he knew, man, he'd be pissed. Jimmy had this theory we was kind of doing the guy a good deed on account of how he loved her so much if he knew she didn't love him no more he'd want to be dead. "Get real," I told him. "The guy just wanted nookie same as you, and if she left him he'd do the same as you'll be doing, a week, two weeks from now. Sniffing down some more."

But the thing is, he never did know. He had this blank look on his face like he's around five years old, watching "Sesame Street," and alls he wants is a bowl of Sugar Frosted Flakes. His eyes—he was like a deer I hit one time in the Pontiac—that's where the big dent in my front fender came from if you wondered. Second before I hit her, I seen her face in my headlights, plain as a target. She don't know she's about to be dead. She don't even know what dead is. She just don't know, period. Don't know what's happening. Don't know what it's all about. Don't know twelve hours from now I'll be roasting her butt over the coals down by the clam flats. Man, you should've tasted that venison. She don't know her heart's about to stop beating, but then she don't know she got a heart.

That was him. Utterly clueless.

PART
III

Dick Petrie

My wife and I were just lying in bed watching "LA Law" when I heard the screaming. You hear this voice outside yelling, "My husband's been murdered!" well believe me, you get up pretty quick and go see what's the matter. Of course I put on my bathrobe first. When I heard her I was just wearing my skivvies.

It was her, Suzanne Maretto, standing out in the cul-de-sac, running back and forth yelling, "Help, someone help me," and so forth. Don't ask me why I remember this but she had high heels on, and she was wobbling when she ran.

"Whoa, there!" I say when I get up close. I put my hands on her shoulders. "What's going on?" I say.

"I've got to use your phone," she says. "There's been a murder. My husband's dead."

Situation like this, you're hoping she's just gone crazy, PMS or some such. You should see my wife at that time of the month. You never know. Only in Suzanne Maretto's case I could kind of tell it wasn't some drug trip or what have you. Even though she's saying these terrible things, and she's obviously upset, she's also what you might call under control. She introduces herself. "I'm Suzanne Maretto from number six," she says. "The one with the Lhasa apso?"

Now I remember, because she was always out walking that dog.

"If only he'd been here tonight this might never have happened," she said. "He's off at the kennel being groomed."

By now my wife's out there with us. "Come on in the house," she says. "You can wait over at our place while Dick calls the police."

So we do. And of course it doesn't take long—a minute, maybe three at the most. Cynthia pours her a shot of whiskey, but she doesn't take it. "I was auditioning for a big television job," she says. "That's why I'm wearing these clothes. It was for arts and entertainment reporter."

What's her husband's name? Cynthia wants to know. "Larry," she tells her. "Oh no," says Cynthia. I guess he used to come over and kid around with Matthew sometimes, when Cynthia'd have him out on his tricycle. "Such a nice guy."

"He managed his parents' restaurant," she says. "Maretto's. We just got married last June."

"Tragic," I say. "Who'd do such a thing?"

I wasn't really expecting an answer from her at a time like that but she gave me one. How she figured there must have been burglars broke in their place. The TV was disconnected from the cable when she came in, and her jewelry all over the place. "I figure it was a case of Larry just coming in to the wrong place at the wrong time," she says. "He must've surprised them." She said maybe they were on drugs or something. It was probably kids that are always listening to tapes of that 2 Live Crew type of junk. It gives them ideas. The younger generation has no respect for human life anymore.

This is when the cops come in. Two cars, blue lights everywhere. Now half the development is up too, everybody out in the street in their bathrobes and stuff, trying to find out what happened. A little later on, after the cops were in there a while, I see this little crowd form near their front door, so I think maybe there's a detective that found some clues, and I try to move in to hear better.

And you know who's in the middle of the crowd, answering the questions? It's no cop after all. It's her. You'd think she was the White House press secretary to hear her talk.

Janice Maretto

I was in Cincinnati that night. Just as we're all coming off the ice after this big final number we do, Pat, one of our stage managers, calls me over and says there's some kind of emergency, and I'm supposed to call home right away. So I run right over to a phone with my skate guards still on and my show outfit. I mean, when they call you on the road like that you know something terrible's happened.

It was my uncle that answered. My parents were down at the police station already. When he said it was Larry I just let out this scream. All these other skaters nearby who were taking off their costumes came running over naturally. But I couldn't even talk. All I could say was "my little brother."

Crazy things pop into your head at a moment like that. There was this Halloween one time when I dressed up like a witch. Larry couldn't have been more than three. When I came out of my room to show him how I looked he didn't even know it was me. He wouldn't stop crying until I washed off all the makeup. "See," said Mom. "It's just Janice."

Sometimes I'd hang around with him and his friends, back when they had this little rock group in junior high. He was a really terrible drummer, but he loved it and nobody had the heart to tell him.

I never liked Suzanne. Even back when they were first engaged and everyone was saying how great it was that he'd found a girl like her, how pretty she was and what great places she was headed. You see girls like that at the rink. They'll kick their blade into your shin and pretend it was an accident. Cut you off in a jump and make it look like it was your mistake. I mean, some people would skate in the middle of a deserted lake, just for the feeling of sweeping across the ice. And then there are the ones that would just shrivel up and die if there wasn't someone out there cheering for them every second, telling them how great they are. That was her.

The next morning, when my flight got in, my uncle told me how they'd found all her jewelry and stuff disturbed, and it looked like burglars did it. But I never really bought that. My first thought, when I heard the news, was Suzanne. I can't say I ever would've pictured some other guy involved. I mean, there was just no reason to want to kill a guy like Larry.

But I had to figure, one way or another, he must've gotten in her way. And like I said in skating, there's people who'd sooner knock you over and leave you flat than move themselves over half an inch. People like that, you just don't want to get in their way. I figure one way or another, my brother must've gotten in hers.

Carol Stone

It was a nightmare, pure and simple. From the minute we got the call, Earl and I barely slept or ate. The first thing we had to do was get to Susie, naturally, knowing what a state she'd be in. Imagine losing your husband to a vicious murderer when you're a newlywed, just twenty-five years old. All I can say is, life can be very cruel. And that's how it seemed even before they began trying to tie her in to the crime.

She was being very brave. That's our Susie. And now, just because she's strong enough as an individual that she doesn't just fall apart, people say she doesn't have any feelings or something. When they don't know her like we do. They don't know how she's dying inside.

So she kept her chin up. That first night they had her on the news, it broke your heart. Her sitting there in my living room, holding on to that little dog. "If anybody out there has any information whatsoever that might assist us in finding the criminals who committed this heinous crime, I beg of them to contact the police," she said. Her broadcasting training really came in handy, the way she knew to look right into the camera and all. She didn't break down or anything. Just kept her dignity. Like I always used to tell her, "You never get a second chance to make a first impression."

Strangers were calling us up, offering prayers, sympathy cards, and so forth. Flowers? We had so many flowers I used up every vase in the house and had to start putting them in Tupperware. I mean you could just feel it, everybody's prayers were with Susie. "It's a weird feeling, Mom," she said to me. "Knowing that wherever I go now, people know who I am. They recognize me." There was this one little boy that saw her in the supermarket who even asked her for her autograph. He said she was the first famous person he ever met. In spite of the tragedy, you had to get a kick out of that.

Those first couple days after the murder it was like we were going around in a fog, there was so much to do. People to contact. Media crawling all over the place. Susie said a lot of people in that situation resent the media for interfering in their grief, but being in that line herself she understood their point of view and she always tried to cooperate. I remember the day we were getting ready for Larry's service, she even pointed out to Angela, his mom, how the striped blouse she was wearing was going to make these vibrating lines on people's TV screens, and maybe something else would be better.

Susie herself looked just beautiful, of course, in a tragic kind of way. Who she reminded me of that day, if you want to know, was Jackie Kennedy after the President was shot. That same quiet dignity and class. She carried this one white rose. She asked the funeral director if Larry could be laid out holding their dog's leash. Unfortunately it couldn't be an open casket. The nature of his injuries and all.

Well, people were just wonderful at that point. And of course, though you'd never know it to see how they're treating her now, the Marettos regarded Susie like their own daughter. So we were all together in our grief. Suzanne told Angela Larry was the only man she'd ever love so long as she lived. Angela told her at least she could take comfort knowing Larry had that one happy year of marriage before being taken away from us. Joe, the father, gave Suzanne Larry's basketball ring from the year his team made it to the state finals. All those years he'd kept it, he said, but it seemed like Susie should have it now.

For days it was all you heard on the news. There were very few leads in the case since the burglars appeared to have worn gloves. There were no fingerprints. No tire tracks. Nobody in their condo development had seen a thing.

Eventually things quieted down. Suzanne wasn't allowed to go back and stay in their home since it was still taped off as a crime scene. She couldn't get her own clothes and makeup, which was hard for her. Not that those things are that important in and of themselves when you've lost a loved one. But I always feel it's important to keep up appearances no matter what. If you start letting yourself go on the outside it works itself in to the point where you're not keeping it together inside either. I mean, sometimes something as simple as a new hairdo can give me a boost when I'm feeling down. And here was my daughter, that had her husband brutally murdered, and she couldn't even wear her own shade of lipstick. We had to go out and buy her all new clothes, toiletries, even underwear. And at a moment like that.

Valerie Mertz

First I heard about it was on TV. They had it on the five o'clock news, you know. At that point I hadn't even laid eyes on Mrs. Perfect there, but I thought I recognized the name. "Hey, Lydia," I said. "That Mrs. Maretto you're always talking about? She have a husband named Larry?"

Liddy's in the kitchen, polishing off a pint of ice cream. I don't know what happened to this rice cake business, but all of a sudden she's eating again like there's no tomorrow. "I guess so," she says. "What's it to you?"

"He got killed," I say. "Murdered. Looks like burglars broke in their apartment and shot him."

Now I never met the woman, so I can't get too upset about her, you know. I mean, sooner or later everybody gets nailed, one way or another. Looks like this was just her turn. And his, needless to say. So the one I'm worried about is Lydia. How she's going to take it, them being so close and all. I try to put an arm around her and think what Ann Landers would say in this type situation.

But she doesn't want to hear it. "So?" she says. "I never knew the guy. I never saw him before in my life."

"I know," I say. "But her being your friend and all, I figured you'd be torn up about it."

"He wasn't that nice to her anyways," she says. "He didn't want her to take this workshop she wanted to go to. I think maybe he took drugs."

"Oh yeah?" I say. "Maybe it wasn't really a burglary then. Maybe it was a drug deal that went bad. Maybe he bought some cocaine or angel dust and then he skunked someone for the money, and they sent a hit man. You hear about that all the time, on TV."

"Search me," says Lydia.

"Well if that's it," I say, "someone should tell the police. That's important information to give them. And they were just saying how if anybody knew anything, there's a special number to call."

"No, Mom," she says to me. I hate to tell you how unusual it is, for my flesh and blood daughter to call me mom. Last time I heard it was probably 1987. Nowdays it's strictly "Hey You."

"You know something about this murder?" I ask her. "Is there something you want to tell me?"

"I don't know a thing," she says. "Will you just lay off me?"

"Well one thing's for damn sure, little missy," I say. "You can bet she won't be coming around here, picking you up to take you shopping anymore. Too many bad memories. Plus I bet she gets a pile of money from the insurance, and goes out and buys a Miata or something. Probably take off for Hollywood."

"You don't know Suzanne like I do," says Lydia. "She'd never leave like that. She's got her friends here."

"Friends. Right," I tell her. "You just see how much she cares about her friends, once she's got a pocket full of cash."

That's when she left. "America's Funniest Home

Videos" was starting, and they were showing this real big woman and she's dancing with her husband at this real fancy place and all of a sudden her skirt falls down. That show slays me.

We didn't talk about the Mrs. Maretto situation anymore that night. But I could hear Lydia in the kitchen, dishes clattering. Sound of the refrigerator door opening. I called out to her to come take a look at the show, figuring if anything will perk up a person's mood these home videos would do the trick. No answer.

"I know one thing," I said. "With cold-blooded criminals like that on the loose, I sure am glad we've got a gun in the house."

Jimmy Emmet

She told me before we done it, after it was over she couldn't see me for a few days. Her parents and the cops crawling all over her and all. So at first I just wait. The next day, on account of all the time she'd been spending at the school, they have it on the announcements that Mrs. Maretto's husband died, and they do this minute of silence where everybody's supposed to be thinking about Mrs. Maretto. Yeah, well I was thinking about Mrs. Maretto all right. But maybe not like they meant.

Four, five days later, when I still ain't heard a peep out of her, I'm getting anxious. She hasn't come round or nothing, which I can understand, but still, you got to think she's got a little time by now to at least contact me. No dice.

Lydia goes to the memorial service. Not me, that would freak me out. So I ask Lydia would she deliver a message to Mrs. Maretto for me. I want to see her. We wouldn't have to do it or nothing. I just got to see her.

Lydia said Suzanne didn't say nothing when she told her that. It was like Lydia was invisible. "She's probably still pretty shook up, Jimmy," Lydia tells me. "Her being a widow all of a sudden."

The next week I go over to her parents' house

where I hear she's been staying, knock at the door. "I got to see you," I say. "I just can't wait one more day."

She laughs. "Oh yeah?" she says. "Why? What do you think would happen if you did?"

I'd bust. I'd yell and scream. Fuck, I don't know. Only I got to touch her skin. Got to put my face in her hair. Got to climb on top of her and ball her.

"Well," she says. "I been thinking. That it's not such a great idea. Seeing you. Considering," she says.

"Considering what?" I say. I'm whispering, but I want to scream.

"Considering you're sixteen and I'm twenty-five. Considering the last book you read was the owner's manual to a Harley-Davidson and the last time you took a shower was probably last Saturday. Considering I'm planning on taking an intensive seminar in broadcast technique this summer in California. I mean what did you think?" she says. "Did you picture us going out to dinner with my folks or something? Did you imagine taking me into the city to a Phil Collins concert or out to dinner at a nice restaurant? Get real."

"What about what happened?" I says. "What was all that about? I thought the whole point was so we could be together."

"Well sure," she says. "Only it didn't work out. Things change. That's the nature of life."

"So what am I supposed to do now?" I ask her.

"That's not my problem," she says. "I'm not your mother."

Bud Baxter

A week, maybe a week and a half after we ran our first story on the Maretto murder I come into the station around my usual time and there's a message waiting for me. Suzanne Maretto wants me to call her up. You've got to understand, in my business a reporter usually has a lot of doors slammed in his face, people see him coming they go the other way. Her especially, who had the press crawling all over her life those first days after the murder, you might think she'd just want to go into seclusion. But it turns out, when I call her back, she has more things she wants to talk to me about. OK, I think. Let's see what she's got. "I can't talk about this over the phone," she says. "But I'll give you the exclusive if you come over." So we make a date for me to come by her folks' house with a cameraman later that afternoon.

When I get there she's all dressed up in this little jumpsuit outfit, high heels, her hair like she's just come from the beauty parlor. She invites me in, asks what I'd like to drink. Lemonade, iced tea, beer, half a dozen different brands of soda, you name it. Would I like a sandwich? Cake?

She wants to know where our cameraman studied his technical work. How does he like the new lightweight minicam? What kind of mike do we have here? She says she saw my report the night before on the couple whose ten-year-old daughter gave her mother a kidney. Good work, she says.

Something about all this makes me uncomfortable. It blurs the lines so you don't know where you stand. She's meant to be the subject. But she's acting like she's the reporter herself.

"So," I say. "What was it you wanted to tell us?"

"Oh," she says. "Well, it's kind of—complicated," she says. After she called me she started to wonder if maybe I'd just get it all mixed up.

"Why don't you just give me a try and we'll take it from there," I say. "Do you have some new theory as to the identity of your husband's murderer?"

"Not exactly," she says. Although she wants to emphasize again that the police have done a fantastic job, beyond the call of duty. "Just incredible. We should all sleep a little safer at night," she says, "knowing there are officers like Detective Mike Warden and his great team watching over our community."

"You didn't have the camera going," she says. "Did you want me to give you a retake on that?"

I tell her I guess that won't be necessary. Not that I'd dispute what she says.

She sits there a second, playing with her earrings. Am I sure I don't want a Coke? How about Rick, my cameraman?

"No thanks," I say. "Really."

At this point I'm just trying to figure out how to make a graceful exit. I mean, with a woman like this who just lost her husband, you never know what could set her off. Maybe she's just lonely. Needed to talk to someone.

"He must've been a great guy," I say.

"What?" she says. "Oh, right. Larry."

"It's just tragic," I say. "So young. When you had your whole future to look forward to. And now it's over."

"Well I'm still alive," she says.

"Right," I say. "Thank God you weren't there with him that night, or it might have been a double murder."

"It was bad enough just finding him," she says. "There was blood everywhere. It was the worst thing I ever saw. Have you ever seen what a person looks like, shot at close range like that? I mean, we're not speaking of some neat little chest wound.

"When they shot President Kennedy," she says, "you know the bullet blew off half his head. Of course that wasn't close range like it was with Larry. But the effect was similar, actually. An unbelievable sight."

I told her how sorry I was. And then I said something like "Gee, look how late it's getting to be. I guess we'd better head back to the station if we still want to be on the payroll Monday morning, what do you say, Rick?"

"I never got to telling you what I called you about," she said.

I say that's OK. We'll be following this story on an ongoing basis.

"The thing is," she says, "as you must know, I'm in your line of work myself. At the moment I'm under consideration for a very big arts and entertainment reporting job in a nearby market, as a matter of fact. Not that I've had much time lately to think about that of course.

"Anyway, I've been working all year with a group of disadvantaged youngsters, making a television special about the hopes and dreams of a group of teenage kids. I finished the project just before, just, you know, a couple weeks back. I was just getting ready to submit it to my station manager, but now, with everything that's happened, I was thinking your own station might be interested in taking a look at it and maybe airing it as a special. You could maybe show a little of our tape, or shoot a little footage of me working on the final edit in the studio. You'd have the exclusive of course."

I told her I'd have to talk to the station manager about that, but it sounded like an interesting idea. What are you going to say? You had to figure the woman must be dazed with grief. Who knows how I'd act, if something like that happened to some family member of mine? You could hardly blame her even if she went crazy. Which clearly she hadn't done.

We've got our equipment packed and we're just loading it in the van when she comes out to talk to us one more time. "I'll tell you another interesting angle on all this," she says. "And that's my dog. I mean, he loved Larry too, and now all of a sudden not only is he away from his familiar home and his old chew toys and everything, but Larry's disappeared, and nobody can explain it to him. You know he's got to be wondering."

"Yup," I say. "Dogs are amazing animals. Got as many feelings as people. More, sometimes."

Angela Maretto

At first it never would've occurred to me Suzanne could be involved. Not in my wildest nightmares would I think such a thing. She was his wife. He loved that girl with all his heart. She was like our second daughter.

Now maybe if I could go back in time and see her at the funeral, or talking to the television reporters, I'd suspect something. But at the time you don't think about that. You're so completely caught up in your grief you don't even know if it's sunny or it's raining. So how would you notice if your daughter-in-law who's standing there with her face in her handkerchief might really be a murderer?

At the time, we just all stayed close together. I felt as long as people were around that loved him, he wasn't completely gone, you know? If it was a big enough crowd, it could seem like he just stepped out of the room for a minute. The times that were hardest were nights, when it was just Joey and I alone, lying in bed holding on to each other and crying so hard you could feel the mattress shake. Those were the worst.

You got through the days, who knows how? I mean at first there was just so much to attend to—the funeral, the police, friends coming by the restaurant, the newspapers. You didn't have time to think, and that was good. I got dressed in the morning, put on my makeup, fixed breakfast. But I don't remember any of it.

It was later, after things quieted down some, that I started to fall apart. They hadn't arrested the boys yet, the investigation seemed like it was at a standstill. I'd go out in the world, and see people going about their business like nothing was wrong, everything was the same as it ever was. That's what drove me crazy. When that happened, sometimes I'd call up Suzanne, say why don't you come on over, have a cup of tea? I just didn't want to be alone. I'd take out the photo albums, write thank-you notes to people that sent us flowers, polish silver, whatever. Having the restaurant helped. It kept you busy.

But I remember this one afternoon. She was over at the house helping me clean out one of my closets. I was getting rid of a lot of Larry's things, and I thought she might be interested in having some.

There was this old school jacket he had from his basketball days. Larry loved that jacket. More than one girl tried to get their hands on it. But there was never anyone he felt that way about.

So there we were reliving all these old memories. And suddenly I open a drawer and there's the jacket. "This should be yours," I said to her. "Why don't you try it on and see how it looks?"

She was wearing a heavy sweater of some sort, so she took that off first. There we were up in my son's old room, Suzanne standing there in her bra and skirt. Which shouldn't be any big deal—we were both women for goodness sake.

Except that's when I spotted it. I mean at first I thought she just had a leaf or something stuck to her chest and I was going to brush it off. But no, it was a tattoo. Shaped like a rose. Right over her left breast. Can you beat that?

Don't ask me why, but I felt a chill come over me, like all of a sudden I knew she wasn't the person I'd always thought. All this time she'd been hiding that, what else was she hiding?

I didn't say a word. Neither did she. But we both knew I'd seen it. And that was the first moment I began to wonder. What if she had something to do with Larry's murder?

I never trusted her after that. Even though I let her take the jacket.

Russell Hines

I'm hanging out in my yard, working on the muffler to the Pontiac. On account of I haven't seen no thousand dollars yet, to get a new set of wheels. Who should pull up but Mrs. Tight Cunt, the grieving widow, in her Datsun. With the radio playing, and that little dog of hers sitting next to her on the seat with a hair bow on, same as hers. She's got the dog belted in, if you can believe it.

OK, I'm thinking. It's about time I got my cash. She leans over, opens the passenger-side door, tells me to get in.

"Hello, Russell," she says to me. "I wanted to give you something."

"Oh yeah," I say. "Great."

Then she bends over and hands me this cardboard box from underneath the dash. Got a Walkman and some tapes inside. Faith No More, AC DC that she never liked, and these tapes about how to get to be a big-shot success just by looking in the mirror every day and telling yourself you're great. "These were Larry's," she says. "I wanted you to have them."

"Whoa," I say. "Wait a second. What about the money?"

"I'm sure you can understand this is a difficult time for me," she says. "Right now I'm still paying off bills for my husband's headstone and funeral service and so forth. And then there's the mortgage on the condominium. We could have purchased life insurance that would have paid it off if he died but for some reason Larry never did that. Don't ask me why. A big mistake."

"Well yeah," I say. I'm not really listening to this crap. Alls I want to know is where's my thousand bucks.

"I'm confident that once everything's squared away, I'll want to make you some sort of gift," she says. "It's just that right now I'm still over-whelmed. I don't know where I stand yet."

"Yeah," I say. "Well I know where I stand, all right," I say. "Knee deep in horseshit.

"We had a deal," I tell her.

"And I'm a person who honors her commit-ments," she says. "It's just, I'm not ready yet."

"Fuck this," I tell her. "I want my money."

"You know, Russell," she says to me. "I've tried as hard as I could to ignore this attitude of yours. But if you're going to use foul and abusive language I'm going to have to ask you to get out of my vehi-cle. I don't want to see anymore of you until you simmer down."

"Don't worry," I say. "I'm leaving. I don't like to hang around places where they're shoveling shit." I'm halfway out the door when she calls me back.

"Russell," she calls to me. "Don't forget your box." And like a fool I take it.

Det. Mike Warden

At first of course it just looked like a burglary where the guy walked in at the wrong time. But it didn't take long before we started asking questions.

For starters, we figured they must've broken in the back door, so why didn't we see some evidence of tampering with the lock? Then there was the way they just disconnected the television set. Left the CD in place, the amp, the color TV. The jewelry we found scattered, that came from all the way upstairs. You'd think they'd have finished with the stereo stuff first before working their way up to the bedroom.

Everyone we talked to said what bad luck it was, the dog not being home. "If he was around when someone tried breaking in, the whole condo development would've heard him carrying on," the father said. Noisy little critter I guess. So it was either bad luck he was off getting his shots, or else good planning.

But the main thing that just didn't jibe with the theory of unplanned assault on a burglary victim was the way they shot him. Point blank, and at close range. Someone held him down while someone else put a gun up to his head and pulled the trigger. And not in the middle of the living room either. This was right next to the door. Right next to where he'd put his briefcase down. Like they'd just been waiting for him.

Of course you had to wonder about motive. Guy had a clean record, no signs of drug abuse, no gambling debts. Didn't appear to be any other woman in the picture. Looking at her, you wondered about other men. And then there was that insurance money. A hundred thousand dollars might seem like enough to kill for, to some people anyway. I worked on a case one time where a guy blew a gas station attendant away for charging him the extra penny when he ran over the ten-dollar mark filling his tank. You figure.

Other than the nature of the bullet wounds, we didn't have much to go on. No fingerprints. No sighting of the perpetrators or a vehicle. No gun.

But then there was the wife. She seemed like a solid person. Real cute, nicely spoken. There was just something about her I didn't trust. She had an airtight alibi of course. At the instant her husband was being shot, she was having an interview for some sort of television reporter job, over in the city. They actually had tape of her there, talking about some movie.

Fact is, it was something she said about this job audition of hers that got me wondering. We're sitting there going over the details of that evening. How she walked in and found him and all. And right in the middle of telling me how he was lying there with the top of his head blown off, she says to me, "Isn't it ironic?"

"Beg pardon," I say. "How's that?"

Him dying on the very night when everything was going so great for her, she says. Almost like that was the price she had to pay for having something go so well like that.

"Have you ever noticed the way every time something really good happens to you, usually something bad has just happened, and vice versa?" she said. "Almost like life just has to balance itself out."

I was thinking it didn't seem to me like much of a balance, getting a job at a TV station maybe, in exchange for a guy's life. But then what do I know?

Dan Jennings

Teach high school as long as I have, you get antenna. I mean, there's days you'll just walk in the cafeteria and feel it, something's up. A week later you find out that was the day some girl got the results of a home pregnancy test and tried to give herself an abortion in the girls' room. Passed out in home ec a week later from internal hemorrhage and infection. That's when the teachers finally get clued in. But the kids—they knew that day in the cafeteria. Which was what you were picking up on.

Now that I look back on it, I can see last February was one of those times. I mean, at first you would've thought it was simply Suzanne Maretto's husband being found murdered. Reason enough for a certain sense of malaise, I'd say. But instead of blowing over after a week or two the feeling grew stronger. By the time vacation week rolled around the whole school felt ready to snap. We're not talking about academic tension, mind you. I'm talking about a crowd that isn't exactly spending their every spare moment bent over their books. And still, you knew they were all charged up about something. You'd walk into study hall and a hush would come over the room. You'd leave the room and feel the whispers starting again the moment you stepped into the hall.

Slowly the rumors began to surface. Someone had seen a photograph of Jimmy Emmet holding Suzanne Maretto on his lap. Someone else heard Suzanne had bought Lydia a pair of sneakers. Someone else said no, it was a CD player. A leather jacket. They said Suzanne Maretto was pregnant. Someone said that video they were making wasn't really about high school life at all, it was a pornographic video in which Mrs. Maretto and Jimmy Emmet were naked, in bed together. They said Jimmy did all sorts of things to her, with shaving cream and cucumbers. Or that Lydia and Suzanne were lesbian lovers. Or that Larry was selling drugs to Russell, and Russell got mad when Larry sold him a bad batch of crack. A girl who'd been having sex with Russell Hines said she'd heard him and Jimmy Emmet talking about how to keep Lydia quiet. Someone else said Suzanne Maretto had a tattoo that said "Jimmy and Suzanne" on her buttocks.

We had a special assembly about AIDS and safe sex sometime in March. When it was time for questions and answers a boy in the senior class raised his hand and asked if it was true you could get AIDS from a tattoo needle. The speaker said she had to admit there were conflicting opinions on that one and she couldn't say for sure. Someone in the bleachers called out, "Let's call up the cable TV station and ask the weather girl." You could almost feel five hundred people gasp. I guess by then everybody knew.

Lydia Mertz

She stopped calling me. She wasn't inviting me over to her house anymore. Of course she wasn't staying at her house at this point, but we could've gone out for pizza. We could've hung out. Just so I could see her.

I brought a flower arrangement to the memorial service. Pink carnations. That color always seemed to fit with her. After the service there was this line you went through, shaking hands with everybody in the family and saying how terrible you felt. Naturally I didn't have that much to say to the parents, but when I got to her, I just threw my arms around her and started bawling. We'd been through so much together. And I felt like it was just the beginning.

"It means so much to me that you'd come," she said to me. Same thing I heard her say to the guy right ahead in the line, and the one in front of him.

Well, I'm thinking, this just isn't the place to talk. She's got to keep up appearances here. It's like she's acting in a play here. Later on, we'll go to the mall and try on silly hats and stuff, blow bubbles, sing songs from *The Wizard of Oz*. We'll just be a couple of crazy girls together again. So I wait to hear from her. I sit around at home thinking any minute now I'm going to see the Datsun pull up and she'll hop out and say, "How about we go over to the mall, Liddy?"

I just sit there in my room, waiting. I hear the TV, one soap after another. Hear that damn Dexatrim commercial nine million times. My mom screaming on the phone to her sister all about what a jerk Chester was. Kid next door playing Super Mario. But never her.

After she moved back from her parents' place to her condo, when the police were done looking for fingerprints and stuff, I went over right away. "I missed you so bad," I say. "My life was just unbearable when you weren't around."

She laughs. Pokes me in the stomach—just lightly, you know? "You hitting the ice cream again, Liddy?" she says. That's Suzanne for you. She knows me so well, she notices everything.

I tell her I was thinking maybe we could go drive around. Like before. There's so much I want to tell her. And naturally I want to know how things are going with Jimmy. And what about our trip to Florida this summer?

"Gee, I don't know," she says. "There's a lot going on right now. It's a crazy time, you know?"

"How's Walter doing?" I say.

She says, "Poor little guy. He keeps sniffing around like he's looking for Larry." The blouse she was wearing the night she found Larry, that got blood on it. One day he dragged it out of the hamper and brought it into her bed. Like he recognized the smell. Another time it was a pair of Larry's old dirty gym socks. She didn't have the heart to wash them.

"So," I said. "Whatever happened to that TV job you tried out for the night Larry, you know. Got killed."

"It didn't work out," she told me. They were crazy to get her on their news team, only the terms of the contract were just too unreasonable. She'd be locked into the same station for two years. She explained to me she had to keep her options more open than that.

"I guess you're going to take that workshop out in California this summer," I said.

"Yeah," she says. "They're going to have this woman there that hosts a morning talk show out of Portland, Oregon. Also some talent scouts who handle placing people like her in some of your mid-range television market cities." Which is the place a person has to start.

"That sounds exciting," I say. "You know," I say, "I don't have to stick around this town." I mean, anytime she wanted me to come be her secretary, it wouldn't matter where, I'd drop everything and do it. She wouldn't even have to pay me, until she was up in the big time.

"I've been reading about Kathy Lee Gifford," she says. "The one that's on mornings with Regis Philbin? And how she married this old guy that was a sportscaster, and even though he was twenty years older than her, they decided to have a baby. She stayed on the air right through her pregnancy and everything. Looked great. She even demonstrated these exercises so women at home who were expecting—which is a big part of your target audience after all—could do them right along with her. The day she came back to work after having the baby—which was like, two weeks after he was born—Regis Philbin got the highest ratings in the entire history of his show. She's doing baby food commercials and stuff. Everything's worked out great for her. Deborah Norville now, she was a different story. Talk about water weight gain. No wonder they fired her."

Cody. That was Kathy Lee's baby's name. Cute.

"How's Jimmy doing?" I asked her. "He hasn't been around."

"James?" she says. "Gee, how would I know?"

I said I thought they were in love and stuff. I figured he'd be with her every second he could now.

"Oh, boys," she said. "They get some pretty crazy ideas. I mean, they really lose their perspective. Someday you'll understand."

"What about—you know," I said. "What happened."

"Let me give you some advice, Lydia," she says to me. "Get back on your diet. Throw away all the M-and-M's you've probably got hidden away in your locker. Throw those dorky glasses out. And if you think Jimmy's so great, go after him yourself. Be my guest."

"He'd never look at me," I said. "He'll never look at anyone else as long as he lives. He told me."

"Well then I guess he's going to have a lonely life," she said. "Because frankly, he's just not my type."

Jimmy Emmet

I can't eat. Don't sleep. Lie there in bed, alls I see
is her face, her body. My hands shake, my dick's
burning. Every time I see a Datsun I start to sweat.

I'm no dope. Like they say, I see the writing on
the wall. And still I can't help myself, acting like
a fucking creep that's crawling on his belly, begging
for it.

Laying there, I get to thinking what I did wrong.
Maybe I came too quick. Maybe I didn't kiss her
enough. Maybe I had bad breath. You read in *Penthouse* all about making chicks come, and how
important that is. Shit, I don't even know if I made
her come or not. I don't know what it looks like. I
seen it at the movies. But it's not like with guys,
where you can tell real easy. You get the idea
you're supposed to know, and you'd seem like an
asshole if you asked. Nobody ever explained it to
me. It's not exactly the kind of thing you sit your
old man down and ask him. Not my old man
anyways.

One time I was with her, the last time, when I
was over at her house, I got this scarf off her. She
used to wear it around her neck. Fastened with
this little pin. She didn't give it to me or nothing.
I took it. I took it because it smelled like her.

So there I am laying on my bed, holding on to

this fucking scarf for chrissake, and jerking off for maybe the tenth time that day. My mom yells up the stairs, someone's here to talk to you, Jimmy. Better get down too, it's a cop.

You want to see a dick shrivel in record time? That'll do it.

Russell Hines

It's—what? Beginning of April? Eleven o'clock at night, eleven-thirty maybe. Chick I know is over, we're making out, watching some show on the tube, nothing special. My old man and my old lady off at the track. Jimmy comes in, doesn't knock or nothing. I remember because I had my hand down Charlene's shirt right around then and I was working on the ground floor. He interrupted the mood, you might say.

"We're in deep shit, man," he says to me. "Cops came round asking all about Larry Maretto. Guy said they aren't buying the burglary angle. Said people at school are saying we hung out with her. Asked what I knew."

"So what did you tell him?" I want to know.

"Nothing," he says. "You think I'm crazy?" But he's worried. Once they start sniffing around there's no telling what could happen.

"Look," I say. "They've been looking into this thing for weeks now and if they don't have a thing by now, what are they going to come up with? We got rid of the gloves, right? Nobody seen us, nobody seen Lydia take the gun. We're cool."

Jimmy says the cop wanted to know how he liked Mrs. Maretto. "She's real pretty isn't she, Jim?"

he says. "I never noticed," says Jimmy. Yeah, right. "Anyways, she's old."

"I hear you're quite the TV star," says the cop. "You really bared your soul to Mrs. Maretto on that tape of hers. Anything else you bared while you were at it?"

"What's that supposed to mean?" says Jimmy.

"All's I'm saying," says the cop, "is I suppose you had to spend quite a bit of time with Mrs. Maretto, working on an indepth piece of journalism like that."

"A little," Jimmy tells the cop. "Not that much. It was more Lydia."

"Well then I guess we better go talk to Lydia," says the cop. And that's when we get worried.

Lydia Mertz

When I got home from school that day there was a police car out in front of our mobile home. First thing I wanted to do was run away. Run over to Suzanne's, ask her what to do. But of course I couldn't do that. They'd probably already seen me. They were just waiting for me.

I walk in and there's three policemen sitting there with my mom. She's got the sound turned off the TV. I mean, why watch the soaps when you can have this in your own house, right?

She's got the photo albums out, a plate of Fig Newtons on the TV table, her macrame. Looked like they'd been there a while. Great, I think. They probably know our whole life story by now. Right up to Chester running away with the manicurist from Pawtucket and the doctor that says she might lose the leg. I wish I could die.

"Hello there, Lydia," says the little cop, the skinny one. "Your mother's been telling us a lot about you. Why don't you sit down and join us?" The way he says it sounds friendly but you know it's not really a question.

"We understand you had quite a friendship with Suzanne Maretto," says the big one. This one isn't such a friendly type. He looks like the kind that everybody thinks is so great because they don't see

what he's like with his wife and kids at home. Kind
that says, "You listen to me, young lady" and takes
a fly swatter to your butt for fun. I know about
them.

"Well I guess you could say I knew her," I say.
Just keep your mouth shut, I'm telling myself. I'm
digging my fingernails in my arm, just to keep re-
minding myself. Knowing I'm not that smart and I
might forget.

"In fact," the other one says. This one's the hardest to figure. He's got a nice face. But he asks the
toughest questions. "We understand she used to
take you shopping. Bought you clothes, even."

"Not really," I say. "I mean, they didn't even
fit."

"You must've got to be pretty good friends," says
the big one. "You and she and Jimmy Emmet and
Russell Hines."

Shit, I think. Now they're in on this too. I'm wondering what they said. What if they told, and now
I'll be in worse trouble for lying. Or they didn't
tell, and I'll get in trouble for telling something on
them. I start to feel dizzy. It's like where the reception goes all fuzzy all of a sudden, or you start
picking up somebody's shortwave on your cable.
I'm getting all these different voices coming in at
once. The little cop telling me there's nothing to
worry about, they know I'm a good girl and not
trouble like the boys there. The big cop that's saying do I know it's a federal offense to withhold
information pertinent to a capital crime. The nice-
looking one, saying where was I the night of February 21. My mom telling them I come from a broken
home, and this has been a bad year for me. And
I'm on this liquid diet, it makes me light-headed.
She knew the minute she heard about Mrs. Maretto

it was trouble. Her living at Number 6 and all. Rice cakes. Whoever heard of rice cakes for breakfast?

"Russell's a liar," I say. "Everybody knows his reputation. He's just trying to get Mrs. Maretto in trouble. Jimmy—I don't know what he's doing. Russell's just got him all messed up, most likely." Then I told them how much Mrs. Maretto loved Larry, had his picture on her desk and everything. I told them how broken up she was after he got killed. "You don't know her like I do," I said.

This cop said he wasn't arresting me or anything, he just wanted to talk. "I'm not going to take you down to the station," he says to me. "Let's just go for a drive. I'll buy you an ice cream." "No," I said. "I'm on a diet."

I didn't want to go, but if I didn't I figured they might get the wrong idea. So the whole time we're driving, I'm telling him about Suzanne and me, and the type person she is. How she bought me the ankle bracelet and stuff. And that we tell each other everything, and it's like we're sisters. "She's such a soft-hearted person she couldn't kill a bug," I tell him. "You should see the way she is with her dog, Walter. It's like he's a person. She'd do anything for him."

"She sure is pretty," the policeman says to me. "I guess Jimmy Emmet probably had a crush on her."

"Everybody thought she was nice," I say. I'm starting to wish I was smarter. I know from TV the way they trick you in these police investigations. I wish my brain worked better, so I could outsmart them if they try anything like that. Alls I can do, I figure, is talk slow and think a long time before I say anything.

"And he's pretty cute too," cop says. "Kind of looks like one of those New Kids on the Block." Even me, I can tell what he's doing saying that. Just trying to look like he's cool about stuff kids like. But you know he isn't.

"She was more of an Aerosmith fan," I say. Just so he doesn't think Suzanne liked Jimmy or anything.

"And probably Larry, he didn't understand her," the cop says. "One of those marriages where the two people just aren't communicating anymore. Happens all the time."

I don't know what I should be saying here. Maybe it would be a good idea to let him know Larry wasn't perfect. Just so they'd understand how hard it was for her, and where she was coming from and stuff. Him not supporting her career and all. How she'd end up homeless if they got a divorce. Lose Walter and everything.

"Maybe," I say. "Everybody has their problems, I guess."

"She probably didn't even mean to get involved with Jimmy," he says. "It was just one of those things that happens when two people spend a lot of time together, and one of them is in an unhappy marriage, and the other person shows them some attention and respect. It could happen to anyone."

"I don't know if you'd call it involved," I say. "We just worked on a video."

"Yeah," he said. "But then Jimmy fell in love with her. And she probably didn't want to hurt his feelings or anything. Her being so sensitive and all."

"She really wanted to help him," I say. "He was the type that never got into school stuff before. She said he had the kind of looks, he could even have a future in broadcasting. Like she could picture him being a sportscaster or a weatherman or something. Or the guy that picks the daily number in the lottery."

"And she was so lonely," the policeman says. "Larry working long hours probably. And not even understanding her when he was around."

"There was this workshop she wanted to take to improve her employability in the media, but he didn't want her to," I say. "And another thing is, Larry used to hit her. But she was always protecting him, so she never let on to anyone. Except me of course. And Jimmy."

"That must have been very upsetting," he says.

"I never thought I'd see a person like her cry," I say. "But it wasn't like she was a TV reporter after a while. It was just like we were a couple of girlfriends. We'd just stay up late telling each other everything, like we were at a slumber party. We never had any secrets from each other."

"And Jimmy probably just helped her forget all her troubles and be young again," he said. "The kids at school say you three used to drive around together to the mall and the beach and so on. There's some wild story going around, about Mrs. Maretto getting a tattoo over at Little Paradise. Easy enough for us to check that out, I guess, when the time comes. Kids are always making up stories, of course."

I didn't know what to say then. So I just sat there a long time. By now we're at the beach, so I just stare at the ocean, wishing I could jump in and swim away. I mean, I loved Suzanne. She was the best friend I ever had. I cared about Jimmy too. I started to cry.

He puts his arm around me, like he's my stepfather or somebody. Well not like that luckily. "You weren't thinking you were doing anything wrong. When two people are in love and their circumstances get in the way, it can be a very tragic situation."

"Like Romeo and Juliet," I said. "We saw the movie in English class. You knew they were meant to be together but their families ruined it. They couldn't live without each other."

"Jimmy said that's how he felt about her. And you can tell she's a very passionate person too. Very sensitive, like you said."

"She told me it was bigger than both of them," I told him. "And it didn't matter that they came from different walks of life, and different worlds and everything. It was like Billy Joel and Christie Brinkley, where he's a rock star and she's a model. Or Van Halen and Valerie Bertinelli. That's another one."

"She was just a very emotional kind of person," he said. "She just couldn't hold back her feelings."

"He said once they'd been together he didn't even notice any other girls," I told him. I mean, I knew it was all over now. Best I could do was just get him to understand. How they were good people and all. They just got confused. They got carried away. It was like a wave that just knocks you off your feet or something. Love will do that to a person.

He said he knew what I meant. He said he could tell I never meant for anybody to get hurt. I just wanted to help my friend. Us being so tight.

"Right," he said. "That's what friends are for. To help each other out in rough situations." I just sat there.

"Incidentally," he said. "I was talking with your

mother today. And she mentioned how glad she is that you and she keep a .38-caliber handgun around the house. Seeing as how there's a murderer on the loose and all. I said I'd like to bring the gun in for ballistics testing. Just a routine procedure of course. We'll be sure and get it back to you soon. So you can feel safe."

All I could think of was, man, I wish I had some ice cream right now. And soon as he let me off at the house, that's just what I did. Went straight for the freezer and cleaned out a half gallon my ma picked up, just that day, at Friendly's. Butter crunch.

Det. Mike Warden

So we go pay a visit to the Hines family compound. Meaning a trailer over by the beach. Half-dozen junk cars in the yard, and a couple of kids sitting there, throwing junk picture tubes against the wall. They tell me their brother isn't home. Their father's down at the clam flats.

This wasn't our first run-in with the Hines family. Russell himself is only seventeen and he's been in the boys' correctional facility twice. Has a cousin doing time in state prison for armed robbery, an uncle in for arson. Quite the family tree. We figure this isn't a family that's so shocked by the idea of a criminal in their midst. These people have got to be realistic. They can't very well expect to see their boy going straight. So maybe they'll be receptive to a lighter sentence in exchange for him agreeing to jump in first with a confession. Especially knowing if he doesn't do it, someone else is bound to. It's like playing chicken, you know? See who swerves first.

We drive out to the clam flats. Wade out in low tide to have a chat. Tell him maybe we can still prosecute the boy as a juvenile. Just because the kid knows how to hot-wire cars and has a two-year-old son, is that any reason to suppose he's an adult?

Guy doesn't say much. But I'm thinking we got our point across.

"Prosecute him as an adult and he's looking at life without parole," I say. "We're figuring Jimmy's the one that pulled the trigger, based on reports he and the Maretto woman were lovers. One kid saw them kissing out behind the dumpsters at the high school. Someone else spotted them at a video arcade at Little Paradise Beach."

And then there's that gold chain the boy pawned in the city last week. Is the father aware that that chain belonged to Larry Maretto?

Father says he'll have a word with his boy. Maybe they'll be paying us a visit down at the station.

Jimmy Emmet

I was out at the clam flats having a smoke when they come and get me. I knew it was coming. Didn't try and run or nothing, when I seen the cop car. I'm not going to walk in. Let them go home to their wives smelling of dead clams I say. But what's the point of running? Where to?

The one cop says, "You James J. Emmet of Number Ten Foundry Street?" And then he gives me the part about "You have a right to an attorney" and blah blah blah. Slaps the cuffs on me. "Hey man," I say, "don't I get to finish my stink-butt?" He guessed not.

They put me in the backseat naturally. Radio's on, and it's me they're talking about. Can you beat that?

I'm thinking, What about Russell? Now do we go get him? And Lydia? Mrs. Maretto, I don't even want to think about what's going to happen to her. I'm not thinking about jail yet, or the trial. Alls I'm thinking is shit, I don't get to make love with Mrs. Maretto this week.

But we don't make no stops to pick up Russell or nobody. Jeez, I'm starting to wonder, they aren't thinking I done the whole thing by myself are they? Not that I'm going to tell or nothing. You

don't skunk on your buddy. Even if he is an
asshole.

There's photographers and everything at the cop
house. TV cameras, you name it. I just duck my
head down low as I can. I don't want my mother
seeing this.

They book me. Take my fingerprints and shit.
Just like on TV. Then they bring me down this
hall—for questioning, is how they put it. "You can
have your attorney present," the cop says to me.
My attorney? Yeah, right.

That's when I seen Russell. Sitting on a bench
with his old man and this other guy in a suit, looks
like Perry Mason. I'm just about to say something
like "They nailed you too huh?" when I finally get
it. It ain't that way at all. Ain't them that nailed
us. It's Russell nailed me. Asshole cut a deal with
the cops to save his own hide. Me, I'm such a dumb
jerk. I don't open my mouth on account of I can't
get Mrs. Maretto in trouble. I'm still thinking she
loves me.

Suzanne Maretto

I was as surprised as everyone else when I heard the police had arrested James and Russell for my husband's murder. You knew the kind of element they were part of, and of course I was aware of the fact that James had this crush on me. But in my wildest dreams I never believed his jealousy of Larry would lead him to murder. In his perverted brain I guess he actually believed that if Larry were out of the way he'd be able to have me for himself.

Naturally the minute the police had their hands on the boys, they started pointing their fingers at me, saying it was all my idea. I should have guessed they'd do that. The part that shocks me is how the police accepted their assertions as credible. When any idiot could see these boys were troublemakers from the word go.

You'd think it was enough that my husband was brutally murdered, and I had to camp out at my parents' house like some homeless person, not even able to get my own clothes or my toothbrush. You'd think people would leave you alone after that, or just try and give you a little moral support. Not charge you with being an accomplice to murder.

As for the girl. Lydia. I never mentioned this before, because she's already got enough problems without adding the embarrassment of this. I mean, I said how she was hung up on James and all. But as a matter of fact, I think the sickness went even deeper for her. I gradually came to understand, from spending time with her, that she had a sexual obsession with me, over and beyond what she felt for him.

Not ever having known someone of that orientation before, it took me a long time to understand. But there was this one day we were at the mall together, when she insisted we go into this store together, Victoria's Secret, where they sell kinky lingerie. It isn't exactly the kind of place you bring a woman friend who's your mentor and big-sister-type friend.

She said she needed to buy some underwear. So she picked out this pair of panties. Red, as I recall. And then later I discovered she'd purchased a present for me there too. A garter belt. She asked me if I'd please put it on sometime, and show her. I just pretended I didn't understand what she was talking about. But then she tried to kiss me and touch me. After that I decided I simply couldn't be around her. I don't have anything against people of that persuasion. It's just not my cup of tea.

So I told her that. And naturally this made her angry and bitter. So angry she hatched this scheme to try and ruin my life. Which when you get down to it, is pretty pathetic. But then, that's what pathetic people do, whose own lives are empty and hopeless. They try to go and mess up someone else's, that isn't. That guy who shot John Lennon, he's a perfect example. He thought he'd get to be a big shot himself, just by destroying somebody important. Same thing with Lydia.

Lydia Mertz

All I could think about after the policeman left was now I got Suzanne in trouble. I didn't tell about her being in on it, of course. I didn't tell about her leaving the door unlocked and telling Jimmy and Russell to wear the gloves. I just got so confused, not knowing what Jimmy told them and what he didn't. I didn't know what to do.

So I called up Suzanne. "I got to talk to you," I said. "I think maybe I said the wrong thing to the police and I'm so mixed up, and I couldn't stand it if you hated me. You're my one friend in the whole world."

I was expecting her to say not to worry. We're friends for life no matter what. Only she didn't.

"What did you tell them?" she says.

So I told her how it looks like Jimmy told them about them being in love. The police knew that. Shit, half the school knew. But that didn't mean everybody was going to think she killed Larry or anything. I mean, everybody was going to find out about her and Jimmy anyways, once things quieted down and summer came and we all went to Florida together and stuff. Her and Jimmy'd be going steady and everyone would see us driving around. But plenty of people fall in love that don't murder their husband. Nobody said anything about her doing that.

Only Suzanne got real mad when I said that. "I should've known I couldn't trust you," she says. "A person that doesn't have enough willpower to stop stuffing their face with chocolate when they weigh a hundred and sixty-five and their face is covered with zits, how are they supposed to have enough sense to know when to keep their mouth shut?"

I didn't know what to say when she said that. I think maybe I'm going to pass out.

"Please—" I say. "You got to understand—"

"Do me a favor?" she says. "Drop dead."

I just sit there holding the phone. And I even wish I could. Drop dead, I mean. That's the first thing I think. I'm going to kill myself. I even think about getting my uncle's gun again. I could leave a note telling everyone I killed Larry. Then she'd be sorry. Then she'd know what kind of a friend I really was.

It was like how you feel when you ate a whole pizza, and then a pint of ice cream on top of that. It was like things would never be OK again for the whole rest of my life. Which is probably true. And I even knew I was too much of a coward to kill myself. That's how bad off I was—not even good enough to kill myself.

I could hear the TV on in the other room and my mom talking to her sister on the phone. I went over to my drawer and took out the silk panties Suzanne bought me that still smelled of the potpourri on account of I never wore them, I was just saving them. I can hear Oprah talking about this woman that was so afraid of dust she couldn't leave her house, and she had to wear this special suit all the time, and a face mask and everything. I mean she used to be normal, and now she's totally crazy. Just to come on the show they had to bring in this whole special cleaning crew and have the carpet shampooed or something. I look at the picture of Suzanne and me I keep next to my bed, and the Gap outfit I know isn't ever going to fit, and I can just feel the waistband of my jeans cutting into my stomach from all the crap I've been eating. I think about going back to school in the fall, and how it will be now that Suzanne hates me, and even Jimmy will be gone, that used to talk to me. I think about how I'll probably never get to Disney World now. I certainly won't be Suzanne's personal assistant, answering her fan mail.

When we were friends was the first time in my whole life I felt important. Just being around a person like her made me feel like there must be something good about me after all, you know? And then all of a sudden there wasn't anything important about me anymore.

Mary Emmet

From when Jimmy was a real little boy—we're talking three, four years old—I always said there was no sense him ever telling me a lie, because I'd always know. He has this kind of face, he just can't pull it off, you know? You'd ask him, "Did you take the money that was laying on the dinette?" "Did you lift that candy from the store?" He'd get this look like he was about to throw up. He couldn't even answer you. "Look me in the eye," I'd say. "Just tell me you didn't do it, and I won't ask any more questions." I'm not saying he didn't get mixed up in plenty of trouble, because he did. But he was an open book. I've seen kids, they could stand there with your wallet in their hand and tell you, "Money? What money? I didn't take any money." Kids that could steal the pope's rosary and show up the next day in church. But not Jimmy. It was like he figured he'd get struck by lightning or something, if he one time told me something that wasn't true. He might say nothing. But he wouldn't lie.

After Larry Maretto was killed, of course I got to thinking. Him being the husband of this teacher Jimmy'd been spending so much time with, and Jimmy taking all these showers and everything, always in a huddle with Russell and that girl Lydia, talking about who knew what. And then when that detective started coming around. You'd be a fool not to wonder.

But I never sat him down and asked, "You have anything to do with this murder?" I could say it was just that I never dreamed he could. But thinking back, I got to say, I knew Jimmy wouldn't tell me a lie. And I was scared to hear the truth.

After they took him away though, and I was sitting here alone, I knew what I had to do. One minute you're sitting there, reading some article in a magazine all about Tom Selleck or someone, the next thing you know they're putting handcuffs on your son and taking him away, like some juvenile delinquent in a show. It doesn't feel like your real life, you know? It feels like you're on a show too. Only there's no commercials. And it doesn't end.

So I had to ask myself then, could it be he did it? And even though I knew this was a boy that cried when you'd pass a dead raccoon on the highway, I knew it was a possibility. He couldn't of killed anybody for money, and he couldn't kill for hate. But love? That could be a different story.

I went down to the police station. They brought him out into this room, just a table and a couple of chairs, the smell of sweat hanging over everything. They sit Jimmy down across from me, and I see his hand can't stop shaking. You want to put your arms around him, but it's not possible, on account of the glass.

So I just sit there, looking at him. I suppose some people, if they saw my boy, all they'd notice would be that crazy tattoo and that Guns 'N Roses shirt. But what I see is his sweet face. He's got his father's eyes, those dark lashes, that blue. He hasn't been shaving long, so the hair on his upper lip is still that fine, soft kind. I'm looking at his pierced

ear, that he never wore an earring in, on account
of after he did it he found out he had them put the
hole in the wrong ear, and he's got the one that
means you're gay. That's when he started wearing
his hair long. To cover it up.

I remember looking at the clock on the wall, looking at the light coming in the window, hearing the
sound of the dispatcher and the voices of the cops
outside. And thinking, remember this moment.
This might be your last hopeful moment. Last moment you still have any shot at all of thinking life
might turn out OK.

Then I ask him. "Did you do it?" And like I said,
Jimmy never lies.

Lydia Mertz

The nice detective, the big one, said to call him Mike. He said he knew how hard this was for me and not to worry because he'd be with me every step of the way. He had a daughter about my age, he said. He knew what it was like, trusting somebody so much you get led down the wrong path. When you're young and impressionable it can happen real easy, he said. The main thing was now I'd come to them. I was doing the right thing.

I didn't even know what the right thing was anymore. All I knew was I had to do something. I couldn't just sit in my house anymore going crazy. At least this way I'd have something to do. Somebody'd be talking to me besides my mom, that never leaves me alone.

So they hooked me up with this tape recorder I put on under my clothes. There's a little microphone, but it's so small you can't hardly tell it's there. Plus it's not like I'd be wearing some skintight midriff top. I always wear these baggy tops anyways.

Then I called up Suzanne, like they told me. At first she just says she doesn't have anything to say to me anymore, and would I please just leave her alone. But then I say no, I got to talk to her. I've been wondering if maybe I should talk to the cops.

I hated saying that—lying, when really I already talked plenty to the cops. But Mike explained to me that sometimes it's like a white lie you got to tell, so in the end the real truth gets told. I was like an operative of the police department. Like a spy. Only I was working for the good side.

I knew when I said that about talking to the police that she'd have to get together with me. "All right," she says. "We'll meet at the mall. Just don't call the police or anything dumb like that." I figure she picked the mall to remind me about all the fun times we had there. Maybe she was even planning on buying me some more underwear. But there wasn't anything I wanted anymore. I don't even wear my sneakers, if you want to know how bad I feel.

She was already waiting when I got there. Mike would've given me a ride only that would've tipped her off. So I got this friend of my aunt's that works at the Wendy's right near there to drop me off. It was a hot day, and I'll tell you, I was sweating so much you had to wonder if maybe it was going to short-circuit the tape recorder.

She was carrying a bag. It was these little gold earrings just like she wears. "I wanted you to have these," she said. "Fourteen-karat gold always has a different look from the fake stuff. It's the little things people notice."

I would've given them back only then she'd just wonder what was up, so I said thanks. I put them in my bag but I knew I wouldn't ever wear them.

"So," she said. "What's this crazy business about talking to the police?"

"Well I was just wondering," I said. "Now that they've arrested the boys and they know about you and Jimmy and everything. You know Russell's going to tell about you putting him up to it, if they haven't guessed it all already. Maybe the best would be to tell them everything and then they wouldn't be so mad, knowing we told the truth."

"Are you nuts?" she said. "It's not like we're talking about shoplifting a pack of gum or anything. You know what the penalty would be for murder?"

"It was only an idea," I said. "I was just wondering."

"Look," she said, "it's important not to panic now. Just because they picked up Jimmy and Russell is no reason for you and I to worry. Everybody knows those two are troublemakers. Nobody's going to believe them. The main thing is the police don't have any evidence against us. No fingerprints. No weapon. Nothing."

"Maybe," I said. "But you can't very well let Jimmy and Russell take all the blame when it wasn't just their fault. The whole thing being your idea and everything. You can't just leave them to rot in jail."

"Look," she said. "They wouldn't even be in this mess if they'd kept quiet. I had everything planned perfectly, if they'd just followed directions and not gone blabbing about it. They fucked up is all. It's not my fault they can't keep their fucking mouths shut. But that doesn't mean I'm going to let them drag you and me down."

"I can't sleep at night sometimes," I told her. "Sometimes I just lay there, thinking about him. Larry I mean. I wonder if he's up there someplace, hating us. I know this sounds crazy, but I even wonder about God. If he knows. And sometimes I think somebody's going to come get me. Punish me, like in that movie *Carrie*."

"The only ones you should be scared of are the

cops, Liddy," she told me. "Don't you know you're the one that would get in the biggest trouble of all if they found out?"

"What do you mean?" I said. "I wasn't even there that night. In the end I even tried to stop you."

"That's not the way I remember it," she said. "The way I remember it is you planned the whole thing. If you hadn't gone and got that gun, Larry would be alive today."

"But you asked me to get the gun," I said. "You asked Jimmy to do it. You were the one that offered Russ the money."

"What money?" she said. "Did Russell receive any money from me? The way it looks to me is Jimmy had a crazy adolescent obsession with me, and he had built up this bizarre idea that if he killed Larry, he could have me. Russell's such an animal he figured he'd come along for the thrill of it. And you were so hung up on Jimmy you'd do anything just to be near him. Knowing you couldn't have him yourself. Seems to me like you were getting your kicks off of thinking about Jimmy and me. Sexually frustrated people do things like that. If they know nobody's ever going to be interested in them, for their own self. And let's face it, Jimmy barely knew you existed, before."

I was feeling dizzy. I wished I had a piece of chocolate to put in my mouth, just to calm my nerves. I remember staring down at those earrings she gave me, kind of like I used to stare at this picture of a kitten playing with a ball of yarn that we used to have on our wall. When Chester was touching me. Just think about the kitten, I'd tell myself. Keep thinking about the kitten.

"I thought we were friends," I said. And the

truth is, even then, even sitting there with this tape recorder strapped to my bra, I was wishing we could just be friends and feeling bad I was doing this to her. Only now it was hitting me, whatever I'd do to her, that was nothing compared to what she'd do to me.

"I was at a job interview the night of the murder," she said. "It seems to me all the evidence points to you."

"You were the best friend I ever had," I told her. "The only friend." I'm crying now. That part wasn't some act for the cops either. I couldn't help that part.

"Yeah, well then," she said to me, "take a little advice from a friend, why don't you? Just keep your fucking mouth shut. It's just their word against mine. And who are they? A bunch of sixteen-year-old losers who grew up in shacks, and their parents sit around drinking and screwing their cousins? I'm a professional person, for goodness sake. I come from a good home. Who do you think a jury would believe?"

PART

IV

Suzanne Maretto

I was doing my exercises in the living room at my condo. I remember because I had a Jane Fonda video on, and we were just at the inner thigh portion of the workout. There's a knock at the door. I go to answer it—I'm wearing my leotard mind you. Weights strapped to my ankles. I must've been a sight.

There's a television camera staring me in the face. That and a couple of policemen. "Suzanne Maretto," one of them says, "I'm placing you under arrest for conspiracy to commit murder. You have the right to remain silent," etcetera etcetera. Just like on some police show, only this was real life.

Still I couldn't believe it. "This is some joke, right?" I said. "I'm a widow. I just buried my husband six weeks ago, and now you're telling me you want to put me in jail?" Even a strong person has her limits.

My parents were down at the station within minutes of course. I knew once my father talked to them he'd get things straightened out. I could just picture him, taking down people's names, making phone calls. I mean, my dad probably sold half these people their car. No way was he going to let me rot in this sickening jail with a bunch of losers on drugs and who knows what diseases going around.

So the real shock came later, when they let my folks in to see me, and my dad had to break it to me that I'd have to stay here until the bail hearing. Ten days before we'd get this mess cleaned up.

I won't pretend I wasn't upset. But then I just switched gears. OK, I told myself. I'm going to benefit from this experience. I'll keep a journal. I'll do exercises. Cut back on my calories—which believe me, once you've taken a look at what they serve here, is not that hard to do. I decided to view my time in the correctional facility kind of like I was at a spa. Well, not a spa exactly. Maybe a religious retreat or a prisoner-of-war camp. Something to broaden my experience. And when it was all over, I'd have some dynamite material to market.

Carol Stone

No comment. That's what I have to say. A person sees their daughter led off in handcuffs to a women's prison and there's some reporter sticking a microphone in my face. What do I know about tape recorders? How do I know the tricks they can do to make it sound like a person's saying something they never said? They twist your words around, I know that much. They make it sound like you said things and did things you never did. They get an image of how they think a person is and then all they care about is convincing everyone it's true. They'll do anything to get people tuning in to their news show. Which might as well be called "Entertainment Tonight."

I'll tell you what I think of television reporters. They're the scum of the earth. They're vultures. First they tear your heart out. Then they play it back for the world to see on the six o'clock news.

Suzanne Maretto

I never liked Jane Pauley. Have you ever noticed how one side of her face doesn't match the other? Next time you see that magazine show of hers, put your hand on the screen so it covers up one of her eyes and half her mouth, and you'll see what I mean. And that hair. I could see it if she was maybe doing the weekend update or something, or the sunrise report. But the "Today" show. It's not like there aren't other people out there.

I have to admit I have a controversial opinion about Deborah Norville. I know people say she isn't very intelligent, but they don't understand the broadcasting business like somebody on the inside. All the things you have to know, and how complex it really is. Which camera to look at. Being aware of your lighting and your monitors, and knowing how many seconds before you have to cut to commercial. They think these people are just sitting around in their living room shooting the breeze or something. They don't know all the talent and training that goes into a production like that. And in my opinion, Deborah Norville was the best in the business.

I wrote a letter about my situation to "20-20." I wrote to "60 Minutes" too, but I'd prefer doing "20-20." Barbara Walters used to be kind of my idol. Now she's pretty old of course. But you have to remember all the people she's met. Billy Joel. Donald Trump and Marla Maples. Tom Hanks. Elton John. You have to respect someone like that.

What we had in mind was an exposé. About the conspiracy these kids cooked up, and how they can ruin a person's life. Only as I said before, I always think positive, so I'm not prepared to say they've ruined my life. All they did was try.

My lawyer was telling me about this play some famous writer wrote. I'm not sure but I think they made it into a movie or a "Hallmark Hall of Fame" or something. It was about this town called Salem, Massachusetts, a couple hundred years ago, where a bunch of teenage girls got the idea of accusing some people of being witches, and everybody started believing them. The girls were just bored or something, looking for something to do, and I mean, in those days, there wasn't much. So they thought it would be fun. Only in the end the people were found guilty and they got burned alive. The writer used to be married to Marilyn Monroe, if that rings a bell.

In my case, it's pretty obvious what happened. The two ringleaders, Russell and James, had some kind of crush on me. Or whatever you want to call it. I won't even repeat some of the remarks they used to make when I'd walk past them in the hall. Just because I'm not a hundred years old and fifty pounds overweight, they think they can get away with their obscene remarks. I have a theory that it has to do with the music they listen to. 2 Live Crew, Guns 'N Roses and so forth. I mean, I don't sit around listening to Lawrence Welk or anything, but these groups are too much. A boy like Russell, listening to some song about killing your mother or your girlfriend all day long, probably just started to believe it. Everybody knew he was already a hood. And then when I didn't want anything to do with them, they figured they'd kill Larry, and then I would. That's the way their twisted brains work.

As for Lydia, well you've seen what she looks like. I mean, I tried to help her. I took her to aerobics with me a couple times and I kept telling her to stay away from chocolate. But she had no willpower. Basically she's just a very pathetic person. And in the end I think she was just so jealous she had to hurt me somehow. So she cooked this up.

It appears the judge understood this. I mean, at my bail hearing the DA tried to give the impression that I might flee the country or something, if they let me out free. Like I'm some desperate criminal. The judge could take one look at me and know I wasn't exactly the type to hotfoot it off, because he granted bail, in spite of all the ridiculous insinuations they were making about me. So at least I'll be sleeping in my own bed tonight, instead of that godforsaken women's correctional facility. Now all I have to do is wait for the trial, to clear my good name.

I'm planning to write a letter to Billy Joel too. Thinking maybe he'd be interested in writing a song about my story. Or maybe even do a benefit concert for costs incurred in my defense. I also wrote to Walter Cronkite and enclosed that picture from the paper of me holding Walter when he was just a puppy. We figured he'd get a kick out of that. I won't be surprised if I hear from him any day now.

Angela Maretto

We went to the bail hearing of course. Not that anything we can do now dulls the pain of losing our son. But you wanted to look her in the eye. You wanted the judge to see you sitting there, so he couldn't forget for a moment this human being that got snuffed out at the age of twenty-four had a mother and a father who loved him with all their hearts, and now those hearts are broken. You didn't want to let him get away with thinking, for even one second, that maybe our son's life didn't matter so much as her precious rights, her precious freedom, innocent until proven guilty, and all that. You knew her lawyers were going to talk about the injustice of keeping her locked up all those months, while the state prepared its case. When the judge heard those remarks, we wanted him to be looking at us, sitting there. Talk about the pain of having to go to jail, I'll give you pain. The pain of going to the cemetery and putting flowers on your boy's gravestone. Pain of walking through the door of the restaurant, still expecting to see him standing there whistling as he polishes the bar. Let the judge see that with his own eyes.

I tried to concentrate on what the DA said, but my mind kept wandering. I know he said something about the gold chain showing up at the pawn

shop. The tattoo. A kid that saw Suzanne driving
with the Emmet boy one time. Position of the body
on the carpet. Didn't fit the MO of a burglary. And
why didn't these so-called burglars take the TV
set?

The big news was the tape of course, of what
Suzanne said to Lydia that day at the mall, when
the police had her wired for sound. We were so
sure once that came out Suzanne would be nailed
for good. I looked over at Suzanne's mother when
it got to the part about her saying "send us to the
fucking penitentiary for the rest of our lives." I
wanted to scream, "Still think your little girl is
such an angel, Earl?" But of course I held my
tongue.

It was what happened next that did me in. Her
lawyers moving in on some technicality about the
way the girl got Suzanne over to the mall in the
first place. I started to go dizzy at this point, but
it had to do with crazy things, pointless things,
how she phrased her questions, the way she put it
when she mentioned the gun. Next thing you know
one of Suzanne's highprice lawyers is making a mo-
tion to rule the tape as inadmissable evidence on
the grounds of entrapment. Next thing you know
the judge is doing it. Bail granted. $200,000. That's
when Joey had to carry me out of the courtroom,
but our daughter tells us the Stones approached
the bench after that, turned over the deed to their
home—which believe me, is well over the $200,000
mark.

My husband and I were long gone by the time
the court adjourned, but we watched it on the news
that night. Her walking out the door of the courthouse, free as a bird, and smiling like she's about
to start giving the weather report. She stops to talk

to a reporter that's sticking a microphone in her face. "Today's decision to grant me bail only reaffirms my faith in the American justice system," she said, and blah blah blah. "I want to thank all the wonderful people whose thoughts and prayers have sustained me during these trying times. The first thing I'm going to do when I get home? Walk my dog." You wanted to throw up.

"How do you plan to spend the months ahead, as you await your trial?" says the reporter.

"I know my husband would have wanted me to go on with my life," she says. "My lawyers and I will be busy preparing our case, naturally. And then, there have been so many television and movie offers to consider. There just aren't enough hours in a day."

Suzanne Maretto

I'm not worried about myself. I know the truth will eventually be heard, and I'll be able to put this ridiculous chapter of my life behind me. I'm a fighter. But how do you explain a thing like this to your dog? Nobody ever thinks about people's pets in a situation like this, but dogs have feelings too. Can you imagine how traumatic it was for Walter, when I was being held in jail? If you want to talk about a crime, I'll tell you one: Animals have no rights in this country.

I have to do something about my hair. The roots are growing in. It looks unbelievably gross. I mean I'm a natural blonde and all, but I help it along. And now with all this business, I haven't been able to do a thing with it. I've got to pick myself up some L'Oreal.

Looks aren't everything. But let's be realistic. When you meet someone, and she's covered with acne or she weighs three hundred pounds or something, do you feel the same about her as when you meet someone that takes care of herself, and has a pleasant appearance? There's a saying my mother passed on to my sister and me. "You never get a second chance to make a first impression." I'll always remember that. I've been meaning to cross-stitch it on a sampler or a pillow or something. It's one of those things that really gets you thinking, you know?

With me for instance. Quite frankly, I know one of the things I have going for me is my appearance. When people see a photograph of a nice looking person in the paper, they're naturally going to think to themselves, Wait a second. She doesn't look like the type to get into this kind of trouble. She looks like somebody we'd like to have living next door. I mean, why would a person that has everything going for them do something like they accuse me of? It just wouldn't make sense.

Of course, there's always that other element. The bitter ones. The ones with the acne and the three hundred extra pounds themselves, that always wanted to be a cheerleader or attain some other kind of goal like that, but they never managed to. There used to be girls like that at my high school, and again at college. The kind that's so jealous, you know they keep hoping you'll get a pimple or something. Maybe those people are happy now. Which is another reason why it's important that I continue to look my best, and not let myself go in any way. Just to maintain my dignity.

I've got to pick some things out to wear at the trial. I'm a perfect size six, there's never any need to try anything on, as long as it's a good-quality label. A couple of little suits, simple yet elegant. Did you see Diane Sawyer's interview with Marla Maples? I love that kind of shirt she was wearing. And some little gold earrings, to pick up the highlights in my hair. Once I attend to my roots.

Some people say they're sure to make a movie about this. If so, I'd like to see Julia Roberts play me. Or that actress that just got married to Tom Cruise in real life—I can't think of her name. I can picture Harrison Ford as my lawyer. Or Mel Gibson. I was thinking they could have Billy Joel do the sound track. I don't think he's ever done a movie sound track before, so he'd probably love it.

I've started writing a book about this. Just the other day I came up with a good title. *Chance of Showers*. It would be kind of a play on words, you know, about my being a weather reporter and all. I'd take the profits from my book and establish a fund in Larry's name for aspiring communications students at Sanders College. My alma mater.

You've got to think like that. Keep accentuating the positive. I believe there's something to be gained from every experience in life. In this case, maybe it's going to establish my career. Although of course this wasn't how I'd planned on doing it.

But let's be honest. Once the trial begins, I'll be on display in a way. Now I know how people like Madonna and Princess Diana feel. You've got to look your best every second. That one moment when you wrinkle your nose or get a piece of spinach stuck on your front teeth or something, you know that's the moment someone's going to snap your picture. So you just have to be prepared every second. My video journalism teacher taught me that.

If I were the prosecuting attorney now, I'd get Lydia on a diet. Not that they'd have any luck. I know, because I tried to help her lose some weight myself, and got nowhere. And of course, the assistant prosecutor is not exactly skin and bones herself. Which to me is a sign of a person that simply doesn't have their life under control. I mean, whose side would you rather be on?

June Hines

You want me to be all bent out of shape because some college girl got my boy to help her off her old man? You want me to act like I'm so shocked. Let me tell you, it takes a lot to shock me these days.

Where I come from, you shit in a hole in the ground until the hole got all filled up. Then you took out your shovel.

I was one of thirteen myself. My mother was sixteen when I came along, and I wasn't her first neither. My dad? Who knows.

Christmastime, growing up, they'd come around from the church with these packages people wrapped up for kids like us with labels on them that said "Boy, seven." or "Girl, ten to twelve." Year I was six I said I wanted a baby doll. In my package was a baby doll all right. Only had one arm though. "What can you expect," says my mom. "Watch out for that Santa in the department store. He's probably just some old man wants to put his finger up your butt." You think I listened for them reindeer? Who had a chimney?

One thing I was always proud of. My hair. I mean, up until I was ten years old, I had this pure gold hair, clear past my rear, naturally curly. Poor as we were, I always kept that hair clean and brushed. Did without my lunch milk three weeks in a row to buy me a hair bow. I always figured, those rich kids over Lancaster, they might have a million dollars and still they didn't have hair like mine. You know what I'm saying. It was my special thing, ain't nobody was going to take that away.

First day of fifth grade, the school nurse does a head check like always. She gets to me and gets this look on her face like she just swallowed a prune pit. "What's the matter?" I say, but she just writes something down on a piece of paper and says, "Here, take this to your mother." She don't know and I don't tell her that my mother can't read.

But I can. It says I got these head lice bugs crawling around in my gold hair. Egg sacs too. I got to use this special shampoo every day to kill them. That plus we got to wash all our sheets and towels (well, that'll take about a minute, I think) and vacuum up the whole house too. And then there's a long list of other what you call precautions.

Now I don't want to tell my mother this, knowing how she'll cuss and scream. Other hand, I got to get these bugs out of my hair. Got to get that shampoo. So I wait and wait, and finally I do it. "Ma," I says. "I got head lice. We need to get this special shampoo or the other kids might catch it. Maybe they got it already."

My ma, she don't say nothing, just goes to get the scissors. I'm hollering "No, don't cut it," but she just gets my brothers to hold me down and they go at it, right at the roots. When it's over, I'm pretty near bald. What's left, she pours kerosene on that. "There," she says. "You just let that set a while."

After a few months my hair started to grow back,

but it wasn't gold no more. Just ordinary brown like everybody else.

It was one of my brothers was the first one to jump me. I couldn't say which one, it was dark.

Thirteen years old, I start to feel like I got some kind of bugs again, only this time they're crawling inside me. I lie there on the floor and there's this wiggling going on in my belly. I didn't notice no missed period on account of I never got no period in the first place. But my ma figures it out. "You're knocked up," she says. She didn't ask me who done it on account of, whoever it was, it was family, so why bother?

That baby was born dead. Strangled on his cord most likely. I looked at him before they took him away. Spitting image of my brother Arnie, so at least I figured that part out.

Once it happened, seems like it's only a matter of time before it happens again. Sure enough, maybe four, five months later, I get that feeling again. This time it's a girl. That's Regina there. Same one made me a grandma herself when she was just fourteen. Thirty years old and I turned into a grandma. Can you beat that?

After Regina, then comes Russell, so quick I still had Regina sucking on my tit when I'm pushing Russell out. One hungry mouth on one tit, one on the other. Seemed like all I was was a bunch of holes. One to put a dick into, two to take milk out. I could talk about my uncle that liked to do it from the rear to boot, but there's kids around.

After Russell comes Sheila, then Roseanne, then Clyde—no, then Vera, then Clyde. Clyde had a twin, but there was this woman over in Greenfield that called me up when she heard I had two of them. Said she heard I had an extra I hadn't counted on—now isn't that the truth—and would I be interested in talking about maybe seeing my way to letting one of them go to this lovely childless couple she was working for, where the woman had one of those operations that make it so you can't have no babies. "Where do I get me one of those operations?" I wanted to ask her.

She gave me five thousand dollars cash, so long as I got this blood test showing Babe was the father, and not no brother of mine or nothing. And that was the truth, it was Babe. By that time my brothers was both over at the county farm, so you knew it wasn't them.

Russell, for some reason he had really took a shine to that little sister of his—Crystal we called her, for the month or two we had her, before they took her away. Search me why, out of all the babies come and go around our place, he had to take a shine to the one that wasn't sticking around, but that's what happened.

Day they come for Crystal, he's sitting on the step holding her. Didn't cry or carry on or nothing. He just holds her real tight until the lady comes that took her away. Don't ever let them tell you money don't matter in this life, I tell him. Money's behind everything. A person got enough money, they can do anything. Go anyplace. And get away with it.

First time he got arrested was throwing rocks at cars down on the freeway. He was twelve. They sent him to a reform school kind of place for a couple of months. That's where he learned how to hot-wire a car.

Fourteen years old, he's back at juvenile detention for holding a knife up to a teacher. Out a few weeks, they have him back for breaking and entering. Then he had what you might call a quiet stretch. That's when Charlene, my cousin's girl, announces she's expecting, and Russell done it. Who knows? The baby come out good anyways, but hasn't been no baby since that Crystal that my boy wanted to hold on to. He's got a look in his eyes now, that boy, like nothing would scare him. I said that to him one time. "Why should I lose sleep over nothing?" he says to me. "What's the worst a person could do to me? Kill me, and alls you do is save me the trouble." Life sucks, and then you die. That's his what you call philosophy, he told me one time.

You ask me, how could he do it? Answer's simple. She was going to have someone kill her old man anyways, it was just a matter of who. If Russell didn't hold the guy down, somebody else would, and then it would of been them got the cash. So if it's going to happen anyways, why not take advantage?

You want to know if I'm wailing in my bed over this here Suzanne Maretto business, the answer is I cried my last tears a long time ago. Maybe he done it, maybe he didn't. If he didn't do this, it's only on account of he was doing something else. I knew a long time ago I wasn't likely to see that boy grow old. Or if I did, the only reason would be they had him locked up someplace out of trouble. So now maybe I'll get to see him grow old after all.

Mary Emmet

On the news they're calling my son an animal. "Teenage thrill killer," the District Attorney called him. But the thing that really got me was when they had some psychologist on, saying what can you expect. The kind of homes these kids came from. And how they weren't raised with any values or morals. "I mean, these boys aren't exactly Vanderbilts," he says. "The kind of homes they come from, they didn't even have indoor plumbing." Like there's some connection between having a flush on your toilet and getting into Heaven.

I did the best I could with my son Jimmy. Just because a person doesn't have some big bank roll don't mean she doesn't love her kid.

He was always a good boy too. Never complained if I couldn't buy him a toy. Never cried. Never asked for much. Give him a pile of dirt and a spoon to dig and he was happy, just making mud. Just tell him not to expect much and he'll never be disappointed, I figured. If you start building up their hopes to get some good job or go to trade school or something, all that happens is they're mad when it doesn't come true.

So my way was, never pretend something great is coming. Just because you blow out all the candles on your cake doesn't mean your wish comes true.

Jimmy grew up knowing those toys they advertised on TV weren't for him, and neither were those beautiful girls they show in the magazines. A person has to be realistic. You try for too much, you just have further to fall.

It's not like now's the first time I heard people talking about what kind of home my kid comes from. All his life people have been telling him, one way or another, he got born with the wrong setup for anything good to ever happen in his life. It's a free country? The sky's the limit? Don't make me laugh. This was a boy that you could've told his life story by the time he was six years old. Like that psychologist said, the kind of home he comes from, he was bound to get into trouble. And the ones that make it come true are the ones who keep saying that.

Basically, the only surprise ever came along in my boy's life was this Suzanne Maretto woman taking an interest in him. To my boy it was like she was some fairy princess that comes sparkling down from the sky and touches his head with a fucking magic wand. Out of all the dumb kids in the entire world, she picked my boy Jimmy to screw with. You better believe he fell all over himself to please her. She was the first person he ever met that told him he might amount to something. Only trouble was, she was just handing him a line. She wasn't just getting his dick up. It was his hopes.

Which only proves my point. Tell a boy like Jimmy that he's got a shot at something good—I don't care if it's a goddam college education or a pretty blonde between the sheets—and you're setting him up to get his heart broken. Which is what happened all right. It was like she took him into this candy store, showed him all the treats, let him taste a few, then locked him out, with his face pressed against the glass. He never knew what he was missing until he got it. Then it drove him crazy.

So now he's locked away for life. He doesn't even get a chance to have a skinny kid of his own, to mess up that kid's life like I supposedly messed up his. But let me tell you this. Just because I don't live in a big house, just because I don't pull up to the state prison in a limousine. You think my heart aches any less?

Suzanne Maretto

Up until now I never wanted to mention this, because I wanted to spare Larry's parents the pain. That, and of course you want to preserve a loved one's memory. You want to see them remembered in a positive light. And not do anything to interfere with that.

But now that they're coming up with these allegations suggesting I was involved in some way, I just don't see that I have a choice anymore. I have to defend myself.

My husband had a drug problem. We're talking cocaine. There—I've finally said it. I mean, he never would have been a wife beater if his head hadn't been so messed up. But I don't want to talk about that part. I want people to remember Larry the way he was before drugs messed him up.

He was already starting to get mixed up with drugs when I met him, only I was too innocent and naive to recognize the signs. Can you imagine me, the one who led our campus Just Say No crusade, hooking up with a coke addict? Well, it happened. Which just goes to show you how pervasive this drug problem is. How insidious a disease we have here, that an honest, upright, Eagle Scout kind of person like my husband could succumb to the temptation. I mean, if Larry could give in to cocaine, that tells me nobody's out of danger. Not you. Not me. Not Tom Brokaw himself.

The way I've finally figured it out, Larry must've got involved with Jimmy and Russell while I was producing my documentary. Maybe he lost his original supplier. Maybe they were just able to get him a better deal than he was finding in the city. Whatever.

They started getting all chummy. Sure it's true Russell's car was parked outside my condo that night. And you know why? He was dealing drugs to my husband. Naturally Jimmy knows his way around our place, but not because of his crazy story about the two of us having an affair. The only illicit activity going on in my home was my husband, snorting powder up his nose.

I began to suspect something last fall. His lack of motivation, etcetera. The way he was letting himself go, and letting go of his goals to really make something of himself. That's why I tried to befriend the boys—build up their trust, make them see they had to leave Larry alone. I was even foolish enough to appeal to their sense of kindness and decency. Told them I wouldn't turn them in, if they would just stop supplying my husband. Finally I even managed to get Larry to admit what was going on.

It was a beautiful, beautiful moment between us. I told him I loved him more than ever, and I'd help him kick this thing. He told me how sorry he was that he let me down. He begged me to forgive him for the times he'd hit me, and of course I said I would. We were never closer than we were that night. He promised he'd go into a rehab program, right after our anniversary. I can still see him, crying in my arms like a baby. And Walter, our puppy, licking the tears from his face. Right then and there I vowed that I'd spend the rest of my life as a journalist doing everything in my power to inform and educate the American public about the terrible epidemic of drug abuse. Just as soon as I got my husband through this hell.

And you know, we would have made it too. Our love was that strong. Only Larry owed Jimmy and Russell a lot of money. We told them we'd do whatever it took to pay the money back—sell our car, refinance the condo, I'd take a second job, anything. But they were impatient. Plus of course, James had this fixation on me, and that just made him hate Larry more.

I think now they must have been threatening Larry for some time before, you know, that night. He just didn't want me to worry, so he never let on. He felt guilty enough already. He figured he'd take care of it himself. Only they got to him first.

I hate to go public with all of this. Now, when Joe and Angela have already been through so much. They'll deny it of course. Who wants to believe their son was a wife beater and a cocaine addict? But the time has come for the truth to be known. And if our story keeps just one young couple like us, with everything to live for, from making the same mistakes that Larry did, then maybe he won't have died in vain.

So now maybe you'll understand what I was talking about in those remarks I made to Lydia on that crazy tape the DA plans to use to build a case against me. Maybe I said some things that sounded pretty strange, but I was just trying to protect my husband's name. Only now that they're dragging mine through the mud, I have no choice but to let my story be heard.

Russell Hines

So now the cunt wants to make like Jimmy and me's some big-time coke dealers. Don't make me laugh.

I mean, let's get this straight. You're not talking to no Nancy Reagan here. Jimmy and me we lit up plenty of weed in our time. If some guy come up to me, said, "Hey, you want a snort?" would I say no? Can't say I would.

But let me tell you, it don't happen to guys like Jimmy and me. We're strictly bargain basement users. A little grass. A lot of beer. Who had the bucks for coke?

Wait'll my ma hears this about me being a big-time drug dealer. A businessman, like. Man she'll be proud—her that never thought I'd amount to nothing, with a son that goes around selling cocaine to the white-collar crowd, wad of cash in my pocket, little briefcase maybe, to carry the stuff. Yeah, right. It'll slay her.

Listen, I done a lot of stuff and I didn't never say different. Sure I balled my cousin. Stole a rubber dispenser down at the Sunoco. And I helped off Larry Maretto, too. I never said I didn't. But I wasn't dealing no cocaine to the poor sucker. If you ask me, the only dangerous substance that guy was hooked on was Suzanne Maretto's pussy.

Earl Stone

All your life you try and protect your kids from pain, make everything perfect. They fall down, you kiss where they got hurt. Some kid at school has a birthday party and they don't get invited, you take them out for an ice cream instead. Maybe they won't win first prize in the twirling contest, you buy them a new Barbie doll. Or the whole goddam Barbie Dream House for that matter. That's your job, to make it right again.

Always before, if a problem came up, I could fix it. Like the time they cut the budget for school buses to away games, and the cheerleaders were going to have to stay home. Suzanne never knew this, but I donated the five hundred bucks so she and the other girls could go cheer. If you could've seen their faces. I mean, how was I going to let her miss out on that, after all the work she put in on those splits?

I'm not saying she couldn't get ahead on her own steam, mind you. Our Susie had the talent and the drive, you knew she'd make it no matter what. But it never hurts to have someone in your corner, helping things along. That was me. The way I look at it, a person should have everything they can going for them. It's a dog-eat-dog world out there.

Take her nose, back when she was little. I'm not

saying this was a Barbra Streisand–type situation. Only you knew, looking at her, that she was going to be a pretty girl. Who could be even prettier once a plastic surgeon got his hands on her. And knowing her aspirations in the television field, it only made sense to pursue that avenue, right? You did what you could. My wife and I were fortunate that we were in a position to make certain opportunities available to our kids. The work on her nose was one such instance.

God knows there were others. We kept a refrigerator in the rec room, filled with Cokes, snacks, and so on. They never had to ask, we just did it. Bought the kids a stereo, Ping-Pong table, the works. Just so we knew where they were. So we knew the kind of youngsters they were spending time with.

Suzanne wanted horseback riding lessons. No problem. Tap dance, gymnastics, modeling, same deal. Faye had her dermatologist, fifty bucks a shot, no questions asked. We got the kids their own TV set, their own phone. Took them to the Grand Canyon and our nation's capital. You buy them braces, give them your charge card, keys to the car, the wedding a girl always dreams about. That's what family life is all about, right? Making sure your kids get everything you missed.

With Faye you had to accept from pretty early on that she wasn't going anyplace big. You had to take her the way she was and love her the best you could. But Suzanne was going places. You knew Suzanne was going to make you proud.

And now this. Listen, I'm not an idiot. I heard that tape. They may not allow the tape as evidence, but I heard it and I know what those words mean, although I never expected to hear them out of my daughter's mouth, that's for sure. And no matter what you think, it's got to make you wonder.

You never mean to do it, but you find yourself thinking, Is it possible she did it? The same little girl that used to ride on the back of your golf cart and tell you when she grew up she was going to marry you?

And once you open the door to that doubt, I tell you, there's no going back. You're thinking about it constantly, thinking about how much you believed in this child, and now maybe it turns out she's not the person you thought she was, or anything close.

Let me tell you. Once you get to the point of believing your precious daughter could have been involved in something like this, it's hard to believe in much of anything anymore. Maybe the sky isn't really blue. Maybe Japanese cars really are better than American. Maybe those people were right that said man never really walked on the moon, and the whole thing was just staged in some TV studio. If my little girl could say the words I heard on that tape the DA played, I guess I don't believe in much of anything anymore. Nothing seems real, except the humiliation.

You know, I still remember the Christmas Eve I stayed up all night, putting together that Barbie Dream House. A year ago I was walking my daughter down the aisle at her wedding. Now I'm posting bail money and hiring lawyers to convince a jury that my daughter didn't arrange the murder of her husband. When the truth is, I don't know anymore if I believe that myself.

Suzanne Maretto

Something I heard on a talk show one time—I think maybe it was Cher who said it—really got me thinking. Just because a person wears nice clothes and shaves her legs more than once a year doesn't mean she doesn't have a deep side, you know?

Obviously, Cher is another example of an individual such as myself, because one thing I learned from this program was what a spiritual person she really is. She said this quote I'll always remember. It was a question actually: "If a tree falls in the middle of a forest, where no one's around to see it, did it really fall at all?"

I thought a lot about that. What's the point of doing something if nobody sees you? That makes about as much sense as seeing this great meal on the table, and nobody's there to eat it. Which reminds me of an article I read in the *National Enquirer*—a publication I don't make a habit of reading, but it was the only thing they had at the beauty parlor that day—about this minister out in Nevada who has been preaching sermons every Sunday for all these years, even though nobody's left in his congregation. Now if you ask me, that isn't holy. It's just dumb.

The way I see it, everything people do in the world, the whole point is having an audience, having someone else see it. I mean, artists like to put their paintings in museums, right? And musicians generally like to have people listen to their music. Not having someone there is kind of like the tree falling in the forest, if you follow me.

That's the beauty of television. It's like an eye that's on you all the time. Watching even if nobody's around and recording what you do. And knowing it's there makes you be a better person in so many ways. Kind of like God, if you want to get heavy.

Say you're in this cabin in the woods and nobody's going to stop by all weekend. Do you have any reason to take a shower and put on your makeup? But now suppose you're going on the "Today" show? Naturally you pull yourself together a little more.

If everybody's house had one of those TV cameras in it all the time, like the kind they have in banks and stores to check on shoplifters, do you think mothers would still scream at their children and hit them? Do you think Deborah Norville was always so nice to her husband as she used to be to Joe Garagiola and Willard Scott and Bryant Gumbel? And why not? There's no TV camera in her living room.

Take Oprah's diet. Look what happened to her. She was fat, then she went on this big diet and lost sixty-seven pounds. She came back on her show hauling a wagon full of sixty-seven pounds of hamburger meat and wearing these tight jeans, looking fantastic. And for a while everybody was talking about how she did it, and how great it was, and it looked like she was finally going to marry Steadman Graham and everything would turn out great.

Then what happened? She started eating wrong

again. Never on television, mind you. You never saw Oprah sitting on her show, eating a plate full of french fries. The problem was, she wasn't on television every minute. Sometimes they turned the cameras off her. That's when she got into trouble. And now look at her, fat as ever.

You can say, oh well, that's her true self coming out, and the person she shows us on television is just a façade, whatever you want to call it. But as far as I'm concerned, what's wrong with a façade, so long as it's a nice one? If being true to yourself means gaining back sixty-seven pounds, I'd just as soon be a little dishonest.

This is why I have always aspired to being on television. Because it brings out the best in a person. As long as you're on TV, someone's always watching you. If people could just be on TV all the time, the whole human race would probably be a much better group of individuals. The only catch is, naturally, if everybody was on TV, there wouldn't be anyone left to watch. Now I'm actually driving my own self crazy. Which can be a problem with me. One time I got so tangled up in these thoughts of mine I forgot all about turning myself over in the tanning booth, and was I ever a mess.

Joe Maretto

We're down at the restaurant. I'm in back tallying up our meat order, Angela's out front, and the news comes on the TV we got mounted at the end of the bar. Nobody called us or anything—we just heard it on the news, same as everybody else.

"New developments in the Maretto case. Details at six." At this point you come over to the bar. Then you have to wait there for ten minutes, through the end of some damn "People's Court" and five or six commercials, to find out what they're saying now about the murder of your son. How do you think that feels?

But the worst is yet to come. Because when the news finally comes on, they're sitting there saying my boy was a goddam wife beater and a drug addict, and those punks shot him because he didn't pay his bills. My son that never finished a bottle of beer in his life, a drug addict. As for hitting her—that guy could never lay a hand on anyone. Least of all her. He worshiped the ground she walked on.

For a minute we just stand there staring at the set. Who knows what the customers are doing at this point? You hear nothing but the voices coming from the screen. Somebody hands me a shot of whiskey—here, Joe, you better drink this. But I just stand there holding it. Can't move.

Then she comes on. Suzanne. Our daughter-in-law. She's sitting on the very couch in the very place where my boy died. Little microphone clipped on her blouse. That little turned-up nose of hers that always looked to me like they took her out of the oven too soon. Looks like she got her hair done for this event. She's got the dog in her lap and she's petting him. And the reporter that's talking to her, he's acting like this is the First Lady or the Queen of England he's got here. "I know this must be very hard for you, Mrs. Maretto," he says. "I know everyone's heart goes out to you."

She looks right into the camera, like she's looking straight at Angela and me. "My husband was addicted to cocaine," she says. "He owed a lot of money to the two young men currently facing charges. He was getting violent, losing control. I believe that's the reason why they killed him."

I can't help myself then. I don't even think, I just pick up the table that's next to me and throw it. I smash my hand on the bar, knock over every drink, every bottle that's sitting there. Then I start in on chairs. Angela tells me I was screaming too. Maybe I was. I don't remember.

When my wife gets me calmed down—quiet anyway—they're just finishing up with the damned interview. "So, Mrs. Maretto, how does all of this make you feel?" says the reporter.

She wipes a tear from the corner of her eye with this piece of Kleenex she's holding. "Well I try to be a positive person, Bud," she says. "I'm a fighter. All through this terrible ordeal I have tried to move forward with my life, hold on to my dreams. I know my husband would've wanted me to. But I have to admit to you that sometimes I wish I had died myself that night. Sometimes I actually wish I were dead."

When we heard her say that, a strange thing happened to Angela and me. Neither one of us said anything, but I knew we both understood what had to happen. I mean, we'd have to work out the details. There'd be time enough for that, but we knew we could handle it. You don't run a bar in the Italian section of town twenty years without making a few friends that can help you at a moment like this. The important thing was we knew what we had to do, and there wasn't a doubt in my mind that we were going to do it.

Suzanne Maretto

I probably shouldn't be telling you this. This is supposed to be top secret. It's not official yet, and they told me not to discuss it with anyone until we had the details ironed out. But just between us, I got a call from a very important New York producer yesterday. They want me to meet with them this evening, and they're flying in today. He's with ABC. They want to do a one-hour special about my story. He said some people at the top of the news division are really excited about this. He didn't name names, but from the way he was talking I got the feeling he meant Barbara Walters.

He said my story has all the angles. Nice-looking young couple, in love, with their whole lives ahead of them and everything to live for. Dreams smashed by drugs. A family torn apart by a bunch of aimless kids, thrill killers, raised without any moral values, who can pull the trigger of a gun as easily as they light up a joint. They might even make us a movie of the week. Plus, he wants me to bring along some of my videos. He said they're always looking for new on-camera talent in New York. And somebody he was talking to from that conference I went to told him I have what it takes.

He said not to tell my parents. Word gets out, people start talking to other people, the whole deal can be ruined, he said. It's better for them to iron out the details with me first, in private. That's why he wanted to meet with me out of town, in a secluded spot. It's funny, but you know, since having my picture in the papers and on the news, it's almost like I'm a celebrity. I can't go anyplace without someone pointing at me or staring. One time this little girl even asked for my autograph. Her mother tried to pull her away, like I'd be offended. I told her not to worry. I thought it was cute.

So I'm meeting him at the beach. I said, "How will I know you?" He said, "I doubt there will be more than one limo around."

Not to get too heavy or anything, but all of this has made me think. About the way life works, I mean, and how strange it is. First something terrible happens. Then, just when you least expect it, something good comes along, that evens up the score again. Kind of like saying, "Every cloud has a silver lining." I mean, Larry dying and everything, that was a tragedy I'll never forget so long as I live. But you have to keep things in perspective too, and remember that if it wasn't for one thing happening, so many other things wouldn't have happened either.

This morning I went over to the tanning parlor. Just to get a little color in my cheeks. I can't say that a few weeks in Women's Correctional Facility does anything for a girl's looks. Plus, if you want to know something, I do some of my best thinking in the tanning booth. It's so quiet and peaceful in there, with the lights glowing. Kind of like meditation.

So while I was lying there, I got this revelation, if you will. That everything that's happened to me so far is all part of a big master plan. It's like, if you get too close to the screen, all you can see is a bunch of little black-and-white dots. You don't see the big picture until you stand back. But when you do, it all makes sense. Everything comes into focus.

Ozzie Ward

Usually I do my raking further down along the flats, but the wind was bad that day, so I figured I'd stay in the cove, closer to the bridge. Wasn't having much luck. I was just lighting a cigarette when I saw it. Something lying on the beach, tangled up in a bunch of seaweed. Too far away to see clear.

First thing I think is maybe it's more of that medical waste that keeps washing up lately. Last month I raked up a shitload of surgical gloves and what-have-you. Bloody rags, used hypodermic needles, plastic tubes, you wouldn't believe the stuff they dump these days. Which is why, when I got closer, and I spotted her hand sticking out, I thought to myself: Oh, great. Looks like now when they amputate someone's arm, they just toss it off the side of a boat, waiting for us clammers to rake it up. This is probably where they throw the dead babies from over at the abortion clinic too. I know for a fact I seen someone's appendix one time.

Only it wasn't a cut-off arm. There was a whole body attached, and a nice one too, or used to be.

I didn't recognize her right away from the pictures they'd been having on the news. I don't care who it is, nobody looks too pretty after they been bobbing around in the Atlantic ten, twelve days.

But then I remembered hearing on the news about how everyone's looking for this TV reporter that's out on bail, awaiting trial for planning her husband's murder. And you got her mother on saying, "I know my daughter would never run away. There must have been foul play." And the guy's old man saying, "This proves she did it. They never should've gave her bail." Ten days, that's all you been hearing is, Where's Suzanne Maretto? Looks like I found her.

She still had most of her clothes on. Her shoes were gone naturally, but she still had on panty hose. There was a lot of seaweed and what-have-you tangled in her hair, but you could still tell she was a blonde. Her eyes were open. Blue.

Now some people I know, if they spotted that wedding ring she was wearing, they would've took it. We're talking a big diamond here. Not that it would've been easy getting it. You'd have had to cut off the finger.

Me, I just laid my jacket over her face, keep the sea gulls from pecking at her anymore, and went for the cops.

Det. Mike Warden

First person I thought about when they pulled Suzanne Maretto's body in from the river was Lydia. All the things Suzanne said about her in the end, everything Lydia went through, and still I knew, Lydia worshiped that woman. This was going to tear her apart.

She was at the house with that mother of hers when I got there. Up in her room listening to rock music. "Come on," I told her. "We're going for a drive, you and me."

"It was all my fault," she says. "If I hadn't got the gun, none of this would've happened. She'd still be alive, and him too. We could all be at Disney World right now."

I said some things, but none of it meant anything to her. "Don't believe it," I said. "If you hadn't got the gun she would've found someone else to do it for her. One way or another, her type always gets what they want."

"Not like me," she said. "I've been a loser my whole life and I always will be." It's funny that you'd be talking about someone they found floating in the bay like she's a winner, but that's how Lydia saw her. And always will.

"You know what her problem was?" Lydia said. "She was too sensitive. She had these high ideals, and real life just couldn't live up to them. Nobody else was as good as her. She was just too perfect. Too perfect for this messed-up world. The only one that never let her down was her dog."

Carol Stone

I hope they're satisfied now. The police. Those low-life boys who dragged my daughter's name through the mud, and that pathetic girlfriend of theirs who called herself Suzanne's friend, and then made it look like my daughter was a slut and a murderer. And the media. They're the most guilty of all, in my opinion, for the way they sensationalized everything, and made it so Susie's face was plastered all over the news every night as a suspected killer.

She was a strong person, but everyone has their breaking point, and finally Suzanne just reached hers. She had managed to deal with the pain of her husband's drug addiction, and even physical abuse. Never even letting on to Earl and myself, she was so brave. She managed to go on with her life, after having Larry taken from her. She managed to keep her chin up, when they put handcuffs on her and took her off to jail. She even managed to deal with the suspicions and abandonment of his family. What destroyed her was seeing herself on the news every night, portrayed as a cold-blooded killer. The way those so-called journalists twisted the truth of her story, for their own sensationalistic purposes. They're as guilty of her death as they would have been if they'd stood there and pushed her off the bridge themselves.

At night, when I can't sleep, I sometimes get out of bed and come downstairs. Sit in the family room, where we spent so many happy hours with Suzanne. Take out the photograph albums. Sometimes I'll put one of her videos on, and watch her doing one of her broadcasts, or singing that song of hers. "High Hopes."

I try to stop myself, but then I picture her getting dressed that last morning. Putting on her makeup, doing her nails. You know she had fresh polish on her nails when they found her? There she was, a couple of hours away from ending her own life, but still she wanted to look pretty. She never would cut herself any slack. Always had to be the best she could be.

She was wearing her favorite dress. The little pearl earrings Earl and I gave her for her twenty-first birthday. Her wedding ring, of course. That meant so much to her.

People wonder why she didn't leave a note. But Earl and I, we understand. There was nothing left to say. Her actions spoke for themselves. Her heart had been broken. The trial hadn't even begun, but already she'd been found guilty in the press.

I can't help myself. I keep playing the scene over and over in my head, like a show I can't turn off. It's like back in 1963, when they kept showing that same footage of the Kennedy assassination, again and again and again. The way they kept making us watch the *Challenger* takeoff, kept showing it rising up in the sky, and then exploding. Only this time it's my own girl that's blown away before my very eyes.

I see her parking the car. I see her opening the

car door, looking out to sea. And then climbing up onto the railing. She hesitates for a second. If only we'd been there to stop her. But we weren't. Then she jumps.

Det. Mike Warden

We had to order an autopsy on Suzanne Maretto's body naturally. Routine procedure. You weren't expecting any more surprises at this point. Just trying to wrap things up. We had our perpetrator. She'd even obliged us by doing herself in, saving us the trouble.

I mean, so long as it was Suzanne Maretto we were going after, it wasn't hard to get our detectives putting out a hundred and ten percent. You couldn't wait to nail a cold bitch like that one.

But when the coroner's report came back, you'd better believe that document had my detectives shook up. And not just because my captain comes from the North End—although it didn't help that half our force is guys of Italian descent. That only helped us to reach our conclusion sooner. To keep the autopsy findings under wraps. Insert the coroner's report into the paper shredder and forget we ever saw it.

It was just plain to all of us that the Maretto family had been hurt enough already. It had to end somewhere, and this seemed as good a place as any. Sometimes justice takes some strange forms that no judge or jury could bring about. This was one of those times.

Let me put it this way: If it had been my boy

Suzanne Maretto screwed over like she screwed over the Marettos', I could've done the same thing they did and never lost a night's sleep over it. Try and find one member of the force that thinks differently. Which is why the first coroner's report will never see the light of day.

As far as the press is concerned, Suzanne Maretto died of drowning, a suicide. That's all they know and all they ever need to know.

Fact is, there wasn't a drop of water in Suzanne Maretto's lungs when they pulled her out of the bay. That woman was already dead when her body went off the bridge. You tell me: When was the last time you heard of someone that did themself in, with their résumé in their coat pocket, and a bunch of eight-by-ten glossies and a couple videos of themself back on the front seat of their car?

Jimmy Emmet

They let Russell work out a plea bargain, thirty-year sentence, with twelve off for good behavior, on account of how he squealed, and him not being the one that pulled the trigger. Me, they put the handcuffs back on and take me to juvenile detention. In the car going over, cop says, "Don't think just because you're sixteen you're going to get away with this. Guy that's man enough to screw, he's old enough to fry." That's the first time they tell me what the punishment is for first-degree murder. Life without parole.

I think I'm going to be sick. I'm scared I'm going to start bawling. Up until then, all I could think of was Mrs. Maretto, and how I just got to see her, but after that it started to hit me. It's not just that I can't ever screw Mrs. Maretto again. I'm never going to get to do it with anyone. Don't ask me why, but I start wishing my mom was here. Not that she's the type that ever made it right before. And she sure couldn't now.

The whole place is fenced in like a fucking chicken coop, barbed wire on top and everything. First thing they do is take your shoes and your belt. Then they bring you in this room where they make you take off the rest of your clothes and shower. I was glad there wasn't any other guys in there. Russell used to tell me what happens in here. You got to keep your eye out every second or someone might come along and stick it in your butt.

They buzz-cut my hair. Give me these work boots that weigh like twenty pounds apiece. Then they hand me this package all wrapped up in brown paper. Inside's a towel, a bar of soap, roll of toilet paper, a couple of disposable razors. Guy takes me down a long hall, past all these guys in cells. Thirty different transistor radios all going at once, you can't hear yourself think.

Someone says, "That's him. Fucked a married woman and blew away her old man." Someone else says, "Asshole."

Guy calls out to me, when I pass his cell, "Was she good?"

Laying on my cot, nights, when I can't sleep, I try to remember. Not all the time, or I'd use it up too quick. I save it for when I'm feeling real bad, and then it's like a treat I give myself. OK, I say. Now you're pulling up to her house. Now she's opening the door. Now she's unzipping her dress. Now you're loosening your belt and taking off your jeans. Here comes her tits. She's doing her cheer. Give me an *E*. Give me an *L*. Now she's laying down on the bed. You've got your tongue in her mouth now. Now you're inside her. Now you're in heaven.

Only it's like a movie you watch, where you don't get cable or something, and the reception's so bad you can't hardly make out what they're saying. It's fuzzy. Getting fuzzier all the time.

Sometimes I feel like I'm some fucking prisoner of war that don't want to lose touch and go crazy. I'm trying to hold on, you know? So I give myself these little tests where I got to remember something. "Was the tattoo on her left tit or her right?" I'll ask myself. "What did she smell like? Was her hair blond, down below?"

I think I used to know. But it's slipping away from me. How do you like that?

Ed Grant

You want to hear something funny? With everything that's happened now, every TV station in the
tri-state area is trying to get their hands on film
footage. Any footage: Suzanne walking through the
door to the courthouse, Jimmy picking his nose, you
name it. And here I am, manager of a two-bit local
cable station, with a three-hour-long video special,
narrated by none other than Suzanne Maretto herself, and featuring all four of them sitting on a
couch and talking heart to heart in the very condo
where she evidently took Jimmy Emmet into her
bed, the very condo where her husband took his
last breath.

I got Russell Hines saying, "Look, if you got a
reputation for trouble and everybody out there's
thinking you're raising hell all the time, anyway,
you might as well raise it." I got Lydia talking
about how much it means to her to have a female
role model she can emulate. I've got footage of
Jimmy Emmet, looking straight into the camera,
and saying, "People got the wrong idea when they
think guys only care about sex, and emotions don't
matter. The person I'm in a relationship with at
the moment, it's not just about getting laid, it's
about love. I'd do anything for this person. And I
mean anything."

Her lawyers put a restraining order on the video. Which is a shame. Not just because it would sure give our ratings a boost. But the fact is, she did a good job with this little project of hers. We're not talking Mike Wallace here, I mean, but I probably would've put it on the air.

I was actually thinking, before all this happened, that it was about time I gave her a try reading the news. Well you better believe she's on the news now. She's a regular goddam celebrity. So I guess you might say her dream came true.

Phil Donahue

Fasten your seat belts, ladies and gentlemen. Joe and Angela Maretto have joined us—and let me say, this cannot have been easy for them—their son, Larry, a young man any one of us might have been proud to know—we are speaking here of the all-American success story, good-looking, popular, up-and-coming young restaurateur—am I right, Joe, that your son was at one time an altar boy? as I was myself—and played golf with his father-in-law, who, incidentally, couldn't make it, but Carol, his wife, is joining us, and may I say, Mrs. Stone, we recognize that not every individual in your position would have the courage to sit here on this podium, facing the very people who accuse her daughter of cold-blooded murder—the daughter to whom I refer being—if you will look at your monitors at this point, audience—Suzanne Maretto, fledgling television newsperson and would-be anchor—and within sight of attaining the great American dream, if you will—a young woman with everything going for her, good churchgoing family—your husband runs a car dealership if I am not mistaken, Carol?—honors student and as you can see, the very sort of individual any one of us might be happy to see our son bring home as his fiancée—which is exactly what Larry Maretto did, on a day that, as his mother Angela puts it—and may I say, my heartfelt condolences to you, Mrs. Maretto, it cannot be easy reliving your family's nightmare on national television—that she wishes with all her heart had never happened, and one which might have been averted if Lydia Mertz—Lydia, thank you for being with us, I recognize you must have had to leave school to come here today, and I believe this is your mother—Valerie tells me she never misses our program—as I understand it, rights to your story are currently under consideration by a major television studio for an upcoming movie of the week—and let me say, in the event that your participation on this program becomes a part of the movie, I'd like to see Kevin Costner playing myself—but all levity aside, let me remind you, two young men are currently serving prison sentences—a young woman is dead of apparent suicide, her husband brutally murdered—life can never be the same for you, Mrs. Maretto, am I correct?—and we gather you all together today out of that uniquely human impulse to know not simply what happened, but why? Carol Stone, your daughter is also dead—and this must be unbearably painful to you, as well as you, Faye—and I say that, having just last week taped a program— many of you may have seen this one—concerning the trauma of being a surviving sibling—as is Janice Maretto—currently on leave from her tour with the Ice Capades—sister of the deceased young husband of Suzanne, also tragically deceased, by her own hand—what could be more senseless than suicide—leading us to ask the question, Why?

Did Suzanne Maretto die of a broken heart, or was it guilt over conspiring with her sixteen-year-old lover that propelled her to take her life, just as

she was on the brink of realizing the very goal—
namely a promising future in television—which
she had pursued with so much commitment and
dedication. Finally we have Mr. and Mrs. Hines—
Mr. Hines, you were willing to set aside your re-
sponsibilities as a clam digger to be with us today,
and Mrs. Hines, I know this isn't easy—I want to
thank you also for coming here today to share with
us the heartbreak of parents whose son, Russell, is
presently incarcerated for thirty years to life for
the murder of Larry Maretto. And I ask you, isn't
it ironic, ladies and gentlemen, that of all the individuals we find on this podium today, the one
whose absence is most felt is the one who perhaps
would have felt most at home here, the individual
to whom I refer being, of course, Suzanne Maretto
herself, who—her mother tells me—always regarded myself as one of her role models and may I
say I am always honored and humbled to think of
young people today holding me in the same kind of
esteem in which I held my heroes, as a youth. On
a personal note may I say that all of us in this
industry hold an awesome power to guide the lives
of young people, and we can only pray we inspire
them in positive directions. We'll be right back
after these messages. Don't go away.

Joe Maretto

Like I told Phil Donahue, I don't care how it happens, any parent who has to bury their child, their heart is broken. That's all there is to it. Broken. Crushed. You wish you could die. Dying looks good. Burying your son is a hundred times worse than if you just died yourself.

But terrible as it is for anybody that loses a child, at least the people that lose their son in a war or something, they can hold on to the thought that there was a point to it. If he was driving drunk, that won't stop you from going crazy with grief. Won't stop you from missing him or loving him either. But at least then you've got to say to yourself, "He made his bed, now he's lying in it."

But this. I go back over and over it, and you know, I could accept losing him. I'd accept never going fishing with my son anymore. I accept it that I'll never again sit in a gym watching him take a foul shot, and then look over at me with that grin of his and give me the thumbs up. Never get over it, understand? Just accept it. The part that makes me so I want to pound my head through the wall—and I've tried it, believe me—is what was the point?

If it actually had been a robbery, and Larry walked in at the wrong time, and some creep got scared and shot him—even then I could maybe say it was like an accident. They weren't thinking about my son, they were just thinking about themselves. They didn't know what they were doing. Didn't know whose brains they were blowing out. Just some guy walking in the wrong door at the wrong time. No face. No name. No life.

But tell me what I'm supposed to think of this? They knew, and they did it anyway. They knew he was a nice ordinary guy that loved his wife, coming home from a long day of work, thinking maybe she's got a beer and a kiss waiting for him, and instead it's the muzzle of a gun.

I can even deal with the two creeps that shot him. They didn't know my son Larry. They were just a couple of losers whose own lives were so worthless they must've figured his was the same. You live in a world of crap long enough and everything looks like crap to you. Don't get me wrong. If I had the opportunity I'd like to spit on their faces and then spit on their parents for bringing scum like that into the world. I could watch them hang and never blink. If they were here now, I could wring their necks with my bare hands. But as much as they disgust me, they're not the ones I think about when I get up in the middle of the night wanting to scream.

It's her. She knew my son. She slept every night in the same bed with him. Knew he would have done anything to make her happy. He handed her his heart on a plate and she threw it in the garbage disposal. She didn't do it because he was unkind to her. She didn't even do it because she hated him. He just got in her way. So poof, she gets rid of him.

She ate at our table. We called her our daughter. Even afterwards, in her grief, whose hand did my wife hold, whose telephone number did she dial when she couldn't stand it anymore and just needed to cry? Hers. The only one we thought could understand the depth of our loss, the only one we imagined that shared the bottomlessness of our pain.

Now it turns out that all the time we were just watching a show. It was all one big performance.

I tell you, she had us going there. We bought it. So did my son.

Kind of makes you wonder what else out there that you think is real isn't really. Like those people that say we never actually landed on the moon, the whole thing was just staged in some sound studio somewhere. People who say Kennedy isn't actually dead, he's just a vegetable in some nursing home someplace. Who do you trust anymore? How do you know anything's real anymore? How do you know who else out there, that you thought was your friend, might just be waiting for the right moment to stick a knife in your throat? Why does a person do something like that? How do you ever get over it?

Like I said on "Donahue," my son gave her his love and promised to stick with her forever. Her, I guess she figured his life was about worth the price of that gold chain we gave him when he graduated high school. "But I tell you how it is for Angela and me, Phil," I said. "Our lives are over. She might as well have put a gun to our heads too. I wish she had, Phil. I wish she had."

Det. Mike Warden

Work in homicide as long as I have, certain themes emerge. You get where you can spot what the crime's about, and mostly it's one of three categories. Money, sex, ambition. This one now, it was all three. Depending on who you were talking to. It was money for the loser that helped. For her, ambition. But for the poor slob that did the husband in for her, it was sex of course.

Sex now. You put sex into a situation and everything changes. A woman wants to get out of her marriage. Her husband doesn't want a divorce. She's got to dump him, but he's holding on. Nobody knows what to do. Then sex enters in. She gets a sixteen-year-old boyfriend. Now she's crossed a line. Broken the rules. Once she's done that, it's an easy step to the next point. Once she's already taken her clothes off, danced for him in her garter belt, once she's let him screw her, anything can happen. After that they both know what an act it is, going around looking like regular citizens. Once you've heard the crazy things a person says in bed with another person and you've thought the crazy things a person thinks when it's happening, it's like you've entered into this other country where no more laws exist. Once sex gets into the picture, you can never go back to being one of those other kind of people that act like they don't ever sweat. I mean, under these clothes we're wearing, we're all just a bunch of animals, aren't we? Once two people have sex they can't pretend different anymore.

So after she screwed him I figure the next step was easy enough. Now that they've done whatever particular odd thing it was that turned them on, what's the big deal about taking him aside one day and saying, "Suppose we get a gun and blow my old man away?" Easy enough to start talking about buying bullets and making it look like a burglary, once you've done the other.

And for his part—we're speaking of the boy now—you might just as well give a sixteen-year-old boy crack cocaine as give him a nice-looking twenty-five-year-old woman to fuck. He's going to be a slave, you understand? A fucking slave. He'll do anything just to get in her pants again. Fix your car? Mow your lawn? Kill your husband? Sure. He's got to have it, you understand? Got to.

Nobody likes to say this, but we all know it's true. Sex is just so bizarre. Here we all are, walking around going to the supermarket, making bank deposits, shooting the breeze with someone over at the barber shop about our car. Acting like we're all normal. Everybody keeps up the act. How's it going? Just great. How about you?

And the whole time we're doing this, we've got this other life going on—the life you live beyond closed doors, alone, or not alone, in the dark, when you're just a naked body, burning up with animal desires. Am I the only person in the world who thinks this is strange? Tell me, am I the only one who notices?

I go register my car. Woman at the Division of Motor Vehicles hands me a form, sticks her pen behind her ear, types up the form. "Another hot one," she says to me. "Think it'll ever rain?" You can tell she's just come from the beauty parlor. She has these little pearl earrings on. Wedding ring. Photos of the kids on her desk.

But what I'm thinking is, What does she look like when she's got her girdle off and some guy on top of her? Does she go home at night, put on cutout panties and a pair of handcuffs, and wait for her best friend's husband to come over? Or lie there alone listening to old Frank Sinatra records and touching herself? Let's face it, once you throw sex into the equation, anyone out there can become crazy. We're all capable of bizarre behavior. Who follows the rules? What are the rules anyway?

Valerie Mertz

We're going to meet Oprah, can you believe it? They called us last week, after *USA Today* picked up the story about Suzanne jumping off the bridge. We were on "Good Morning America," "Evening Magazine." That's not even counting the local shows. I tried taping them, but we were on all three channels at the same time, so we could only get one. It's OK though, because this is just the beginning. Sally Jessy Raphael wants us to come on her show too. We're also talking to Geraldo. Suzanne Maretto would die if she knew. Turn over in her grave, I mean.

First thing we did after the people called from Oprah was run out and get a big can of Ultra Slim Fast for Lydia. Like Suzanne used to tell her, the TV camera puts ten pounds on a person. But we have eight days to work on taking some weight off, if she sticks to the Slim Fast and maybe a few rice cakes. We're going to the mall for something to wear on the show. Not stripes they told us. But Lydia already knew that too. From Suzanne.

But that's not the most incredible part. Yesterday this woman comes to see us. From Hollywood. She's a producer. Did you ever see that made-for-television movie about the girl with the deformed face that had to go around with a bag on her head all the time, until this fashion model with terminal cancer gave her money for an operation? She was in charge of that one. Also the boy that turned out to be allergic to his own family. I never saw that one, but it starred that kid from "It's All in a Day." The cute one.

She wants to buy the rights to Lydia's story. We already signed a contract. They're paying Lydia $10,000 right away, and a lot more if the network goes ahead and puts the movie on TV. Which Ellen—that's the producer—says is basically a sure thing, on account of how our story has, like she says, all the elements they go for in Hollywood. She loved it when Lydia told her the part about walking in on Suzanne and Jimmy that time. And her doing her cheering routine in just her garter belt.

At first, after all this happened, I guess Lydia's head got pretty messed up. Thinking about how Suzanne never really liked her at all, and Jimmy going to jail, and having to face all the kids at school that talk about her all the time now, and nobody wanting to sit with her at lunchtime, like she's an alien.

But now it looks like things are really working out. This producer, Ellen, says they'll even fly us to LA when they start filming. To be consultants. Meet the stars and everything. Those kids at school that won't be friends with my kid—do they get to be in *People* magazine? Do they get to meet Oprah? I ask you.

Which gives Lydia motivation for her diet, naturally. Like Suzanne always said, evidently, you never get a second chance to make a first impression.

Faye Stone

Believe it or not I used to be skinny. Back when I was in preschool, before Suzanne was born, people used to say I looked like one of those Walter Keane paintings—you know the ones I mean, of some little girl with big eyes and toothpick legs that look like she just got out of Biafra or a concentration camp?

My parents were always trying to get me to fatten up in those days, if you can believe it. Mealtimes, the two of them would sit with me through the whole entire Huntley-Brinkley news, plus "Newlywed Game," one at each end of the table, and me in the middle. "Now the airplane's flying into the hangar. Here's one for your Aunt Pamela. One for Uncle Roger. We'll buy you a Skipper doll if you finish your vegetables. . . ." Nothing worked.

Then they brought Suzanne home from the hospital, and everything changed. Suzanne this, Suzanne that. "Have you ever seen a more beautiful baby?" "Listen, I bet she could be in commercials. Gerber or Beach-Nut. Pampers, maybe. That's how Brooke Shields started out, you know. And look at her now." I remember this one time, when we took her out to the supermarket, this woman stopped my mother and asked her if she'd thought of sending Suzanne's picture to Ivory Snow. For the box. She said she'd never seen anything so cute in her life as Susie in that little bunny dress of hers. Then she must have noticed me, because she said I was cute too. "But for goodness sake, get a little meat on her bones," she said.

I started making myself eat my vegetables. I joined the clean plate club. I even asked for seconds. Thirds. Dessert. Snacks. Yes, I will have a potato. Butter or sour cream? Give me both. Please.

I thought then they'd be happy, but you know, they never noticed. When I went to the doctor, and he said I was in the ninety-eighth percentile for weight, I thought they'd be proud. But by then they were just worried about Susie being underweight. Now all they did was keep making that plane fly into her mouth. One for Aunt Pammie. One for Uncle Roger. They told Susie they'd buy her a ballerina doll, if she'd stay in the clean plate club for a whole week. "What about me?" I wanted to yell. But I didn't say anything. I kept figuring any day now they'd notice what a good job I was doing, how big I was growing.

I started eating more and more. It got to where I knew I was too big. The only clothes I fit were chubbettes, and even then, I could always feel the elastic on my panties cutting in around my thighs and my stomach. My undershirt left little red marks in my armpits, from rubbing. But I couldn't stop.

Evenings, when my dad came home from the lot, he'd stand in the doorway and put his briefcase down. "Who's my big girl?" he'd call out. We'd both come running. But the one he picked up was Susie.

"I'm the big girl!" I wanted to yell. "I'm the biggest one of all." Only I didn't.

Saturday mornings, he took her with him on his

golf game. She rode on the back of his cart at the club. I stayed home and watched cartoons, with a big plate of pancakes and lots of syrup. As long as I had food in my mouth, things felt OK.

When you've got two sisters like that, it gets to where people always look at you like you were half of a set. She was the blonde, I was the brunette. She was the baby, I was the big sister. She was the skinny one. I was fat. She was the star, center stage. I was her hairdresser. She was popular. Me— take a wild guess.

When the whole business started, after Larry was killed, at first it looked like here we go again. Suzanne on TV every night, getting interviewed, having her picture in the paper. Everybody feeling so sorry for her. My mother went out and bought her a whole new wardrobe, for goodness sake. On account of how her old clothes would probably remind her too much of how happy they'd been, and so forth.

Wherever we went after that, it was always "How's Suzanne doing?" "Poor Suzanne." "Is there anything we can do?" "She's been so brave."

After the boys were arrested, my parents still kept it up. Talking about how unfair it was, the hatchet job the media was doing and so forth. And of course, if anyone had thought to stick a microphone under my nose I would've come out with the same lines. Only nobody did.

But since you've asked, I'll tell you what. She was my baby sister, and it's true, I worshiped her. You know what they say—when in Rome . . .

She was irresistible. Look at me, when I was four years old she moved in and wrecked my life, and still I adored her. She had this ability to manipulate a person. Like one of those commercials you see, where you know they're handing you a line, you know they're working on you, and still you can't help it. When the commercial's over, you've just got to get up and pour yourself a Coke, or put Dove with Moisturizer on your shopping list. Listen, I'm a beautician. I know hair-care products. And still, when I'm finished watching Cybill Shepherd tell me why she uses L'Oreal, I'm ready to run right out and buy myself a bottle. Suzanne had that kind of power over a person. My dad couldn't resist it. Larry Maretto couldn't. You think a sixteen-year-old boy could say no to a person like that?

I'll tell you a story. When I was ten—Suzanne was six—my grandmother sent me this locket that used to be her mother's. Me being the oldest girl and all. That was one thing Suzanne could never take away.

This was a wonderful locket. It opened up so you could put a picture inside. And on the outside, etched into the gold, it had the word *Daughter* in very flowery script, with a little circle of diamond chips around the edges. First thing I did when I got the locket was get a really little picture of my mother to put inside. And I never took that locket off.

It drove Suzanne crazy. I mean, just about every special treat we'd get, there'd always be two of them. A brunette Madame Alexander Cissy doll for me, a blonde for Suzanne. A blue organdy dress for me, pink for Suzanne. We had matching Easter hats, matching Schwinn Traveller bikes with streamers, matching Princess phones for our rooms, not that I had much use for mine.

But with this locket, there was just no way to even things up. Not that my father didn't try. Even though it was my birthday present, he told her, when he saw how upset she was, that he'd buy her a new locket, and have the word *Daughter* engraved on that one too. When she said that wouldn't be the same he bought her a charm bracelet with all these sterling silver charms of all her favorite things: a ballet slipper, a miniature telephone, a sportscar, even a miniature TV set with dials that actually turned. She still wasn't happy.

She said why didn't I trade her the charm bracelet for the locket. And it was a neat charm bracelet. But it was also something you could go out and buy at a store, which was different from a locket your grandmother gave you, handed down to the oldest daughter in the family for three generations. And anyway, the charms fit with her life, not mine. So I said no.

Two, three months after I got the locket, we took a trip to Cape Cod, and I left it home in case it got lost in the waves. When we got home, I searched everywhere, but I couldn't find it. I turned my room upside down looking for that locket, and for years after, I kept hoping it would show up, but it never did. Finally I just gave up. I even forgot about it.

You know something? After Suzanne died, my mother asked me to clean out the condo. It would just be too painful for her, you know? So I was cleaning out her drawers. And what do I find, tucked under a whole stack of Victoria's Secret bras and panties, but my grandmother's locket. I opened it up. But instead of the picture of my mother that I'd put inside, it was a picture of Suzanne.

Funny how things work out, isn't it? Me being the only child again. Sunday nights now I always try to have dinner with my parents, who have been nearly destroyed by all of this business. So there it is, just the three of us again. I'm not the big sister anymore. Just the daughter. And incidentally, I've lost eighteen pounds. Stress, you could say. The funny thing is, I'm not even dieting, and still the weight keeps falling off. What do you know?

Jimmy Emmet

So that's it. You want to know what I got to look forward to? A hundred years looking at these four walls, if I live that long. I never thought I was going to get elected President or nothing. But I didn't figure I'd end up like this neither. My dick might as well get petrified and drop off, for all I need it now.

The other night, I can't say which on account of they start to blend together, I'm laying there and I decide to count the times we done it. Starting with that time at the beach. Ending with a night at her condo. That was the last time.

You know what? It added up to fourteen. Fourteen times, total. Maybe two hours of fucking, max. And the part that kills me is, I can't hardly remember anymore what was so great about it. I know it must've been. I used to say I'd die for it. But I can't even remember what it felt like anymore.

AUTHOR'S NOTE

The outline of the story told here was suggested to me by a recent, highly publicized murder. I used, in a novelistic way, those facts made known to me through television and newspaper reports. But when those facts contradicted my imaginative and fictional necessities, I chose to pursue my own imagination.

The story I really wanted to tell is not about a specific set of characters and circumstances. I wanted in some way to explore questions of fidelity, love, sexual obsession, ambition, violence, and how our thoughts about these things are created and manipulated by television, movies, popular music and magazines. The question that interested me most was: Where do our motivations come from for self-fulfillment, for sexual attraction, for compassion and, finally, for love? I imagine all writers share these kinds of concerns.

So this is not a book about a specific murder case, or any individuals connected with such a case. It would be unfair to align the characters in this novel with those beings who gave me some inspiration. A frequently quoted line from Flaubert comes to mind: "Madame Bovary, c'est moi." Madame Bovary, that's me. To some terrible extent, all the characters in this and every other novel I'm ever likely to write represent elements of my own self. Names, places, characteristics, personal histories, ultimate guilt, ultimate responsibility, are all my own invention.

ABOUT THE AUTHOR

JOYCE MAYNARD is a former reporter for *The New York Times* and wrote the syndicated column "Domestic Affairs." Her nonfiction has appeared in most of America's major magazines, and she is the highly acclaimed author of three previous books, *Baby Love, Domestic Affairs,* and *Looking Back.* Joyce Maynard lives with her three children in Keene, New Hampshire.

SPELLBINDING THRILLERS . . .
TAUT SUSPENSE